Readers love *Fish Stick Fridays*
by RHYS FORD

"*Fish Stick Fridays* is a sweet and spicy romance contemporary with some delicious suspense, a pinch of mystery, and some hot steamy loving."
—Smexy Books

"I am a huge fan of Rhys Ford's writing and would recommend her to anyone, and this story is one of my favorites."
—Joyfully Jay

"I could rave about this book for days, but I think instead I'll just go read it again."
—QUEERcentric Books

"I had a rollicking good time reading this and will be looking forward to more stories set in Half Moon Bay!"
—Gay Book Reviews

By RHYS FORD

Clockwork Tangerine
With Poppy Dennison Creature Feature 2
Grand Adventures (Dreamspinner Anthology)
Murder and Mayhem

COLE MCGINNIS MYSTERIES
Dirty Kiss
Dirty Secret
Dirty Laundry
Dirty Deeds
Down and Dirty
Dirty Heart

HALF MOON BAY
Fish Stick Fridays
Hanging the Stars

HELLSINGER
Fish and Ghosts
Duck Duck Ghost

SINNERS SERIES
Sinner's Gin
Whiskey and Wry
The Devil's Brew
Tequila Mockingbird
Sloe Ride
Absinthe of Malice

Published by DREAMSPINNER PRESS
www.dreamspinnerpress.com

HANGING THE STARS

RHYS FORD

REAMSPINNER
PRESS

Published by
DREAMSPINNER PRESS

5032 Capital Circle SW, Suite 2, PMB# 279, Tallahassee, FL 32305-7886 USA
www.dreamspinnerpress.com

Hanging the Stars
© 2016 Rhys Ford.

Cover Art
© 2016 Reece Notley.
reece@vitaenoir.com
Cover content is for illustrative purposes only and any person depicted on the cover is a model.

ISBN: 978-1-63477-897-8
Digital ISBN: 978-1-63477-898-5
Library of Congress Control Number: 2016914706
Published December 2016
v. 1.0

Printed in the United States of America
(∞)
This paper meets the requirements of
ANSI/NISO Z39.48-1992 (Permanence of Paper).

To the San Diego Crewe who help me hash out things from pronouncing Angel's name to book titles over Korean pastries and Vietnamese Coffee… whether it be iced or hot.
And to Mary, who I should probably just declare the Queen of Half Moon Bay.

Acknowledgments

TO THE FIVE! Darling Penn, Lea, Tamm, and Jenn, always here in the words. And to my darling sisters, Ree, Lisa, and Ren.

To those at Dreamspinner who make me look good: Elizabeth North, Lynn West, Grace McCullough, and the rest of the editing team, as well as lyric, Amanda, Tammy, Naomi, and everyone at DSP.

One

FOUR IN the morning was way too early to die.

Angel Daniels was sure of it, and getting shot wasn't even a good way to go at that.

In fact, if there was any good way to die, standing in the middle of a former pizza shop while holding a five-pound bucket of cranberry-jalapeno-almond muffin batter wasn't it and wouldn't have been Angel's first pick. Mostly because he'd spent way too much time making the damned batter the day before, and after being woken up following only three hours of sleep by his too-stoned-to-make-it-to-work Tuesday baker, he'd stumbled into the Pizza Shack Bakery with the small consolation of knowing the muffins would be a hit with his morning customers.

That was until some asshole busted in the back door and pulled a gun on him.

He was going to die with a two-day-old scruff because he'd forgotten to buy razors, and his long brown hair was pulled back into a ponytail with the only tieback in the apartment, a bright pink fuzzy thing he'd found tucked into the back of the bathroom junk drawer. They'd have to find something nice for the mortuary. He ran through what he had in his closet and couldn't come up with anything better than what he was already wearing, an ancient Temple of the Dog T-shirt and a pair of loose jeans, both worn thin from washing and work. At least his underwear was clean. He had that much going for him. Nothing to wear to his own funeral, and he'd leave a hell of a lot of work behind, including whomever was going to be saddled with Roman.... God help them all... but his briefs were clean.

No, four in the morning wasn't even the *time* of day Angel planned to die.

He'd spent a good hour at the bare-bones gym he belonged to, sparring with a few guys the night before, mostly to burn off his frustration at yet another note from Rome's school about his attitude and alarming lack of completed homework. His arms hurt, and there felt like a bruise was forming on his left cheek. Even though he'd worn a guard, something always seemed to get through. He was too tired and worn out to deal with another piece of crap looking to stick itself to his life.

Besides, Rome was dead asleep in the front where Angel'd left him, sprawled out on one of the thickly cushioned sofas Angel got for twenty bucks at a church thrift store. He didn't need his eleven-year-old brother to come in and watch him die. The kid already had too much to deal with, and Angel couldn't add to it.

He also didn't *want* to get shot, but better him than Roman.

"Are you going to get on with shooting me?" He glanced down at the bucket, hefting it for the gunman to see. "'Cause if you are, do it soon, because this is getting kind of heavy."

The young man holding the gun said nothing, just stared at Angel's face as if he'd seen a ghost.

The broken door was letting the sea-salt-kissed fog into the oven room, carrying with it the tarry stink of the rain-damp parking lot and exhaust-stung air from the nearby highway. Somewhere in the outer streets, a misfiring truck was making its early rounds, its brakes squealing as it went by. A few glowing dots penetrated the thick fog, a line of soft yellow lightbulbs running along the edge of the motel's second floor. A slight ghost of aqua blue with a splash of red along the edges of the door, the light from the motel's broken street sign leaking in. The cold followed the fog and lights, creeping in with a slithering intent to steal the heat from the hot kitchen.

Angel squared his shoulders and stared down at the young man trembling at the door with his hand wrapped tight around the very deadly looking handgun. Shit, he was just out of his teens, barely old enough to get a thick peach fuzz on his chin, and the fear in his swollen, bloodshot blue eyes was intense. If the boy was more than twenty, Angel would eat his left boot.

The guy holding the gun was half a foot shorter than Angel's five eleven and so skinny his collarbones cast shadows across his skin from the overhead fluorescents. His hand shook, the gun's muzzle doing a salsa in the air. The boy's sun-brightened blond hair was matted into uneven dreadlocks, tangled in with bits of debris and twigs, and his nose was overbaked, peeling up at the edges of a very painful burn. A pair of filthy Vans and Dockers held together by sheer will and dirt was enough of a clue that the kid was sleeping rough, something Angel was all too intimate with.

Talking a kid off the ledge was already a daily chore, but at least Roman didn't have a gun in his hand while he fell apart. And from the looks of the boy, he was only going to need a slight gust of wind to push him right over. He couldn't save the world. He'd tried often enough in his thirty-one years on the earth, and nearly every single time, it'd come back to bite him in the ass.

Or in his brother's case, his throat, but old habits were hard to break, and no matter how strong he'd gotten tossing around bags of flour and tubs of finished batters, he was going to have to put the damned bucket down soon enough.

Lifting the bucket up to his hip, Angel stared the kid down. "Seriously, you sure you want to do this? Easy enough for you to take a step back out that door and we can call it done."

"I... can't." The gun bobbled again, and the kid's face scrunched, his lower lip trembling. "I just... I'm sorry, dude, but they want—"

"I got a kid sleeping out in the front of the house," Angel cut him off. Terror clawed at his throat, and Angel quickly shut it down. Panic wouldn't do him any good. If anything, he'd make a stupid mistake and they'd all be killed. He needed his nerves to be steady. "My baby brother. So I'm going to make it really simple for you. You take what I've got here and move on. There's maybe a hundred bucks in small bills and change for the opening crew, but that's about it. Unless you want something to eat, it's all I've got to give to you."

"Ange? What's going on?"

Angel's already chilled blood turned to ice when he heard shuffling footsteps behind him, then Roman's sleepy grumble.

"And why do I gotta sleep here? I'm not a baby—"

"Rome, go back up front," Angel barked, not taking his eyes off the guy with the gun. Roman was near, too near, and Angel spotted his eleven-year-old brother's reflection in the oven's inset glass panels. The fear he'd tamped down broke free, running through his blood and turning his nerves to an icy slick. "Roman! Get the fuck out of *here!*"

"They didn't say there'd be a kid," the gunman stammered. "Shit, I—"

Something sharp and dangerous tickled the cold air, a metallic snip of alarm pinging his nerves, and Angel wasn't listening anymore, drawn to a movement framed by the open door, then a low rumble outside.

Headlights cut through the fog, a brief flash of white through the open door, and the sound of an engine rattled the back room's jalousies.

The beams cut off, the twin slices of light quickly extinguished in the thick shadowy morning, but the car's motor continued to rumble, its menacing growl seemingly rising with each passing second. The dark outside turned black, the ambient light from the motel and street suddenly cut off by a tall, solid shape. A squeak of glass against rubber bounced into the kitchen, and the young man pivoted, his eyes widening and half-crazed. The boy's hand shook, flinging outward probably from surprise, and the gun flew from his loosened grip. Angel wanted to lunge for the weapon, grabbing it away, but there wasn't enough time. Not after he saw what was going on outside through the broken-down door.

There was a glint, something metal and deadly catching on the light coming from the door. He'd felt the heft of that kind of gun in his hand, knew exactly the shape of that particular familiar blunt silhouette in the choppy darkness. There wasn't going to be any time to grab the weapon lying on the floor where it landed. Not if he wanted to keep his little brother alive.

Flinging the heavy bucket at the blond, he lunged for his younger brother and caught Roman up in his arms. His brother smelled of sugar, Ivory soap, and the powdery bitterness of slightly grubby little boy. Angel's chest ached with his fear, leaden and heavy. It pressed into his heart, jabbing into his throat, and Roman began yelling for Angel to let go.

Running for the front would mean dodging around the bank of counters and putting Angel's back to the action, making him and Roman a target. The kitchen was a narrow space, the ovens set up against the fireproofed wall between the cooking space and the front of the bakery. The walk-in refrigerator was out, and besides, Angel didn't want to trap them in a dead-end box. It was too far to get Roman to the other room, not in time anyway, so Angel cradled his argumentative, panicking brother and dove down between two heavy steel mixers, praying the machines' thick bodies would give them enough cover.

"Stop it!" Roman fought being shoved between the machines. "Fricking cut it out—"

"Get down!"

Angel ignored his brother and shouted at the young man, but the blond didn't move. Staring at the gun on the floor, the blond's mouth moved silently, a goldfish smack-smack of his lips, and Angel found he could taste his own fear, as thick and rank as spoiled milk in his mouth.

"Fuck! Roman, stay here."

The young man who'd broken in was still standing in the middle of the kitchen, oblivious to the world, when the gunman in the car began firing.

The *pop-pop* was surprisingly small considering the terror running hot through Angel's blood. Rome was screaming, Angel tangled around him, arms flailing wildly as Angel dropped him to the floor. Catching an elbow across his chin, Angel saw stars, and his rattled teeth sliced through the edge of his tongue. The pain was intense, enough to keep him focused on the screaming kid he'd inherited from his lackadaisical father. There was a splash of something hot and wet across his face, and the kid's shrill yells cut off sharply.

"Rome! Fuck, are you hit?" He turned in the tight space, his hands skimming over Roman's body as he looked for a wound. His brother stared up at him. His face was white from shock, and his gray eyes—so much like Angel's own—were nearly black from his blown-out pupils. Gulping, Rome shook his head. Then they both ducked as another blast came from the vehicle's rolled-down window.

Hit, the young man jerked forward, and a burst of crimson blood splashed.

"Dude, stay here," Angel told his shaking brother. "Don't move unless I tell you to. Got it?"

Roman whimpered when Angel began to pull away. Digging his fingers into Angel's shirt, he held on tight. "Don't go out there, Ange."

It hurt to see Roman so vulnerable, especially after they'd battled over every little thing in the past two weeks. He wanted nothing more than to hug his baby brother and tell him life was going to be okay, but Angel promised Rome he'd never lie to him. People always break their promises. Rome'd spat at him when Angel reassured him their dad would be back. From the moment their father dumped an angry nine-year-old Rome at Angel's front door, Angel'd been trying to prove Roman wrong—hell, he'd been trying to prove anything to Rome, but the kid wasn't buying any of it—and now, when lying was oh-so tempting, Angel stuck with his word and told his younger brother the truth.

"I'm just going to see if I can get that guy safe, okay?" Angel gave his brother one last quick hug, pulling away slowly. "And I need to get that asshole outside to leave. Somehow. 'Cause if I don't, we're all dead, buddy, and I'm not ready to die. So stay *right* here and tuck yourself in."

Rome nodded and set his jaw, rolling up as tight as he could into the space. Angel stuck his head out, as low to the ground as he could, and surveyed the damage. The kitchen was a mess, but the young man who'd come in hot through the bakery's back door was a bigger concern than a few shot-up walls and batter buckets.

There was blood everywhere, and a large black hole punctured the young man's ribs. His chest heaved with his struggling breaths, the wound sucking in air. Turning him over onto his side, Angel got the young man as far behind the bakery's large metal mixing drums as he could. Then he fumbled for the dropped gun.

And came up with a plastic toy handgun with its orange tip filed clean off.

"Mother—" He bit back his frustration. The bullets seemed to have stopped, but the car's rumbling engine roared loudly in their absence. Frantically, Angel looked for his cell phone where he'd left it on the metal prep counter, but it'd been turned into a few plastic pieces now lying on the floor next to the oozing shot-through bucket. "*Shit.*"

There'd been a time when he'd have had weapons stashed in places he could easily get his hands on them, but other than the kitchen knives they used to break down ingredients, the Pizza Shack Bakery was sadly lacking. Regret wasn't going to do him any good. He was going to have to find something quickly or they both wouldn't last for very long if someone else with a gun came through the door.

"Okay, they done?" Quickly reassuring himself that Roman was out of sight, Angel then risked a quick peek around the corner of the back door. None of it made sense. Why send a young guy in with a fake gun, then blow the place up with real bullets? "Okay, dude, I'm trying to get you out of here. I just don't know how the hell to do it."

If Angel'd thought things had gone to hell before he came up empty in the weapon department, whoever was in the car decided to bring out the big guns.

Literally.

Another shot, but this one boomed, rattling the jalousies, and pebbled shot filled the kitchen, sending Angel back down into a crouch. The smaller of the Shack's two ovens took the hit with an angry crack of punctured glass. The blast hurt Angel's ears, and he ducked down, rubbing at the sides of his head to ease the ache. A quick check of the kid assured him his first problem was still breathing, but the larger, more menacing one was still outside, and from the sound of the next echoing blast, the asshole was just getting started. Roman yelped, then shouted he was okay just as Angel's stomach nearly burned its way up his throat.

"Stay. *There*," he shouted back.

Looking up, Angel groaned at the demise of his newer oven. Then a gurgle from the kid behind him yanked him back to reality. There wasn't anything he could use as a long-distance weapon, but the arm-length mixing hook was hefty enough to do considerable damage.

"If I don't get my head blown off," he muttered, grabbing the detached dough hook. It was unwieldy, but it was all he had, and an ear-shattering shotgun blast peppered the oven's already damaged front. Standing up, Angel took a deep breath and squared his shoulders, making sure he had a good grip on the hook's square end. "Fuck it, Angel. It'll be just like being back with Dad in the bus."

He leaped out of the back door, screaming at the top of his lungs, and nearly caught his heel on the edge of the cement pad the Shack rested on. His shoulders tensed, Angel swung at the black SUV idling a few feet away from the bakery. He couldn't see in, it was too dark, and the window the driver shot out of was quickly being rolled up, its rubber guide catching on the glass in jerky squeaks. Catching the edge of the hook against a rear window, Angel struck it, turning his face to avoid a splash of glass pebbles when the pane gave way.

The damned thing bounced off of the glass—*bounced*—and Angel lost his grip on its end.

It tumbled over his forearm, an edge on its attachment end catching on the jute bracelet Roman made for him in art class. Twisting around, he grabbed at the hook, wrapping his fingers around the metal shaft. Getting a good purchase, Angel let the hook's bulbous end rest against his clenched hands and he swung again as a howling shriek cut through the air.

For most people, the sight of a six-and-a-half-foot-tall golden-skinned, bright penny-haired man in curlers and a leopard-print onesie would be unique, perhaps even alarming. For Angel, it was simply Tuesday. More importantly, Justin, the curler-sporting ginger Viking in red bedroom slippers, wielded a crowbar and did not appreciate the Pizza Shack Bakery being shot up like a stationary paper-duck target at the county fair.

The crowbar came down on the roof of the SUV nearly the moment the driver gunned the engine and its tires tried to grab at the damp asphalt.

The back end of the car hit a ridge in the lot's uneven surface, and Angel threw himself back toward the Shack, grunting when the bumper grazed his thigh. The hit spun him around, and Angel landed hard on his hip. Scrambling to get his legs out of the way as the SUV hydroplaned sideways, Angel hit his shoulder against the doorframe, then folded his knees up into his chest, praying the car wouldn't jump the cement slab and hit him.

The SUV's massive tires chewed up the weeds growing along the edge of the bakery, grinding them into a choppy mess. Justin flung the crowbar at the retreating vehicle's back end, and the bar struck the rear window. It hit hard, its edge leaving a spiderweb across the glass, but the window held. Another roar of its engine, and the SUV shot out into the fog, spitting loose gravel and torn-up greenery into Angel's face.

They were left with a moist silence, fog-damp and echoing, punctured through by their frantic gasps for air and the wail of police sirens in the distance. A gurgling cry startled Angel out of his pained fugue, and he reached for Justin's outstretched hand, letting the tall man drag him to his feet.

"Rome, I'm coming in now," Angel warned his brother as he headed into the kitchen. "You okay, dude?"

"Yeah." Rome's voice shook. "Can I come out? Is Justin out there?"

"Yes, he is, but no, you stay there." He wasn't sure the SUV wouldn't be back, and honestly, Angel didn't want Roman to see what was left of the young man who'd held him up just a few minutes ago. "I'll let you know when. Just stay there and be safe."

Angel grabbed a handful of bar towels from a bin. The pool of blood under the kid wasn't much larger than what Angel remembered, but he had no way to gauge the time they'd spent beating at the SUV. He was stretched out where Angel'd left him, his eyes closed and his mouth open, his body shaking under Angel's own trembling hands.

"Justin, use the landline and make sure there's an ambulance coming," Angel ordered over his shoulder, pressing the thick pack of towels into the injured man's wound. The blood was still hot, and the guy moaned under the staunching push. "They shot this guy who came in before they got here. He needs a doctor something bad."

"Shit, one of the baker bunnies? Wait, who the hell is that?" Justin craned his head in, the thick spray of freckles on his cheeks standing out as the blood left his face. "Oh God, honey, he looks… *dead*."

"I hope not," Angel said, checking over the young man's too-still body. His chest was moving, much to Angel's relief, but his breathing was shallow and troubled. "Because the last thing he did in life was something pretty stupid. I'd hate to face God and have to explain I died holding a bakery up with a fake gun."

Two

A DAY-OLD San Francisco regional paper was waiting for West when he climbed into the backseat of his town car. Its front page shouted in large black letters about a political scandal West Harris couldn't have cared less about, but he knew his assistant, Agnes, left it on his town car's backseat for a reason. Turning it over so he could see the stories under the fold, he was drawn to the column-wide color photo to the right of the lead story. It was bright, or as bright as news pulp could get, an achingly familiar face from the past come back to haunt his present in the worst possible way.

Angel Daniels definitely wasn't the same sixteen-year-old boy he'd spent a teenaged summer with. Not by a long shot. It was somewhat hard to tell from the photo, but West could see Angel's long-lashed eyes were still a smoky gray, and his silken gold-streaked brown hair, while darker now, was still a bit of a wild mane around his hard-angled face. He'd filled out quite a bit, his lanky frame broader, with muscled shoulders and sculpted arms, while his once-cute features were now strong and deadly attractive. Still, no matter how many years they'd gone through, Angel Daniels still looked like he was a mouthful of trouble and a hell of a lot of dangerous. Exactly the kind of trouble West needed in his life when he'd found himself adrift and lonely one sweltering Half Moon Bay summer and definitely not the kind of trouble he needed now.

West really could have done without seeing Angel Daniels's face before he'd finished his first cup of coffee. Maybe even not before he'd had his fifth.

"Shit, I didn't need to see this," West muttered to himself, settling into the car as Marzo, his bodyguard and driver, closed the door behind him. Angel'd gotten prettier—no, handsome now, West supposed as he tried to study the photo with a detachment he didn't quite feel. "Definitely haven't changed, have you, Daniels? Although I'd have thought by now you'd be dead from a drug deal or something. Instead, you're now just a thorn in my side I've got to work to get out."

"You say something, boss?" Marzo asked through the slightly open window separating the front from the back. "Need me to get you something?"

"No, I'm good, Marzo. Thank you," West replied, folding the paper back before he fell into a stupid, useless melancholy over idiotic things.

The newspaper was open again nearly as soon as they took their first corner.

It was hard not to look for the boy in the man, but there were definitely traces there. The stubborn tilt of Angel's half grin and the quirk of a dimple so prominent on his right cheek it showed up even in newsprint. It hadn't just been Angel's storm-cloud eyes to catch West's hormone-enraged attention. It'd been the way Angel'd sucked a tear of pink cotton candy from his long fingers. West spent the night trying to hide his arousal, finally resorting to shoving ice down his pants to cool himself off, but it didn't help much. Not since his eyes kept finding the lanky young man manning the Ferris wheel booth, and he'd memorized every worn spot and tear on Angel's jeans before he'd gotten up the nerve to say hello.

But God, that mouth. West'd known that mouth, tasted those lips back when they'd both been young and stupid, sharing an anger at the world and sheltering themselves in the disgruntled emotions that came with being a teenager. There'd been a lot of firsts with Angel, too many to count, and most were now regrets.

Or at least that's what West tried to tell himself as the town car pulled away from the curb.

San Francisco was a dreary wash of grays and beige, lost in a lackluster downpour thick enough to wet the roads and feed the fog but not quite strong enough to wash away the metallic stink of a grimy city street. West stared out of the town car's window for a moment, lost in contemplation as a crowd trudged across the intersection, a sea of bundled-up bodies spotted with weathered umbrellas carried by the less foolish. The stench of something drifted through the partially open window, a sour-green odor, possibly rotten vegetables or even a whiff of a neglected pond of water. It was difficult enough to parse out the caustic taint from the rest of the heavy soiled stink creeping into the sedan's interior.

Still, for all its stench, San Francisco's busy streets were a damn sight more interesting than the cookies-and-milk existence his twin lived in.

The car turned and then climbed Grant, passing under the dragon gate and the tourist foam at its base pillars. Frowning, West took a sip

of his coffee, searing his tongue. Gasping at the hot bubble of air in his
mouth, he cleared his throat to get his driver's attention.

"Marzo, did Agnes reschedule where my first meeting is?" West
asked the thick-necked Italian man driving the sedan. The window
partition rolled fully down, letting the scent of Marzo's Earl Grey
mingle with the strong black coffee West set back down in the cup holder
between the backseats. "I thought we were at the office at nine for that
deal with the fusion restaurant?"

"No, boss. They were moved to tomorrow. This is the start-up tech
place. Changed over to their Russian Hill office so they can do a demo.
Agnes rescheduled their afternoon to this morning. Folder's in the back
with the paper and your coffee." Marzo craned his neck to gauge the
oncoming traffic at the intersection, straining the collar of his button-up
shirt. "Aggie pinged me before I got the car out. Said to tell you to have
IT look at your phone or something because she tried texting you, but
nothing was going through."

"Strange. Seems to work for my mother." West frowned at his
phone's screen. "But then knowing my mother, she'd send me messages
via pigeon if she thought it would get her what she wanted."

He'd gotten at least six texts from his mother, mostly about
needing money, and one from Lang asking him to join Lang's family
for dinner that weekend. His mother he'd simply ignore, leaving Derry
to issue her funds, but Lang he'd call back personally, once he figured
out which excuse he hadn't used yet to avoid sitting at a table with his
deliriously happy twin brother, Lang's grease monkey of a husband and
the hellspawn of a little girl they were raising.

"Maybe a Sunday dinner isn't out of the question." Lang was in
Half Moon Hell, but West wondered if he couldn't be useful in reaching
out to Daniels. Hell, he probably knew Angel on some level. If there
was anyone who'd know a rebellious baker thumbing his nose at a resort
development, it'd be his tree-hugging twin. "I need to—"

His phone chirruped, and West briefly glanced at the screen before
answering. "Morning, Derry."

"See the paper I left for you?" His former college roommate and
current CFO of Harris Investments growled through the phone line. "Did
you see that piece of shit on the front page?"

"Really, Derr?" He took another sip of the coffee Marzo'd left for
him, better prepared for its heat. The brew punched him in the face, dark

and peppery with a hint of sugar. Tucking the phone against his shoulder, he asked, "Paper? You actually use the paper to get your news?"

"Yeah well, sending you a text with a website link doesn't have the same dramatic effect," Derry argued. "You kind of need that slap of paper when bitching about a pain in the ass you've got over there in Half Moon. Now, how about if we talk about what's really important—like getting that asshole out of there so we can develop that damned property."

"The lawyers say we can't touch him," West reminded Derry. "That contract my grandmother cooked up pretty much lets him manage that fleabag motel until he decides he doesn't want to anymore. And he flat out owns the parking lot and bakery. Have you had any luck with him about selling? You said you were going to reach out to him last week."

"Yeah, sure." Derry's snort was loud across the phone line. "I had about as much luck with him as you did dating that quarterback in college. And we both know how that ended up."

"Very badly," he conceded. "Hazards of growing up with private schools and tutors, I wasn't good at reading social cues. I'm much better now."

"Better? You just don't give a shit now, Harris," Derry replied. "Fucking some twink up against a bathroom wall in a club doesn't count as a date. You actually have to go out for dinner or maybe a movie. You're just as bad now as you were in college."

They'd been outsiders, both out of step with the other boys living in the freshman dorm, a requirement West'd hated down to his teeth. His soon-to-be best friend arrived at the Ivy League's hallowed halls wearing a too-shiny polyester suit and sporting the broadest hayseed accent West'd ever heard. There wasn't any sign of that corn-fed farm boy in the sleekly groomed man who sat across of him at board meetings. Derry's unruly blond hair was now ruthlessly cut short, and his speech was more of a mimic of West's own private school tones than Lang's. West still rather missed Derry's old nose, but a childhood brawl left it bulbous and broken, not the image Derry imagined for his life away from the farms and fields.

Now Derry Washington was everything West would have wanted in a lover—in control, influential, and just a little bit eager to keep West happy. It was just a damned shame Derry was as straight as West's black hair and about as different from Angel Daniels as a man could get and still have a dick.

"You listening to me, West?" Derry tsked.

The sharp click jerked West back to the conversation, and he blinked, realizing he'd been staring at Angel's picture in the newspaper.

"Did you read the article? Asshole's place got shot up, and he's more interested in making sure his customers get their damned cupcakes than getting the hell out."

"It says they lost some equipment in the shooting, but a suspect was shot. Probably shut the place down for a day or two." West skimmed through the article, putting his thumb over Angel's face so he could read in peace. "Daniels could find it difficult to regroup. Didn't you tell me the bulk of his business was wholesale? He might be ripe for selling after this."

"Might be. I'm going to see if I can get one of the girls to work him over. He might be more—"

"Not going to work," West cut his friend off. "Plays on my team."

"And you know this how?" Derry's sigh was long-suffering and exasperated. "Never mind. Let me guess. Bathroom wall at a club or idling car in a park?"

"Neither of which I do, I'd like to point out." West returned Derry's sigh. "Go for the loss of equipment angle. He can't have a lot of cash on hand to replace that stuff or he wouldn't be living in a motel."

"Could be he's there because it's close to work. Right across a parking lot he owns," his friend reminded him. "That's like what? A two-hundred-yard commute? And free rent for managing the motel. How shitty of a life is that? Might as well be in jail. Three square and a cot is better than this kind of crap."

"He's used to shitty lives." The coffee in West's stomach turned sour, and he reached for the roll of antacids he'd tucked into his jacket pocket that morning. "The motel is probably an entire staircase from where he came—"

West didn't see the delivery truck until its grille filled the window on Marzo's side of the car.

The hit came hard, slamming West against the divider. Glass pebbles struck his face, scraping at his shaven cheek. Then a wave of hot coffee splashed over his arm, the cup ripped from its holder as the car was pushed across the road. The smell of burning rubber choked West's lungs, and he tried to grab at the armrest, but he couldn't seem to find it. His mind caught Marzo's rain of curses; then the world faded into a buzzing din.

Caught in the truck's grille only for a moment, the sedan began to spin, lurching suddenly when its rear struck a hydrant, snapping it from its moorings. A gush of icy cold water pushed through the car's torn back end, blasting at West's twisted body. His bones rattled from the hit, and his stomach curled in on itself as he lost his bearings. The sedan tilted, its tires hitting something with a shuddering stop. Then West braced himself against the remains of the backseat as the car flipped over.

Light and dark stuttered across West's vision, the seat belt digging into his belly as he caught flashes of the street and buildings between the shadowy clips of the sedan's crumpling roof. West tasted blood, his mouth filling with his swollen tongue and bits of glass. One caught against the roof of his mouth, and his only thought was of terror and of dying in a knot of metal and plastic on the side of a rainy San Francisco road.

The world stopped churning around him, and West gulped for air. His chest hurt, and he couldn't breathe around the fluids in his mouth and nose. All he could taste was the metallic burn of blood, and his lashes were wet, spangled with water, but his face hurt too much for him to try blinking. There was a great creaking, and it took him a good long moment to realize the mannequins in a clothing store's windows he was staring at were sideways.

No, his brain sludged a thought through the pudding of his mind, *you* are sideways.

Then the mannequins disappeared, replaced by Marzo's bloodied face.

It was good to see the Italian man he'd hired to watch his back. Less good to be coughing up red foam, but West was less concerned about what he was spitting out and more worried about the long trail of blood on his bodyguard slash driver's forehead. He tried to find something to wipe it off with, but his arms weren't working properly, and for some reason he needed to throw up.

"Need another coffee, Marzo," West mumbled around the glass he couldn't seem to get out of his mouth. "Spilled this one."

"Yeah, don't try to talk, West," the man grunted. "Ambulance is going to be here soon. We're going to get you out of this car and looked at, okay?"

"The truck." West blinked again, not liking the scratchy feel of his lids against his eyes. "Driver okay?"

"Driver's long gone, boss. Did a runner."

Marzo sounded far away, lost in a rush of crackling. West shook his head and instantly regretted it.

"Don't do that, man. Looks like you bashed your head in. Just wait, all right? And once we get you looked at, I'm going to find the guy driving that truck and rip him a new asshole."

"Just an accident, Marzo," he ground out.

"No, boss, this wasn't no accident," Marzo corrected him in a gentle voice at odds with his rough face. "Someone's trying to kill you, sir. *Again.*"

"OVEN'S A loss, Angel," Frankie said, wiping his broad-knuckled hands on a rag. "Cost you more to repair than it would to buy a new one."

He was a big Southern man, tall and round but nimble on his feet and a lifesaver for Angel. Frank'd resurrected the Pizza Shack Bakery's equipment from certain death so many times, Angel truly believed there wasn't anything the older man couldn't lay his hands on and heal. Hearing his oven had gone to meet its maker shocked the hell out of him. Angel studied the remains of his oven and let loose the word he'd been holding on his tongue since early that morning.

"Fuck."

He was tired. Dead to the bone tired, and the day wasn't even half-over yet. The Shack was finally empty of cops, the bakery was given the go-ahead to cook in, and he'd conned Justin into taking Roman back to the motel with him for the afternoon, something his younger brother did not want to do. Yesterday, school was ruled out for Roman at nearly the exact same moment the blond faux gunman kicked in the kitchen's back door, and Rome oddly enough vehemently disagreed with the decision until Angel figured out he'd used the morning for bragging rights.

And God only knew what story Rome told his classmates. Angel half expected to find himself in the school's front office explaining to the principal and CPS that no, they hadn't taken down a ninja troupe or terrorists, and yes, his brother had a very vivid imagination. It'd been a bit of a relief when he hadn't gotten yet another call to go down and pull Roman's head out of his ass.

"I don't have the money for new, Frank," Angel said, rubbing at his face in the hopes it would scrape his brain off of his aching skull. "Shit, I don't have money for *used.*"

"What about insurance?" The repairman looked around the shot-up bakery. "Tell me you've got insurance."

"Yeah, but they're not covering a lot of it. The guy laughed when I told him how old this thing was. Said I'd be lucky to get five hundred for it." Angel tallied up what he had in his emergency funds and winced at the number he came up with. "I've got no idea where the hell to pick up a used oven. They make classifieds for old broken-down ovens looking for a new place to call home?"

"I might have a line on one. A guy I know is selling off his equipment. Going down to Florida to chase old women with sagging tits and big bank accounts." Frank stood, stretching his back out in a long popping crack. "Rotating. A little bit bigger than this one but definitely newer. Gas, which would be good, considering you've already got lines."

"Frank, there are stone tablets with Scripture on them that are newer than this oven. How much?"

Angel braced himself. Frank named a price high enough to take the wind out of Angel's lungs.

"Shit, there's no way I can swing that. That's like… shit, might as well ask for a unicorn."

The older man took his ball cap off and ran his hand through his thinning hair. "Now don't take this wrong, and hear me out all the way before you say anything."

"You start off like that and my gut reaction is to say no," Angel warned, leaning against a prep counter. "But sure, go ahead."

"I know this guy," Frank hedged. "And I know you. The oven's a good one. Cheap at that price."

"Yeah, I just don't have anyone to give my left nut to so I've got the cash to buy it," Angel interjected.

"What I'm telling you, son, is that I'll float you the oven. Now shut up and listen before you talk."

Frank held his hand up, and Angel swallowed the no in his throat.

"He'll take payments for it if I speak for you. We can work something reasonable out between all of us, and that way, you stay in business, and that sweet girl Justin works for gets those peach cobbler muffins she likes so much. And let me tell you, that alone is worth the price of that oven."

"So you're going to help me get an oven just so you can continue to bring Yvonne in after church and get peach muffins?" Angel scoffed. "Pull the other leg, Frank."

"Never underestimate what a bit of sweet can do between two people, son," Frank countered. "Now, you know you're not going to get a better deal than this. No bank'll touch you. And not like that scum father of yours is going to extend his hand with some cash. I'm the best you've got."

"Even if my dad was going to extend his hand or anything else on his worthless body, you're still the best I've got, Frank." He hated the idea of being in debt to the man, but Angel didn't see any other way out. Even used, a good oven cost thousands more than he had on hand. "We have to do it legally. Contract with interest, and I turn the insurance money over to you."

"If that helps you sleep at night, kid, sure." Frank grinned at him. "Now, tell me there's some dobash left over from this morning's run, and I won't even charge you for coming out."

"Maybe a couple left. I made cupcakes out of the batter this time around. Shake and we'll call it a deal on the dobash." Angel held his hand out as a man cleared his throat from the back of the kitchen. Turning, Angel frowned at the silhouette at the door. "Sorry, we're closed."

"Thanks, but I'm looking for Angel Daniels," the man replied, shaking an umbrella off at the stoop. "I take it that's you?"

Angel frowned. "Yeah, but I wasn't expecting any deliveries. We're shut down for the day."

"What you've got there is cop, son." Frank stiffened and tucked the rag into the back pocket of his work pants. "Thought you all were done here."

The man stepped out of the watery afternoon sun and into the kitchen. Around Angel's height and with roughhewn Irish features, he looked more like a rugby player than a cop, but the badge he flashed was real, as was the authoritative stance he took once he got inside.

"Detective Montague. I've been assigned to a case involving a Weston Harris. Do you know who that is?"

"Oh yeah. Can't seem to shake him off of me." It was a shame what they'd come to. He hadn't seen West since Angel's father stole out of Half Moon Bay with Angel and a roadside diner's Saturday-night take. West was long gone by the time Angel'd been dumped back onto Main Street, left with nothing but a backpack full of dirty clothes, a few books, and a couple of bucks he'd made playing poker at a truck stop. "He owns the Moonlight Motel out back behind the bakery. Why?" A chill ran through Angel's blood. "Something happen to him?"

"You can say that. Someone in a delivery truck rammed the car he was in this morning."

Montague's smile was thin and cold, a sliver of ice on the heat of Angel's worry.

"And one of the head honchos at Harris's business seems to think you might have been the one to do it."

Three

WEST HARRIS.

It could have been the tired in his bones or maybe the stress of being shot at and being scared for Roman, but *hearing* West's name brought Angel's heart to a shuddering, clenching stop. It wasn't like he didn't see West's face a few times a month. Hardly a week went by without him dropping by Lang's store, Between The Lines, so he'd seen West age over the years.

No, he corrected himself, he'd seen Lang age and only hoped he could find glimmers of the angry, hurt teen he'd lost his heart to more than a decade ago. West wasn't there. Not in Lang's amicable expressions and shy smiles. West's edges were sharper, his hunger and thirst for knowledge deeper, and they'd share secrets under the warm summer skies lying on the beach with only the stars and the ocean to keep them company. Even now, after life slapped at Lang, then handed him someone to love, Lang's face still had fewer shadows, fewer secrets than his brother's.

"Is he okay?" Angel found his voice, a scraped whisper in his too dry throat. "West. Is he okay?"

"He should be fine, Mr. Daniels. Mind if I call you Angel?" Montague asked. "Is there somewhere we can talk in private?"

"Angel's fine," he said softly, trying to find his heartbeat again in the middle of his sharp inhale. The relief filling the space his fear left made him sick, a sugary gloop of emotion Angel wasn't sure he deserved to feel. "Sorry. I just—fucking hell. *West.* Um… private. Yeah, the front—"

"Hold up. Why do you think the man's got something to do with Harris getting hurt?" Frank edged in close, his booming voice harsh and loud in the wide space. Frank's tone lacked menace, but there was a definite steely thread in his words. "He's had some shit come down on him, and instead of the cops going out and finding who shot his place up, they send you to poke him over some rich dude who's been making problems for him. You all ever think maybe this Harris guy sent someone to shoot Angel and that they're now trying to cover their asses?"

It was interesting watching the standoff between Frank and the cop. For all his bluster, Frank was a solid, large, older black man, easygoing until he came up against anyone of authority. Then his heels dug in, and he stonewalled with the best of them. Montague seemed... amused, while oddly, Frank hovered on belligerent. The cop wasn't small, thickly built, and probably had more strength than Frank expected under his button-up shirt, red tie, and beige duster, but a brawl would mean Frank getting arrested, and when push came to shove, Angel needed that damned oven.

"Frank, it's okay." As much muscle as Angel'd put on over the years, Frank still could probably pick him up and slam him into the ground without so much as sweating. Pulling on Frank's arm, Angel tugged him back. "The cop and I've got to talk. Someone fucked Harris up, and they came up with probably a bunch of people *they* think want to see Harris taken out. Cops don't know me, so they've got to ask. Might as well be here and now so I can get back to work."

Jutting his chin out, Frank stared down Montague for a long minute, then turned to Angel and said, "Need me to stick around? In case you need a witness or something."

As endearing as Frank's protectiveness was, it was odd to have someone hovering over him. His father was more a look-out-for-number-one, and from what Angel'd seen growing up, it was pretty much how the world operated. Half Moon Bay was different. *He* was different here—a better person, a kinder person—and it was the main reason he'd fought his way through the hell his father'd put him through just to come back. Then just as Angel thought he was finally free of Linus Daniels and his fuckery, his father'd stopped by his apartment long enough to dump his scared brother, then took off for parts unknown, leaving Angel to deal with Roman alone.

If only trying to keep Rome's anger and troublemaking contained as tightly as possible counted as dealing.

So Frank's paternal adoration was a perplexing, welcome mess of affection Angel didn't quite know what to do with. He hadn't been expecting to find a father figure in his thirties—although *father* was a bit of a stretch. Uncle maybe. Or at least an older disgruntled cousin with a really good left hook.

"What am I going to need a witness for?" Angel scoffed. "Not like I did anything to him. And he just said Harris is okay."

"Cops lie, kid," Frank asserted. "It's how they trap you. They don't *have* to tell you the truth. It's not entrapment if you give up stuff they can twist and use against you. Hell, Harris could be dead for all—"

"Harris is fine, by all accounts," Montague reassured them. "This is just routine follow-up, and since I'm here, we can touch on what happened last night because it's probably going to land on my desk. Harbershaw's going on vacation in a couple of days, and I'll be handling most of the heavy stuff."

"There you go, no witnesses needed. Frank, it's okay. 'Sides, you've got one more job today, right?" Angel reminded the mountain of a man looming over them. "You go do that, and I'll let you know what the insurance guy says. Maybe I can talk them into giving me more than a few bucks. Had to have learned something from my dad about getting people to do what I want."

"Angel, you are nothing like that asshole. I'll get back to you later about the oven, kiddo. Should be able to get in tomorrow or the day after. I've got a guy with a truck." Frank fixed a steady hard glare on the detective, tugging his T-shirt down over his belly. "We'll have you up and running in no time."

"Okay… and thanks. Really. I don't know what else to say." Angel found himself caught up in a brisk, hard hug. The man smelled of unfiltered cigarettes, oil, and the cinnamon candies he kept stashed in his pocket to suck on while working. Gasping to tease Frank when the man finally let go, he choked out, "Want some of the cupcakes?"

"I'll swing by later and grab them. Next job should be easy. I'll be back in an hour." Grabbing his toolbox from the floor, Frank nodded at the kitchen's back door. "If you need help fixing that, wait till I come back, and we can knock it out."

"Thanks. I'll see how far I can get without nailing my hand to the wall or something," Angel replied as Frank elbowed his way past Montague, then closed the temporary back door as tightly as it could fit into the newly built-out frame. "Love the man but…. *Jesus*."

"Your friend there seems a little uptight." The detective chuckled. "Doesn't seem to like cops a lot. Anything I've got to worry about?"

"Nope, you're fine. Frank just gets… intense. He'll tell you he was an angry young man in the sixties and didn't have a lot of love for cops." Giving Montague a shrug when the detective grunted at him, Angel continued with a laugh. "And then he'll tell you he's a cranky old man in his sixties, and he *still* doesn't like cops. Says it all the time so don't take it wrong. This questioning thing going to take long? 'Cause if it is, I'm going to need some coffee."

"I wouldn't say no to coffee," Montague replied, pulling a notebook out of his jacket pocket. "If you're offering."

Montague's deep brown eyes looked as tired as Angel's felt, and there was a sadness to them stark enough to make a stone ache in sympathy. A pale stripe of skin on Montague's tanned ring finger was recent, the grooved edges of a missing band still denting the detective's flesh. There was a simmer there, something tangible Angel liked, especially when the detective's wide mouth quirked to the side into a sardonic grin. The cop was handsome enough for Angel to wish he felt up to flirting with anyone, much less a straight cop. Hell, he couldn't remember the last time he'd even kissed anyone, other than Justin on the cheek when he offered to keep track of Rome.

"Coffee and a cupcake. That's what I'm offering." It was safer to keep to what he knew, and Angel slung down two mugs from the shelf behind the register. "Maybe a muffin or a scone. Depends on what we've got. Come on to the front. There's at least places to sit there."

The Pizza Shack Bakery's windows needed cleaning, Angel noticed as he led the detective to the front of the old building. Dust from the road and the rain left leopard-like rosettes on the glass, and it was something he could get Rome to do in exchange for a few bucks. He'd yanked the blinds up, letting in what little sunshine he could pull from the overcast day. The kitchen door opened up to behind the counter space and the bakery's oddly empty display cases. Set on the short right side of the long space, the cases were angled to show off sweets and pastries to passersby and customers, but while the setup worked great for pulling in walk-up business, it was hellish to get around with a full tray. Or, as Angel stepped around a box of coffee Justin'd left on the floor, around the case itself.

Several love seats and couches were placed around low coffee tables, with a few padded wooden chairs thrown into the mix to keep things interesting, and considering he'd been scraping to get by back when he'd first opened the bakery, Angel liked how the front room ended up looking like a place people could sit and talk. The broad room's golden walls were nearly gilt under the afternoon sun and a decent enough backdrop for the landscapes he'd found at the dump and paid Justin to add mythical beasts to.

"Pizza Shack Bakery?" Montague held up one of the shop's flyers. "I remember getting slices here after school. Kind of weird name, though."

"Hey, that sign on the roof's expensive. It was easier to just add Bakery to it than get a new one." He shrugged off the detective's chuckle. "I was running cheap back then, and everyone knew where this was. Seemed like a good idea at the time."

"You make anything pizza-tasting?"

"Empanadas on Friday." He laughed at Montague's curious glance up. "Like tiny calzones. Easy to make and sell like crazy but a bitch to keep stocked. The crew's got to deep fry all day with those bastards. Just coffee or something to eat?"

"Coffee for now," Montague replied. "Maybe something later? I don't know how much money—"

"Don't want the money. It'll be day old in a couple of hours, and I can't open tomorrow, so can't sell them. They might as well get eaten. I'll see what's left later," Angel called out to the detective wandering around the bakery's seating. "Coffee's a medium roast, if you don't mind. I get a great deal from a family on the Big Island. Just got a shipment in this morning, so I can at least say the beans are fresh."

"If it's hot, relatively a dark color, and better than the crap they give us at the station, I'm calling it a win," Montague shot back. "Never been in here before. It's… nice. Like it's a living room or something."

"That's what I was aiming for. Mostly people like to sit on couches, so they stay longer. And if they stay longer, people going by think it's a busy place and want to stop," Angel confessed as he brought the full coffee mugs to the front. "I read it in a business magazine. I don't know if it works, but it sure as hell looks nicer than plastic lawn chairs. Cream or sugar?"

"Black's fine." The detective took the mug Angel offered him, then sat down. "You said you've got a history of sorts with Harris. Anything to be concerned about?"

"Something of a history. We did stupid things together when we were kids… teenagers. Then I left, and he… did whatever it is rich kids do when they're done with their playthings after a summer." The velvet sofa was a lot more comfortable than Angel'd remembered, or he was a hell of a lot more tired than he'd realized. Either way, it felt good to sit down, even if it was to get grilled by a cop. "I haven't seen West in… shit, years. Not since me and my dad drove off. I know his brother—friends kind of—but it's been a while for me and West."

"How would you say you guys left it? Okay? Bad? Good?"

It'd been hard to get into his father's van that early-fall evening. There hadn't been time for more than a quick good-bye. He'd been over sixteen, or near enough for a court to count him as an adult if some asshole in a suit wanted to. There'd been tears for both of them, and he'd gotten one last sweet kiss before his dad grabbed him by the hair and threw him toward the car. Gutted and in pain, Angel snuck off the first chance he got and called West, only to be told in a cold, rigid voice he'd been nothing more than someone to fuck around with during a long, boring summer at the beach.

Nothing had ever hurt Angel more than West hanging up on him that night. Not before and not since. He'd forgotten how much he hurt inside and was surprised to find himself bleeding still.

"It wasn't... great." He sounded empty, an echoing vastness stretching inside his mind, but the sear of pain was oddly too intimate, still too raw to share with anyone, much less a cop. "There's issues with the properties here, but he hasn't been involved. Most of the time it's a lawyer or one of his corporate guys... um, Washington or something. Where'd the accident happen?"

"Washington was who'd mentioned you." Montague sipped at his coffee, then put it down to take out his notebook and pen. "Considering it's only a half an hour or so from where he got hit to Half Moon, the investigating officer asked me to chase you down and get back to him. Anything you want to tell me?"

"Well, from about seven to noon, this place was crawling with cops. So I've got a stack of cards with names you can run down if you want. Just... hell, West." Angel leaned back, his coffee forgotten under a storm of memories fueled by the mention of West's name. "Between digging out bullets from the wall and trying to get my baker squared up before he headed to go use the pizza ovens over at Joey's, I don't think I was alone enough to do more than piss out the coffee I drank after I got up."

"I'll just need someone's name." The detective tapped his pen against the edge of his pad. "What about this history you've got?"

"Dead history. Been a long time since... well... seriously, is he okay?" Angel asked softly, then clarified when a frown creased Montague's forehead. "Do you know what happened?"

"Not a lot of details other than the car was T-boned when he was heading to a meeting. He and his driver were taken to the hospital with moderate injuries. From what I hear, he'll be fine. Banged up a bit and maybe a broken bone or two," Montague replied. "One of his management guys tossed your name into the pile of people to look into. Said you guys were butting heads over a property but nothing about anything personal. Want to talk to me about that?"

"Pretty simple. I manage the Moonrise."

The detective gave Angel a blank look.

"The motel behind the parking lot. His grandma used to own it and hired me to look after the place while I was trying to get the bakery going. She died, and West inherited the motel, but she sold me the Shack and the parking lot for cheap. He wants to build some condos because housing prices out here are insane, but he needs all of it—the motel, the bakery, *and* the parking lot—or his company won't have enough land for the project."

"And you're not willing to sell it?" Montague's thick eyebrows rose at Angel's nod. "Not enough money?"

"Not enough *everything*." The sofa's velvet shone in places where it was rubbed down to the weave, shiny spots dotting the plush rich fabric. Angel ran his thumb around one of the spots, gathering his thoughts to explain to the cop why he'd never sell.

"I know housing's tight here. I've got lucky with a foreclosure, but I'm going through hell putting it back together." Montague eased back, opening the space between them.

It was an old trick, one Angel'd seen his father pull to draw people into conversations. The detective didn't seem like the kind of guy who'd use old con psychs, but like Frank said, cops lied all the time. Sometimes without even saying a word.

"Okay, let me explain a few things. First, this bakery's all I've got. Well, and I've got Roman. He needs stability, Detective. His life's... our dad pretty much fucked it up. He's on medication to help him deal with some of the shitty genetics we have, and it's a damned struggle to get him to stay in school.

"I've had him for not even two years, and shit's gone from crap to worse since then, but I'm the best chance he's got to make it out of the other side of puberty a halfway decent human being," Angel explained. "He's waiting for me to dump him. Just like our dad did. Just like his mom. Here he's got his own room, and the price is right for me. I don't pay to live there. I can dump any money I make into this place and him. And fuck, kids are expensive."

"Tell me about it." Montague grinned at him from across the rim of his mug. "I've got kids of my own. Girl's about to be a freshman in high school. Talk about expensive. You probably were offered a hell of a lot of money, right? Why not take it? You can set up the bakery anywhere."

"That goes to the second bit. A lot of us living there don't have family, and we sure as hell don't have enough money to live anywhere else. I made a deal with West's grandmother to keep that place clean and open to people who need a safe place to get on their feet." He didn't want to scrape open all of the wounds the motel residents had when they arrived, but Angel'd seen the bone-numbing surrender in their eyes when a case worker or shelter employee dropped them off at Angel's door. "She worked my employment contract so the asshole lawyers he's got can't push us out. There's people who need the motel to stay open.

"So, the Moonlight's got a purpose, and I gave my word to keep it open." Angel shook his head. "Bottom line is, I can't yank my brother out of the only home he's ever had, and I can't shut down a place where people feel safe for the first time in their lives. Yeah, the money would be great, but I'd be selling my soul to the Devil."

"So that's why Derry Washington coughed up your name? Do you think he called the cops down on you to force you into a corner?" Montague's pencil flew across the page of his notebook, and Angel forced himself not to read the man's upside down scribbles. "And let's talk about what your angry friend said before he left."

"Frank says a lot of things." He smirked into his coffee, then took a sip, washing away some of the bitterness on his tongue. "Oh, about Harris's company shooting this place up? I don't know. I don't think so."

"Do you often have a lot of violence around you, Angel?" Montague struggled with the pronunciation. The detective's phone beeped at him before Angel could answer. "Hold on a second. This is the station."

"Not a problem." Angel picked up his now empty cup. "Need more coffee. And I promised you a cupcake or something."

"Hold on that for a second," Montague said sharply, then turned his attention back to his phone for a moment. Grunting a few times, he hung up, and every scrap of friendly cop bled from his face. "The kid who broke in here last night didn't make it, so this is now an official murder investigation. So I'm going to have to ask you not to leave town for a while, Angel, because they found a recently fired gun tossed into the bushes by the motel about half an hour ago, and oddly enough, it's registered to *you*."

Four

"I DON'T see why you can't stay with us."

Lang's voice was thick with amusement, and West resisted the urge to smash his twin's wide, bright smile in with the cane he was leaning on. As if expecting the hit, Lang stepped sideways to let West into the beach house, holding the door for his brother to walk through.

"Watch your—"

"I was walking before you were, Lang," West snarled as he edged past his twin. "I think I know what I'm doing."

"He sounds like an old woman," a less than cherubic voice muttered behind him. "Like he's going to yell at me to get off his lawn."

"If I had a lawn, brat," West grumbled back. "I'd yell at you for even looking at it. And who dressed you this morning? You're wearing every color known to mankind and possibly a few human beings can't even see...."

"The girls at school say I'm cool." Zig preened at the cascade of pink and blue feathers in her caramel curls, then tugged at the red crinoline skirts she wore over her purple leggings. "Something you wouldn't know about."

"Okay, you two," Lang called out after them. "I can't believe I'm breaking up a spat between my twin brother and my daughter. Zig, be nice to your rotten uncle."

"How come he gets to be a dick and I have to be nice, Dad?" She turned, walking backward a few steps and grumbled at Lang.

"Because you're ten, you know better, and West is hurt. People get pissy when they're in pain." Lang grabbed a case from Marzo's hand, hefting it over the threshold. "Keep it up, though, and you'll be picking up the whole neighborhood's dog poop because—"

"Yeah, rule number one. Sure. Got it." Zig sniffed. "Yeah, I liked it better when we had the swear jar."

"I think we all do." West's ankle ached, twisting under him as he took a step. "Or I might have to get a very big dog that poops a hell of a lot. Grab that duffel, hellspawn. There might be something in it for you."

Five steps—painful steps—and West was into a house he never thought he'd come back to.

Even though he'd had Agnes call ahead to have the house aired out, it smelled of stale air and canned fake citrus. There were streaks on the living space's massive windows, wide foggy swaths blocking the view to the ocean below. Dust motes sparkled through the long streams of sunlight pouring into the high-ceilinged room, dancing on the heat-fueled air currents. The main room's stuffed-to-the-gills poppy-red couches were slightly at odds with the house's modern clean lines, soft curves blunting the structure's cold white edges. The discordance continued in the space's artwork: brash splashes of graffiti art painted on drywall sheets and hung from long black cords.

At the time he'd picked everything out, West thought the bright colors would warm the harsh lines of the almost-too-stark house, but its icy depths remained frigid, untouched by even the splash of hot colors across its rooms.

Perched on a cliff above the rocky beach below, he'd been drawn to the jut of hard white walls and glass expanses, an architectural quartz formation nestled into the wild, windblown California bluff. It was a fortress of sorts, one of solitude and quiet, and when that thought crossed his mind, he'd laughed, a bittersweet chuckle, thinking back to a lighthearted argument he'd had with Angel late one hot summer night about superheroes and dreams.

Buying the house on the bluff had been irrational. West had no intention of ever living at Half Moon Bay. It was too full of memories—painful ones at that—but the house was... perfect. Even if he'd been the one who'd preferred a stately manor with a deep, dark cave in its bowels, the bright white crystalline house on the shore seemed like destiny.

He'd thought it funny how dreams died quietly, their passing unmarked until the moment when he'd stood in the middle of a hard-angled castle, and it made him long for a gray-eyed, sweet-mouthed love he'd turned his back on.

"What'd ya get me?" Zig plopped the bag on a backless couch set in front of the wall of windows. The sun flirted with the gold in her hair, teasing out the brightness in her curls. "Can I open it?"

"Yes, you can open it, brat," West murmured. "Just let me get settled. Forget someone tried to run my car over with their truck?"

"Yeah, kinda." Zig bared her teeth at him in a mockery of a smile. "I just figured you were moving slow 'cause you're old."

"Nice. I'm sure Lang loves to be called old by someone younger than most of his socks," he teased back.

"Crap." She grimaced. "You just don't look alike. Kind of. You look different."

"Same face, same body," West reminded her. "I just got more of the personality and brains."

"Says the person who regularly pisses enough people off he needs a bodyguard," Lang shot back as he took off his jacket. "And Zig, you can't just—West is…."

"Take what's offered and then take more when no one's looking?" Zig parroted West back at her father. "What? *He* says that's what you do."

"Good to know someone's listening," West drawled. "Leave her alone, Lang. She's busy right now."

As much as he reluctantly liked Lang's adopted daughter and mostly tolerated the grease monkey his brother'd married, their happy, all-smiles family was a little much to take. To be fair, it wasn't all smiles. There were dark days, struggles when Zig fought with her fear of every adult in her life leaving her alone. Lang's marriage hadn't been a magic cure for that. Her changing her name to Zig Harris-Reid helped, but there were still times when the world pressed in too close for his niece, and from his point of view, spoiling the hell out of her seemed to make her smile.

Her fathers were not so pleased about it, which made West even happier for some age-old sibling perverse reason.

The couch seemed too far away, but West was going to be damned if he let anyone see how much it hurt to move. The painkillers he'd been given rattled about in one of the bags Marzo was carrying in, and his jaw hurt from clenching his teeth. The cushions collapsed around him when West finally eased onto one of the couches, and something sharp dug into his back, probably his wallet or phone in his pocket, but he didn't care. He was off his feet, and the pounding in his head faded a bit as he closed his eyes and blocked out the sunlight.

He didn't know what the hell he'd been thinking buying a house made up mostly of windows. Everything was so damned bright, and the white walls burned lines into his vision. His head was beginning to pound again, and Zig's curly hair grew sideways, then shrank back down when West blinked. Another dip of his lids, and the world splintered, pseudo-glass fractures forming across his eyesight.

"Hey, so can I open it?" Zig plopped down next to him, her slender body barely denting the couch's fluffy cushions, but the slight jostle made him nauseated. Her hair was everywhere, having escaped a woefully ambitious hair tie, but she smiled achingly sweet at West, turning on a charm she could only have learned from her once-uncle, now-father, Deacon. "Can I? Huh?"

"Zig—" Lang's less than subtle reprimand sounded far away, and for some reason, squeaky. "You're killing me here, West."

"Lang, this has nothing to do with you," West verbally poked back at his brother. "This is between Zig and I. You go do… whatever you and Marzo are up to. We'll handle our own affairs here, thank you very much."

"He's going to call you a dick later," Zig whispered softly. "To Dad One. Deke. Just so you know."

"Yes, I know. And when he leaves, I'll probably call him an asshole because that's what brothers do." West risked a nod but instantly regretted it when his world tilted forward, then to the side, leaving him unbalanced. "You really need to have better names for them. You can't keep calling them Dad One and Dad Two. It makes them sound like failed *Cat in the Hat* characters."

Zig's grin was evil and sly. "Does that make you the fish?"

"As if I'd ever be a fish." West snorted lightly at her. "Open the bag. It's on top."

He could smell the leather as soon as she unzipped the duffel. Hell, anyone within a five-mile radius probably got a whiff of the finely tooled black leather biker jacket as soon as Zig opened the bag. She clutched the opening tightly in her small hands and gaped at West, her fawn eyes wide with excitement.

"Are you perhaps waiting for it to crawl out on its own?" he prodded. "You're going to have to hurry up. My pain pills are in there, and that thing's in the way. It's going to have to come out sooner or later."

He'd never understood the joy of giving someone something before. Or at least, not since… Angel. In the years since he'd first gotten a glimmer of sunshine and a tug of bright on his face at the sight of someone else's glee, West hadn't seen it since. Not until Lang insisted he bring something for Zig's first Christmas at Half Moon Bay and he'd watched her go from wary to explosively delighted in a matter of seconds.

He'd never known a five-foot-tall stuffed unicorn with a shimmery rainbow mane and golden horn could bring so much happiness. Or hugs. He'd gotten a lot of hugs from Zig that day, mostly sticky from too much candy but still adoring, tight embraces that'd been punctuated with a round of appreciative swear words so bawdy an aged-out prostitute would blush to hear them.

Amid the sappy music and twinkling lights, West coughed up the two-dollar fine for the swear jar, gaining another hug and a whispered *Thank you, Uncle West* that nearly broke his heart in two.

As she pulled the black leather biker jacket out, Zig whispered softly, "Oh—*damn.*"

There was reverence in her young voice, a slither of disbelief West never experienced growing up. The little girl wasn't used to presents, not yet. Maybe never, but West was going to give it his best try to change that.

Because if anyone needed to know they deserved getting just-because presents, it was Zig Harris-Reid.

Not long ago, there'd been tears in his twin's eyes when Lang confessed to finding cans of food stashed in Zig's closet, tins of corned beef hash and gelatinous pink meat the young girl and her uncle ate cold, much to Lang's horror. It'd been an adjustment—a hard adjustment—as they all discovered ingrained prejudices about foods, clothing, and oddly enough, shampoos. His naïve, sweet brother's shock at what his husband and now-daughter couldn't live without amused West at the time. He and West grew up wanting nothing, and Lang was suddenly in love with a pair of people who'd dive for change under a couch cushion to buy an overboiled hot dog from a convenience store.

And despite all the battles Lang'd fought in his life, he'd still remained… innocent, and Zig's hoarding rattled him to the core.

"Just tell her she's okay," West'd told him when his brother called him to share his pain at the stack of cans and a lost little girl. "And maybe give her some of those canned sausages. They're disgusting, but Marzo seems to like them."

Since then, West was determined to give Zig anything he felt she deserved. Surprise gifts without any occasion attached to them because he'd wanted to be surprised like that when he'd been young and his father'd returned from a trip. There'd been nothing spontaneous in the Harris household, no sudden flights of fancy guaranteed to slough off the boredom of schoolwork and manners. For all the distance he'd wanted to put between himself and Lang's new family, West simply couldn't walk away from the little girl who dreamed of ruling the world but still hid tins of food under a pile of stuffed animals just in case her world fell apart... again.

"It's so pretty. And nice. And the inside—the fabric's got *cats*!" Zig held the soft leather up to her shoulders. Rubbing at its sleeves, she snuck a glance at West through her lashes. "West, the dads won't let me—"

"They'll let you keep it." West eased off his left hip, feeling every bruise under his skin. "Of course they will. It was made for you. Now try it on. It's probably going to be a little bit big, but that's so you can grow into it."

Her hug was as tight and sweet as the first one she'd given him, and West wrapped his arms around her, grunting at the fresh wave of pain running over his ribs and spine. Keeping his face as calm as he could, he patted Zig on the back, then let her go.

"Go find a mirror, hellion." West caught up the duffel before it slid onto the floor. The rattle of pills was a siren call, and his body was begging to answer it. He smiled as Zig ran up the stairs, probably heading toward a bathroom with a full-length mirror. Digging out the pharmacy bottle, he muttered, "Marzo, I'll need some water, please. I need to take a handful of these things."

"Of course, boss." The bodyguard put down the case he'd been carrying. "Let me see what's in the kitchen. Told the agency to stock the place up."

West bet himself Lang would wait until Marzo was out of the room before growling at him, and as usual, his twin did not disappoint. His brother was nothing if not predictable and rigidly against making anyone feel uncomfortable.

"You can't keep giving her things, West." Lang ran his fingers through his shaggy hair. "We're trying *not* to spoil her."

"And that's your choice." His hands were shaking from the pain, but West kept them hidden. The weakness in his body alarmed him, and he didn't want Lang to find yet another reason to pick at him. "It's not like our mother or sisters are going to surprise her with gifts. And if there's one thing I've learned from Agnes, little girls adore just-because presents."

"You think of your sixty-three-year-old assistant as a little girl?"

"No," West sniffed. "She has granddaughters. Agnes is a fine well of knowledge in dealing with someone like Zig. I'd be a fool not to make use of the resources I have."

"You shouldn't—"

"That's where you're wrong, Lang," he cut his brother off. "I should. Because no one did for us. Other than what infrequent affection we received from our grandmother, we were raised on an emotional glacier. You raise her how you need to, but someone has to be... our grandmother for her. It might as well be me, because it sure as hell won't be *our* mother."

The resignation in Lang's eyes signaled West's victory, as did the soft frustrated sigh he let out in one long shuddering breath. Tossing his hands up, his twin finally conceded the only way Lang could give up on a fight... by changing the subject.

"I was going to take Zig out for some pizza. Deacon's working late on a bike, and I don't want to cook. Do you want to come with us?"

"No." Keeping a smug smile off his face was harder than West expected, and a bit of it must have crept out because Lang's deep blue eyes narrowed. "Thank you. While pizza sounds great, I can't stand to be in a car right now. I just want to take a hot shower and maybe nuke something the shopper left in the freezer. Marzo's heading back to the city tonight, and he'll want to make sure I'm set up here before he leaves. So, sadly, no pizza in a loud, noisy restaurant with plastic chairs and fuzzy-backed vinyl tablecloths for me."

"You, brother, are an asshole," Lang pronounced with a disdained sniff. "And a snob."

"Hah." West poked at Lang's side, hitting the ticklish spot they shared just beneath their third rib. "And here Zig thought you were going to leave before calling me an asshole. I should have bet her on it."

"You'd have lost." Lang stepped away from his brother, keeping himself out of West's reach. "Because one, she said I'd call you a dick. And two, if there's anything Deacon's taught me, it's never to wait to call someone an asshole to their face. You never know when you'll have a second chance. So you, brother mine, are a massive, raging asshole."

"Even if I spoil your damned kid?" West teased, waving Marzo over before the man headed back into the kitchen holding a much-needed bottle of spring water.

"Especially because you spoil my damned kid," Lang grumbled. "Because she loves you, West, and I swear to God, if you break her heart, I'm going to fucking kill you and feed your body to the seagulls."

"HEY, ANGEL," Joey called out from the front of the pizza parlor. "Wanna do me a favor?"

After loading the last couple of buckets of batter into the restaurant's fridge, Angel was tempted to crawl onto one of the frosted-over shelves and hibernate until his brother was done with high school. After dealing with the cops, Frank's assessment of his shot-up oven, a long protracted fight with his insurance company, and then a growly detective who'd practically accused him of murder, the last thing Angel wanted to do was a favor for Joey.

Since he was pretty much standing in the middle of the biggest favor one restaurant owner could give another, Angel knew he was on the hook for whatever it was Joey wanted him to do. The bakery would have been dead in the water without Joey letting his crew come in at three in the morning to complete their wholesale orders, and the damned man refused to let Angel pay for any of the utilities, preferring to take payment in the form of a wedding cake for his youngest daughter sometime in June. It was hardly a fair trade for Joey and his brother, the restaurant's owners, but they'd insisted, and Angel wasn't in any position to argue.

Now, with as tired as he was, Angel heartily wished he'd put up a bit more of a fight.

"Yeah, sure," Angel growled back, slinging a tub of guava-habanero batter up onto a rack. "Whatcha need?"

The short, balding Italian man padded into the hot kitchen, deftly avoiding the line cooks as they assembled pies and heated up pastas. Wiping his sauce-smeared hands on his apron, Joey gave Angel a crooked, apologetic smile.

"I hate to ask you, but I'm kind of in a bind here." Joey jerked his head toward the front of the house. "Place is packed, and I'm down a driver. Can you drop a pie off for me? I'll slide you a ten for it."

"No, it's fine." Angel was afraid to nod in case his head snapped off his neck and rolled across the floor. "In town or further out?"

"No, no. Close by. Down by the beach. Along the bluffs." Joey's face broke into a wide grin as he patted Angel on the shoulder. "Thanks, kid. I appreciate it."

Kid. Angel figured he outweighed the slender man by at least one hundred pounds and had almost a foot on him, but Joey'd known him since Angel'd been about the size of a straw and about that bright, so he'd earned the right to call him kid.

"I'll box up the pie and get you the address. There's a tip on the tab, so you'll be taking that with the ten I'm giving you." The man was shaking his head before Angel could protest. "Take it, son. You've got bills and a boy to raise. Pride doesn't put potatoes on the plate."

"That's the truth," Angel muttered. "Thanks. Just let me finish up here, and I'll run it over."

"Thanks." Joey grabbed a cardboard box, then slid a hot, steaming pizza into it. "And don't forget the money. My wife is going to have my balls if my daughter doesn't get that cake 'cause you're out of business."

"Hey," Angel snorted, closing the walk-in door behind him and shaking off the cold on his skin. "Not like I couldn't come here to bake it."

"That's not going to help me, kiddo," he replied, folding the lid down. "You go out of business and she can't get those chocolate cupcakes she likes so much, I might as well not come home."

THE SMELL of cheese, pepperoni, and tomato sauce ruthlessly teased Angel all the way to the slender side street leading off of the main road. His stomach growled, reminding him the last time it'd been fed was hours ago, and a few bites of an oat-bran muffin washed down with a mouthful of cold coffee wasn't going to sustain him for very long.

"Screw it. I don't care if it's cold. I'm rolling down the window," Angel muttered to himself. "This damned pizza is killing me."

Leaving the bakery's modified VW van for Justin to use for deliveries in the morning, Angel was left with his old Range Rover to load up the walk-in for his morning crew. It needed new… everything, but the beat-up old green beast was reliable and fairly easy to fix. Although, when his ass hit a hard edge in the seat frame when the Rover's tires rambled over a large bump in the road, Angel figured the damn thing could use a better suspension.

"Yeah, that's happening when pigs fly," he sighed. His cell phone chirped from its perch in the truck's console, so Angel hit the button on the one new thing he'd gotten for the Rover—a stereo he could talk through when he drove—and answered. "Hello, Pizza Shack Bakery."

"Dude, it's seven o'clock. Where the hell are you?" Roman's voice cracked, reaching for manhood, then crumbling into a squeak that was more aluminum foil on teeth than gravelly baritone. "Joey Junior just dropped off some pizza for us 'cause he was heading home sick and said you're out making deliveries for him."

"One delivery," Angel corrected. "And did you thank Joey Junior for the pizza?"

"Justin did. I was taking a shower. When are you coming home?" His younger brother sighed heavily. "Stupid Justin won't let me play any games until you're here, remember?"

"Yeah, because he doesn't want to watch you leave blood splatter all over the TV screen. Won't be more than forty-five minutes tops. Leave some pizza for me and you can stay up an hour later."

"Dude, it's Friday. I can already stay up an hour later." Roman snorted. "And we've got three pizzas."

"I meant an hour on top of what you've already got." Angel maneuvered around a bend slowly, not liking the blind curve. His lights caught on something alive in the brush, a pair of eyes reflecting yellow back at him for a brief moment, then disappearing into the windswept grasses. "But if you want to be a dick about it—"

"No! Shit, sorry. Okay? I just want to play tonight, and Justin's a weasel-dick."

"Justin's doing us a solid by hanging with you. Don't be an asshole about it." Angel sighed. "Get some food in you, watch some TV with him, and I'll be home as soon as I can. Did you do your homework?"

"Bro, it's Friday."

"Bro, get it done before I get home and you can play games all fricking weekend." He'd been told by the counselor to pick his battles. The idiot woman just hadn't told him which ones to pick, and it seemed like the one war he constantly waged with Roman was about schoolwork. "All of it, Rome. I've got the list from your teachers."

"Fine, but if I'm dead from boredom when you get home, it'll be your fault."

Roman hung up before saying good-bye and before Angel could hit the End Call button.

"It always is, dude." Exhaling hard, he muttered to himself, "It always fucking is."

A rise in the road hid the house from view, but Angel could see its lights shining over the hill's edge. A few hundred feet and the place's jutting angled white spires emerged from the darkness, its crystalline windows and crisp lines a vivid brightness against the star-filled sky. The home was a quartz fortress rising from the gold-and-gray coastline, a massive, profane slice of modern architecture set down in the middle of a homey California beach town.

"Damn, this place is nice," Angel whispered, carefully balancing the pizza as he got out of the Rover. "And Jesus, it's huge."

The door was pretty hard to miss. A tall, wide plank of heavy black wood, it dominated the house's front face, competing with the expanse of long windows above it. The doorbell took a while to find, and Angel was only certain the button he'd pressed was a chime because he could hear it echo through the house's massive interior. A few seconds later, the door opened, and he found himself staring straight into his past. Angel's breath stole from him, sucked out by the shock of the achingly pretty man with weary bright blue eyes and short, ruffled black hair standing awkwardly in front of him. He'd kissed that bruised mouth and suckled on those long, trim fingers. He knew the taste of the man in his throat, a sensual echo strong enough to flavor his memories even after all the years they'd racked up behind him.

"Well, fuck me," Angel heard himself say. "It's *you*."

Five

UP UNTIL the moment he'd opened his door and spied Angel Daniels standing on his front walk, West *knew* time was something a human could only experience in a line. There was no deviation from the thread spun out by the Fates, no knot in the cord large enough to fling a person back to an earlier point in their lives.

So West was alarmingly unprepared for the sudden jerk back in time and the sudden resurrection of a summer he'd buried behind him more than a decade ago.

The photo in the paper didn't do Angel justice. Shorter than West by an inch or two, Angel filled the doorway, the breadth of his shoulders and the power in his long jeans-clad legs leaving West breathless. He didn't want to be affected by the soft tousle of sun-kissed dark hair or the man's stark storm-gray eyes, but the sight of him—Angel—punched a hole through West, pushing aside every bit of control and detachment he'd built up since the day he'd told Angel not to call him anymore.

"Well, fuck me," Angel rasped, taking half a step forward. "It's *you*."

"Unfortunately, I never got around to fucking you," West muttered. "But that can certainly be remedied. There's plenty of places in this house I'd love to bend you over. Take your pick."

Angel snorted. "Think that's how it's going to go? Like we're just going to pick up where we left off? Like it was just last week?"

"You were the one who kept telling me to live in the moment, Daniels." West leaned forward, pushing himself into Angel's space. "Miss me?"

"Like a hole in my head." Angel's pulse leaped at his throat, the small tickle of movement under his skin drawing West's attention. "Miss me?"

"Never gave you a single thought," he lied smoothly. "Delivering pizzas now? Thought you owned a bakery."

"Did. Still do. Had a little problem with the place, though. Some asshole shot it up." Angel assessed him, his changeable gray eyes cool and steady. "You know anything about that?"

"Not a damned thing. If I had something to say to you, I'd say it to your face. I'm not the one who runs away from things."

"No, but you're the one who cuts things out of his life if shit gets too real."

West nearly winced at the jab—probably did if he was going to be totally honest—but honesty was lost in the swirl of emotions crashing over him. There was too much to feel, too much to sort through, and it was made all the harder as he stared straight at the source of all the heartache.

"That was shitty. I'm sorry." Angel's voice softened, but the anger West heard—the pain throbbing in his voice—was still there. "Fuck, you still piss me off."

"Yeah, you piss me off too," West agreed. "And damned if I know why."

"You're not pissed off at me." He squared his shoulders, leaning into West a bit. "You're mad at yourself, for being an asshole back then and for being a fucking dick now. You're just too fucking much of a coward to admit it."

Something broke in West, a small whimpering shred of longing with teeth sharp enough to fight its way out of the bramble inside of him. His tongue stuck to the roof of his mouth, but his brain took the thought it'd dragged up from the storm brewing in him and tossed it out, damning West and any consequences.

"We were good together," West muttered. "Damned *fucking* good."

"A long time ago, Harris, like you said." Angel's face, his open, erotically handsome face, was suddenly shuttered, eyes hooding as he spoke. "So, not one single thought? Nothing? But we were good together?"

"Maybe a couple of thoughts," he confessed softly. "Just not... *shit*, Angel. I missed you. Damn me to hell if I didn't... don't miss you."

"You haven't seen me in years, and you're trying to shut down my life because, what? You want to build condos?" Angel's gray eyes turned stormy, a hurricane of pewter and ebony caught in their depths. "You don't get to miss me, Harris. Not now. Now when—"

"Just... listen to me, okay?" West wanted to find the words to explain away the stupidity of his youth, of how he couldn't look at cotton candy without thinking of Angel or hear the crash of a wave against the shore and not think of his first kiss, a salty, sweet explosion of sensations when their lips finally touched.

Numbed by the pain pills and his heart bleeding out from regret, anger, and pain, West did the stupidest thing he'd done in his entire life since he'd slid down the banister of his childhood home and launched himself through the massive windowpane at the end of the stairwell. Instead of slamming the door in Angel's face, he stepped in closer, ignoring the sharp sting of pain twisting through his ankle and knees. The pizza fell, and while his stomach grumbled loudly at its loss, his mouth ached to be filled with sweeter, lovelier things.

Angel Daniels.

"The motel… that's just business. I didn't mean for it to get as ugly as it has."

"I live in that business. Not once did you come to me to talk. You knew I was there, but you let that asshole Washington turn the screws," Angel accused.

"Look, we can talk about all of that. I just never… crap. I just want… for us to be okay," West whispered. He was flayed open, his mind reeling with the impact of Angel standing in front of him. He *missed* the man. As stupid as it sounded, as it was, he'd missed the soul he once shared everything with. "I don't know how else to say it."

"You don't get to decide we're okay, Harris. You don't have that right," Angel muttered into West's ear. He leaned in close, close enough for West to smell his skin, an odd mélange of sugar, spices, and a hint of masculine sweat. "Give me one fucking good reason I shouldn't make you eat your own teeth."

"Because my parents paid a hell of a lot of money for these teeth," he replied hoarsely. "And if I remember correctly, you were always so *very* practical. Even as you were getting into that van and waving good-bye, you made damned sure you knew how to get hold of me. Or at least that's what it seemed like at the time."

"That what you think? I was going to use you?" Angel rubbed his jaw against West's cheek, his faint stubble leaving behind a raking burn. "Like I used you all summer? Like all of the times I asked you for what? Oh, wait, I didn't ask you for jack shit, Harris. Not then. Not now."

West refused to step back, knowing he needed something from the man he'd left behind. He just didn't know what.

No, he reminded himself. He knew exactly what he wanted from Angel Daniels, what he'd wanted from Angel all along, and with the numbness creeping through his mind and the pills rattling around in his empty stomach, West discovered he no longer cared what the hell happened that night so long as he got a taste of Angel.

One single taste and he'd be able to walk away.

Like he'd done before.

But this time it wouldn't hurt, West promised himself. This time it wouldn't be his heart left in a smear of ashes across his soul. This time it would take away the anger he had raging inside of him and maybe soothe the sharp, hard prickle of hurt Angel seemed to carry in his heart.

"I wasn't expecting you, Angel. And I sure as hell wasn't expecting you to… hit me as hard as you do," West rumbled back. He wanted Angel. There was no mistaking the hardness of his cock or the ache in his heart. The years were melting away, leaving behind the rocks they'd probably flung at one another in the time they'd spent apart, but damn him if Angel didn't still make West want more than a quick fuck and a good-bye. "You always told me to grab what I wanted and hold on. Right now, *this* is what I want."

His mouth found Angel's, and there was a brief hiccup of time when West was *afraid*. Scared he'd gone too far or maybe not far enough when he should have. Either way, his fear ran slick, bitter spit over his teeth, and his throat closed up, leaving him speechless. His world hung on a fraying thread, a risk West knew better than to take but a cliff he was going to jump off anyway.

And damn the rocks below.

"Fucking hell," Angel muttered. "*Jesus Christ*, you make me nuts."

A touch of Angel's tongue on his lips and West knew he was destined for a painful crash, but he'd be damned if he didn't enjoy the fall. Because God, the man tasted like someone'd poured Heaven and all the stars into West's mouth, and he couldn't drink it all in fast enough.

Angel's hands were rough, long fingers harsh with calluses and scrapes, and his touch burned serpentine trails of desire along West's skin. His mouth was hard, taking from West more than he was giving, and West's lungs ached, trapped between wanting more of the man pushing him back into the house and inhaling a sweet sip of the evening air so he could dive back down into Angel's mouth again. Their tongues fought, teeth striking once, then twice before they found an angle both of them liked. West dove in again, catching a brief suck of wind. Then he was tasting the masculine sweetness of the man he'd never wanted to toss aside.

He'd had no choice, some part of his brain reminded him. Their lives were too different, and West's father—his goddamned, controlling father—promised to break Angel in every way possible if he didn't walk away from the wild, gray-eyed almost-lover he'd fallen for in those brief summer months.

Angel came up for air first, gasping as if West took everything from him, leaving him parched and sucked dry. His hands were still clenched around West, his fingers shoved down past West's belt, digging into his tender flesh.

West's cock *hurt*. Not in the way his spine ached or his ribs throbbed from being thrown about the car but in a delicious, hot, needy tightening of skin and nerves he'd not felt in forever. West couldn't get his hands on enough of Angel's skin. He'd tangled his fingers into the man's T-shirt—some banged-up, faded black piece with a grinning kirin on it and a name of a band he'd never heard of—but it wasn't enough to drag Angel in tight. He needed more of… everything… kisses, tongue, and sweat. There was something raw growing between them, a desperate hunger brought up by the slightest touch of Angel's lips to his.

"We can't do this. I *can't*. This is stupid. Too fast. Too *stupid*," Angel growled into West's mouth. "God, I fucking hate you right now for making me want you."

"Yeah, I'd hate me too," West confessed around Angel's tongue. "But I wasn't the one who dropped the pizza."

"I'm tired, and you're… crazy," he muttered.

"Stoned really. Pain pills." West smiled faintly. "We're both emotionally and physically compromised."

"I should walk away."

"I should let you go."

Angel sighed. "I don't see either of that happening. Do you?"

"No, I don't," West agreed. "But damn, it's good to see you, Angel."

"It's been years—"

"Feels like yesterday, love."

The world… shifted. That was the only word West could come up with for the odd change in dynamics he felt when Angel pushed him into the foyer wall. His shoulder blades hit the hard plaster, rattling some faux-metal thing with tentacles the designer hung next to the door and called it art. West used it to hang his jacket on, but oddly enough, it wasn't attached firmly enough to hold any significant weight.

West found that out when he grabbed at it—grabbing at *anything*, really—so he could anchor himself as Angel tore him apart with his mouth and fingers.

God, those fingers. That tongue. Those lips. Angel was everywhere on him and still not where West needed him to be. With his scalp aching from Angel clenching his hair, West fought back a mewling gasp when Angel's teeth raked a welting score down his throat.

The tentacles shattered on the foyer's tiled floor, dragged off its perch by West's weight. He couldn't breathe, and his skin tightened over his muscles, reminding him in a brief slap of pain of what he'd lived through yesterday. But the bitter sweetness of Angel's mouth was too damned… good to push away.

Even if he was the one being held against the wall and kissed senseless.

A moment later, the simmer turned to ice, and West was free of the hot, hard length of Angel's body. He hung there, unbalanced and adrift for a moment as he realized the man'd let him go—fucking let him go—in the middle of *everything* they'd been doing to one another. Angel's shirt was torn open, an uneven rent through the collar and down the front, exposing a tanned stretch of skin and hard muscles.

The air was cold on West's belly, the buttons from his shirt popped off and scattered over the floor. He'd somehow worked the tang from Angel's belt loose and undid the top button of the man's jeans, pulling them open enough to stroke at the soft, silken dark hair below Angel's belly button.

Angel's hands were in his own mink-and-gold mottled mane, his fingers pulling the strands away from his sharp, sculpted features. The mouth West'd savaged moments ago was swollen, a blush of pink flesh marbled with teeth marks and wet from West's tongue.

Then it all fell apart.

The pills West'd taken weren't strong enough to withstand the rush of blood pounding through his veins, or perhaps Angel's heady taste drowned out any narcotics, because West took one step toward the muscular, rough man pacing off his foyer and his knees buckled under him, pitching him onto the floor.

Angel caught him—a cradle of firm flesh, regrets, and an anguished need so sharp it cut West open from the inside out.

He *hurt*. He hurt inside his soul, places he thought he'd deadened so long ago they might as well have belonged to someone else, but the flare of pain in his heart, in his chest, down to his very soul blazed bright enough West knew he'd only been blind to the misery he'd buried inside of him.

"Angel, I—" West grabbed at the man's shoulders, needing to lever his hips up before his sprained joints splintered apart. The pain in his limbs hit West hard, stretching out until his gums were tight on his teeth. "Shit, my ankle—"

"I've got you," Angel muttered in his rough burned-caramel voice. "Just hold—"

West never found out what he was supposed to hold onto. As Angel hooked his arm around West's back, a gunshot broke through the heated silence they'd built up. The bullet hit the light fixture hanging down from the foyer's tall ceiling, shattering it into a million pieces and raining shards of glass down upon them. The light's heavy black frame plummeted, and West tried to throw his arm up to protect them, but he was too late. It glanced off his temple, leaving behind a spark of pain.

Already rattled, his skull creaked, blossoming into red swirls and staccato jabs. His eyes were working furiously, blinking to clear away the swelling clouds. Then the world tilted and Angel's face shifted, jagging to the right, then the left.

West swallowed hard, tasting blood again, a too familiar flavor on his tongue considering the past couple of days. Then he mumbled at the man holding him up in the remains of his foyer, "This is *not* how I wanted us to meet again."

Then all West heard was Angel's fading shouts for him to hang on while he succumbed to a thick, rising darkness.

"SO YOU didn't see anyone outside? No idea of who shot at the house?" Montague eyed Angel with equal parts suspicion and incredulous doubt. "Nothing? Gender? Height?"

"It was dark outside," he confessed. Running his hands through his hair, Angel was quickly made aware of his torn shirt by the gust of cold wind hitting his bared nipple. Bringing his arms down, he then crossed them over his chest. "Look, I wasn't… outside isn't where I was looking."

The house was overwhelming, rising up around him, and Angel felt more than a chill when the cops arrived with an ambulance in tow.

West remained passed out right up until the moment the blond medical technician put her hands on him. Then he woke up swinging. It was definitely not a good sign for Angel, who'd been trying to convince the cops he and West weren't arguing when the gunshot rang out, and Montague didn't seem to be buying what Angel was selling him.

"You've got to admit, it seems odd. From what I see, it looks like you've been tangling with each other, and then there's bullets flying around, but you see no one?" The detective's eyebrows seemed permanently raised onto his forehead, where they'd gone nearly as soon as he'd heard Angel's take on what happened. "And didn't you just tell me you and Harris hadn't seen one other in years, but I'm supposed to believe you found enough common ground to suddenly tear your clothes off in the middle of his foyer?"

"Would I have dropped a pizza from Joey's place on the floor for anything other than a hot piece of ass?" Angel growled back. "Look, I didn't say it made sense. It *doesn't* make any fucking sense. We sure as hell didn't leave things on a good note between us, and tonight… fuck, tonight just kind of happened. Maybe because I'm as tired as shit and my brain just said why the hell not? He's on pain pills, so he's not thinking straight either. It was stupid and… just… stupid, but I didn't plan on it. And I sure as hell wasn't paying attention to anyone outside who got it into his fool head to shoot out the light."

"Are you on something, Mr. Daniels? Is there something you're not telling me?" Montague looked up from his notepad, his dark eyes deadly serious as they fixed on Angel's face. "Did you come here to hurt Mr. Harris? Maybe in retaliation for what happened at the bakery the other night?"

"I'm not on something." It was never a good thing when the cops suddenly called you mister. That step back from friendly was a long one, distancing the police officer from their quarry. "Look, if I shot the light out, where's the gun?"

"You're a strong guy, Mr. Daniels, and that's a whole hell of a lot of brush out there," the detective replied. "You'd have had more than enough time to chuck it up the hillside or hell, even over the cliff. Might have even been able to hit the ocean if your aim was good enough. Then there's that matter of that gun we found. The one registered in your name."

"I don't own a gun," Angel ground out between his teeth. "I've got my kid brother living with me. I'm not having a gun anywhere he can get his hands on it. And your guys just scraped some of my skin off at the bakery and here. That'll tell you I didn't shoot anyone. Hell, West is right *fricking* there. Ask him."

From the irritated grumbles coming from the living area, West wasn't very keen on the emergency medical staff poking at him. Angel chanced a look over his shoulder, and their eyes met, a flash of tangled somethings wrapping around Angel's gut at the blood splatter on West's cheek. The EMT took West's distraction for acquiescence, and she daubed something wet across his wounds, drawing a long hiss out of West's slightly bruised lips. Turning back to the detective, Angel tugged at his shirt and said, "Look, if you're going to keep me much longer, I've got to call home. I've got a friend sitting up with my brother. I don't want them to worry."

"Sure, go ahead. Give me a few minutes with Harris. Then I want to touch base with you again before I release you." Montague tucked his pen into his jacket pocket. "Don't go anywhere, Daniels. You're not cleared to leave."

"Yeah, okay, like I've never heard that before."

Angel dug his phone out, then wandered off to find someplace quiet to talk. The cop's eyes were hard, glittering and sharp when he passed the small clusters of uniforms in the front of the house. Finding the kitchen empty, Angel ducked into the cool, shadowy room and dialed his brother's phone.

"Where *are* you?" Roman's voice was tight with worry. "You said you'd be home by now."

Angel intimately knew the particular panic drowning Roman at that point. He'd swallowed more than enough of that metallic-edged fear in his life, so much so he'd grown up thinking everything in the world tasted slightly of rancid blood and oily threads. They'd both been tossed away too many times before. Their father conveniently forgetting he had a son whenever the mood struck or when money got too tight to stretch to cover two mouths. He couldn't count how many streets he'd roamed, looking for someplace warm to sleep or at least dry. Dry went a hell of a long way, and food was something he could easily live without. It'd been a blessing to finally stop moving. To have a bed in a room with solid walls.

He still wasn't quite used to waking up in the same place after nearly eight years, so he didn't have much faith Roman was settled either. And in the middle of the night, in the dark while his younger brother battled nightmares with little whimpers and tangled thrashings under his covers,

Angel was beginning to wonder if either one of them ever would truly believe they were home.

"I'm here, Rome. Some shit went down at this guy's place, so now I have to wait the cops out." Angel spoke calmly, slowly, more for his brother's sake than anything else. Cops was a dirty word for them, but honesty went a long way with Roman. Knowing the police were keeping Angel from coming home would shift his focus for a second, long enough for him to shake off any paralyzing fears. "They said I can leave soon. I had to talk to them about some idiot shooting a gun off by the house, but I'm okay. Everyone's fine. Well, except the guy's pizza."

"Justin was about to call you, but I wanted to do it. Then you called instead," Roman muttered.

Then Angel heard words he never ever thought he would hear come out of Rome's mouth.

"I was scared you weren't coming home. I thought you were going to be like Dad and… just leave me."

It was stupid to cry, even stupider to cry while standing in an expensive house owned by a guy who'd broken his heart, but Angel felt his tears burn across his eyes, then fall, hitting his cheeks and the counter he'd leaned against.

"I will *never* leave you, kid," Angel swore, pushing as much of his love for his brother into his voice as he could, anything to make Roman believe him. "No matter where you are, that's my home, okay? No one's taking you from me. No matter what. I will *always* come home to you. Understand me?"

The line was silent, too silent and too long, but finally Angel heard Rome sniff. "Okay."

"Good. I'm going to see if the cops will let me go, and you tell Justin I said you can hook up a game." He snorted as Roman began to scream for Justin as if he hadn't just been sniffling into the phone. "I'll be there to put you to bed, dude. Don't give Justin a hard time. Got it?"

He suffered a few more seconds of Rome's shouting, then took a few minutes with Justin, assuring the redhead he was okay and would be back to the motel in a bit. After hanging up the phone, Angel hitched himself and leaned back against the upper cabinets, taking in the cool quiet.

"The detective said you can go, but he wants to talk to you tomorrow. I told him you had nothing to do with this… or the car crash in San Francisco, but I don't think he was convinced. I guess it's hard to take a man who's been knocked out by his own lamp very seriously."

West's voice startled him, and Angel banged his head on the slick wood behind him. West hobbled in and stood at the counter near Angel's knee.

"You okay?"

"From you scaring the shit out of me? Or hitting my head?" He rubbed at the spot.

"Either." West shrugged. "Both. But mostly about... what happened out there."

"I don't know who shot your place up, West," Angel sighed. The day was not only catching up with him, it was wringing him dry and making him its bitch. "I just... don't fucking know."

"I'm not talking about that, Angel." He moved in closer, his hands parting Angel's knees with a gentle push. Sliding in between the V he made, West leaned in, his palms flat and hard on Angel's thighs. "I'm talking about what happened before some asshole used my front hall light for target practice. I'm talking about us."

Six

"WEST...." ANGEL'S habit of biting the tip of his tongue as it peeked from his slightly parted lips hadn't changed. "I can't... *fuck*. I can't stay."

His gorgeous face was a mural of emotion, broad strokes of bold, colorful expressions. If West's heart hadn't been lodged sideways in his throat, he could have watched Angel chew around his words all day. As it was, the beleaguered organ stammered and shook as West schooled his face into a well-worn cold mask.

"I understand." If there was one trick he'd learned from his glacial father, it was a rigid control over his voice. Brittle anger was a good choice for that moment, a wall of something hard and glittering to shove aside the knife plunged through his chest. "Of course, you can't stay."

"You don't understand... I've got...." Angel raked his fingers through his already wild hair, pulling the long strands from his face. The shadows under his eyes were wells of bruised fatigue and stress. "I've got to get home to Roman."

"Roman. I didn't know you were seeing anyone." The burn of Angel's hot kiss lingered on West's skin and throat. His head throbbed, and there were still stars on the edges of his vision, but nothing hurt more than hearing another man's name coming from Angel's lips. He clearly loved *Roman*. Angel could never mask his feelings. They ran through his voice, brightening away a bit of the bruises in his eyes.

That *light* in Angel's voice... pissed West off.

"You're seeing someone and you... come at me like that?" The pain in his chest turned into a firestorm, charring his throat. "Guess you've changed more than I'd—"

"Roman's my kid brother. Dad dumped him on me and split," Angel cut him off. "You know how that is. Except this time, Dad's not coming back. Sometimes things get too tight around him. Last I talked to him he was doing okay, but I promised I'd be there soon."

Angel slid off the counter, his body a long hot slide against West's chest and legs. He dominated the space, pushing West back with the sheer power of his body and intense stare. The shadows did interesting things to Angel's features, casting him in a bronze light and gilding his cheekbones. His fingers trembled when they skimmed over West's jaw. Then Angel brushed over West's lower lip, a delicate feathering whisper of flesh and nails.

"If I could, I'd stay, because we've got a lot to talk about. Hell, I'm not even sure what happened back there by the door, and I'm not saying it was a mistake, but I don't know if it ever should have happened. I just don't know," Angel murmured, his breath sweet on West's face. "But Rome's a kid waiting for his big brother to come home. I'm all he's got, and I've got to be there when he reaches out. I'm sorry. I am."

"Like your father wasn't there for you when you needed him?" His words weren't meant to be a jab, but even to West, it sounded like he'd sharpened them on a bitter whetstone and aimed for Angel's jugular. "That… wasn't… I'm sorry. How old is he?"

"Eleven going on… six, I think. Sometimes sixty." Angel's chuckle lightened the sour between them, but the edge of West's words remained. His hand dropped, leaving a trail of fading warmth along West's mouth. "I'm sorry. I am. Because I'd like to hang around and deal with this… with us but—"

Most fires were doused by water, plumes of steam and hot currents. In this case, the simmer between West and Angel mewled and died with an exasperated gasp, with a flick of a light switch and a worried man wearing West's face.

The kitchen's recessed lighting flared to life, bright enough to leave spangles across West's sight and, if he wasn't mistaken, certainly more than adequate to perform emergency brain surgery if anyone needed it. Blinking away the tears from the sudden drench of white, West stumbled back, pulling away from Angel's welcome heat and into the evening chill pouring in from his still open front door.

"West, are you okay?" Lang grabbed at him. He sounded concerned, a flick of panic perhaps hovering at the upper reaches of his tone, but West couldn't be sure. He couldn't remember the last time anyone other than Marzo sounded concerned about him, and *that* was mostly job security. "The cops called me. Said you were shot."

"It was probably just some idiot in his backyard and didn't realize the house was here. I'm fine, other than the aches and pains I'd already had, just a small lump on my forehead. I might have twisted my knee.

It hurts a little bit." Pushing his brother off, West shook his head, then winced at the clanging of bells in his brain. The nausea was back, digging into his throat and reminding him he'd taken a beating the day before. "That metal monstrosity in the foyer hit me on its way down. I'm going to instruct my designer to stop using such heavy pieces. I might as well be asking to be murdered by my own house."

"I'll see you around, Harris." Slipping past Lang, Angel neatly made it to the kitchen doorway before West could tell Lang to get lost. "Sorry about the pizza. I can ask Joey's crew to send out another one."

"Angel, wait!" West turned and nearly lost his balance, caught on his brother's foot. "Lang, get out of the—"

"Why is Angel here? And what pizza?"

Like their birth, Lang was wrapped around him, making it difficult to move. He was also a lot stronger than West remembered, his upper arm bulging under his sleeve when he grabbed at West to stop him from following Angel. "Crap, Joey must have asked—"

"Lang, I swear to God, if you don't let me go...." He yanked himself free, his knee twisting under him as he hurried out of the kitchen. "Daniels! Damn it.... *Angel!*"

It was already too late. A deep-growling engine started up outside, and Montague was shouting at someone to let Angel leave. West made it to the edge of the foyer, and then the room began to swim. His knees buckled, and West tried to grab at the wall to steady himself before he toppled forward.

This time Angel wasn't there to catch him, and West hit the floor, twisting so he struck the hard surface with his shoulder. He made a loud thump and rattled every single inch of his already banged-up body when he landed. Someone nearby shouted something, probably one of the cops, but West was more concerned about not hitting his head even as fiery tendrils of snaking pain grabbed at his joints and squeezed down tight on his spine. There were black leather shoes stomping around near his head, and West turned over onto his back and gently lowered his head to the floor.

It still hurt. Resting there and breathing hurt. Much like the empty space Angel'd dug up out of him throbbed, and he felt his soul keen at the gaping void stretching through it.

"God... damn... it," West ground out, ignoring the buzz of voices flittering around him. "Fucking goddamn it all."

Lying in the ruins of his foyer, West stared up at the ceiling and began wondering about which moment his life'd gone from manageable to pure chaos when a sweet-faced imp of a girl with tears in her soft brown eyes popped her head in front of his face and stared worriedly down at him.

"Ah, that must have been it. Probably the second I met you, hellspawn," West murmured softly as he reached up to hug Zig against him. "You bring the chaos, little girl, and it's okay."

"I thought you were *dead*." She tried to keep her bottom lip steady, refusing to be drawn. "You are such a fucking *dick*."

"There's going to be a hell of a lot of dog shit in your future if your prettier dad hears you, kiddo, and at least I'm not a dead dick," he pointed out, tugging at her again. "Come here. It's going to be all right. I'm okay, brat. Totally okay."

"You only think he's pretty because he looks like you," she sniffed. "*Fucker*. Don't tell him I swore."

She flopped, boneless, across his chest, pushing all the air out of his lungs, and her arms came up to choke his neck, ensuring him a long, agonizing suffocation in his near future if he didn't dislodge her. He heard a tight sob. Then his neck was dampened by a brush of tears and blubbering. Stroking her curly hair, he sighed when Lang crouched down next to him.

"Zig, I'm fine, and I declare you're exempt from punishment because things said in battle and stress shouldn't count against us," West reassured her. "But once I get up to my feet, I can't say your Daddy's going to be okay because I am going to kill him for sticking his nose into my business."

"I'd say it's the last time I ever worry about you, but we'd both know that's a lie," Lang sniped back. The hardness and worry in his face softened, and he reached for Zig, stopping only when West shook his head. "Come on. You two need to get up off the floor. You about gave Montague a heart attack there. I think he thought someone was shooting the place up again. Where the hell is Marzo?"

"Marzo headed back to the city tonight. He'll be back in the morning. *And* Montague can go fuck himself, brother. Right now, the terror princess and I are going to have a damned good cry in the foyer, and then…." West tightened his hold on Zig as she hiccupped with another bout of tears. "Someone is going to get me another handful of painkillers and another pizza, because right now, I'm not quite sure which I need more."

"ABOUT TIME you got home." Justin opened the door just as Angel fit his key into the battered knob's lock. Screams were coming from the mini-apartment mingled with the sounds of gunfire and tires squealing, making it hard to hear Justin, but Angel caught enough of it. Shrugging, his friend said, "He's fucking losing his mind."

"Shit." Angel pushed past the redhead, then stopped short when he saw Roman sitting cross-legged in the middle of the room, his elbow working hard to jostle Violet, the older woman living in a room down the walk, as they did battle on the screen.

His brother was still in the clothes he'd worn that day, a sure sign he hadn't taken a bath, and a couple of open pizza boxes were on the credenza, their lids tossed back and their contents sucked down with only a few smears of oil as evidence of food. Violet barely glanced over her shoulder long enough to give Angel a nod hello, but it was enough of a distraction for Roman to gain an edge. Dragging her attention back to the screen, she began to swear in Hmong.

Since Violet wasn't quite five feet tall, ancient, and weighed about eighty pounds only after eating five large bowls of pho, Angel wasn't too worried about Violet taking his baby brother down.

Roman, however, had a whole bunch of shit to be concerned about because Violet was wiping the floor with him.

"I'll give you another ten minutes. Then wrap it up, Rome." His reflection dominated the screen, and Roman yelped when Angel loomed over him. "You two find a save point and shut it down."

"Just go to bed," Violet shouted over an explosion. "It'll be fine. We'll mute!"

"We're *in* his bedroom," Roman grumbled, but he reached for the remote, then turned the volume down. "Hold on. Let me find a spot so we can regen there."

Roman's acquiescence was shocking, but Angel wasn't above embracing small miracles. Not when his pillows and sheets were already stacked up at the far end of the foldout sofa, a tantalizing promise of a few hours of sleep dangled in front of him, but the day's grime clung to every pore of Angel's body, and he wanted it off. Still, after driving home in a panic at being late, he'd have expected a bit more than a taciturn grunt or two from his younger brother.

"Oh yeah, he's really worried about me," Angel grumbled to Justin as he toed his sneakers off. "Look at the angst all over his face."

"Hey, he was stressing a bit before I called Violet to come over." Justin leaned against the wall. He looked as tired as Angel felt, his mouth tightening at the corners. "Took a bit to get his meds in him. He wasn't going to take them. Then the pizza showed up, and I told him he couldn't have any until a pill went down first. Pepperoni is apparently a great motivator."

"Yeah, food rules. Speaking of pizza, any left?" Angel pulled out one of the wooden chairs from the small dining room set near the room's large window, then sat down with a heavy sigh. "Although I don't know if I'm that hungry."

"At least get something in you. There's garlic bread too, but I kept that and a small mushroom and olive from the locusts over there." Justin straddled the other chair, resting his arms on its back. "You doing okay? What took you so long to get home?"

"West Harris." There was a stack of envelopes on the table, and Angel sifted through them quickly, looking for any bills. "I kind of... kissed him. Sort of."

Justin's hand slapped the bills down onto the table, trapping Angel's fingers. Hissing, Justin leaned in. "Shut up! You kissed Voldemort?"

"Don't call him that. And yes, sort of. Mostly." His stomach and brain definitely wanted nothing to do with the pizza in the fridge and everything to do with lying down. Scrubbing his face with his hands only left Angel with a queasy roil in his stomach at the garlic-tomato odor on his palms. Leaning his head on the back of the chair, Angel slumped down, stretching the muscles in his lower back. "It was stupid. I just... someone just shot his house up, and he just seemed... scared."

"He's trying to kick you out of your home, steal your business out from under you, and you go and feel sorry for the asshole?" His friend snorted. "Did you hit your fricking head?"

"Not much of a home," Angel said, looking over his shoulder at his brother. "Maybe I should sell the damned bakery—"

"You told me to slap you if you said that," Justin retorted. "Not that I'm going to because you could crush my skull in with your bare hands, but I'd like to remind you how fucking hard you worked to get that bakery going. And sure, this place isn't a mansion, but it's... cozy."

"I sleep on a fold-out couch in a motel built only a little bit after the Flintstones came out. Cozy it ain't." The game was still loud, a barrage of booms and shouts, but it masked their conversation from Roman's often prying ears. "I just wonder if I'm doing right by him."

"You're the only one who ever has, Ange. Probably the only one who's ever going to," Justin replied, bending forward across the table. "Talk to me about you kissing the Snow Miser."

"How many nicknames you've got for him?"

"Man, too many to count, and most of them start with fuck or end with ass." Justin poked at Angel's shoulder. "Where is he? Why is he here? Did he come find you to harass you? 'Cause if he did, that asshole needs to die."

Angel gave a quick rundown of his night, from Joey asking him to deliver a pizza to the tangle he and West got into, then the bullet going through West's open front door. Laying it all out, it seemed… ridiculous. He hadn't seen or heard from West Harris in years, but he'd blinked and the burned-up seconds between them faded away, leaving him wanting West's hands and mouth on him, just like that summer they'd spent together.

"He just looked… scared and angry, Just. Really fucking scared, and I felt like shit for hating him." Angel stared out the window at the shack a few hundred yards away. "I guess I wanted to kiss and make it better."

"You don't kiss a gator on the nose, Angel. It's a good way to lose your lips… and your head." Justin sighed. "God, why the hell aren't we attracted to each other? It'd made life a fuck of a lot simpler."

"We don't do simple, dude. Just not our style." He shrugged. "So there you go. I danced with the devil, then told him to call me. Now I'm going to get them to turn off the game and go grab a shower. Thanks for staying with him, Just. I owe you big time."

"Hey, free pizza and a complaining kid, what's not to love?" The redhead shooed Angel toward the bathroom. "Go get defunked. Use up all the hot water and relax. I'll stay and make sure they shut this thing off in a few minutes. Then I'll kick myself and Violet out so you can get some sleep."

"Yeah, because we're doing this all over again in what?" Angel glanced at the clock. "Six hours? Good times. Okay, five minutes, Rome! Then it's say good-bye to the crazy people and lights out for you."

ANGEL LEFT the black-out curtains open, using the lights from the parking lot and nearby houses to illuminate their rooms. The sounds of Roman loudly brushing his teeth drowned out most of the soft murmur coming from the streets, with a backbeat of a barking dog somewhere off in the distance. It was late, and tomorrow wasn't looking any shorter, but Angel was reluctant to hurry Rome off so he could crash.

"Perfect damned time of the day," Angel sighed, picking up the cup of coffee he'd made himself to relax and settled into the couch. "Absolutely damned perfect."

As a whole, the apartment wasn't much. Legally, it probably couldn't even be called an apartment, but they'd done what they could with it. An end unit situated as close to the driveway as possible, the manager's apartment was a cubbyhole barely large enough for two roaches to dance a tango, but it'd been home since Angel signed the purchase contract on the Pizza Shack's ramshackle building. He'd torn out the industrial carpet, sealing off the concrete below, and thick carpet remnants took care of most of the cold. In the summer, they were easy to roll up and store in the motel's stock rooms, so the apartment stayed cool from the chilly slab.

The kitchenette boasted two burners, a garbage disposal, and oddly enough a fully functioning dishwasher but no working oven when he'd moved in. First thing Angel did before moving in was rip out the dishwasher, replacing it with a stove-oven combination big enough to cook a twenty-pound turkey. At the time, he thought he'd use the oven in case something blew at the bakery. Now it did double time during the holidays and cookie duty on the weekends Angel could spare time to mix together a batter.

When Roman appeared on his doorstep, Angel'd moved out of the small bedroom to crash on the sleeper sofa. The first few weeks were a grueling slog of nightmares, fights, and tantrums, but they'd weathered the storm. Or at least it calmed down enough for Roman to trust him enough to talk about the things bubbling up in him. It was all Angel could hope for. In the end, he'd call it a win if Roman had enough tools to cope with the crap living inside his brain and to want to do something more than con people out of their money.

It was more than what their father'd done with his life… more than what he'd given them both… and Angel could only hope it was enough.

"I'm done!" Roman never did anything by halves, and coming out of the bathroom was no exception. "Stick a fork in me, bro!"

His brother shouted when he spoke, stomped when he walked, and sang when he yelled. A bundle of noise, contrariness, and stubborn tempers, his brother shoved his way through life, used to taking what was in front of him whether he needed it or not. People were disposable, and money was king with nothing else in between mattering.

It was the hardest habit to break, Angel discovered, learning how to give a shit about anyone else besides yourself. He hadn't known that when his father dumped him in Half Moon Bay, but he'd sure as hell learned it before the summer was out. That summer changed *everything* for him. He'd hated every single damned second of his life right up until the moment he'd met West Harris and learned he was worth more than being bait for a con and a decoy for shaking someone down.

No matter what West did from that moment on, he'd given Angel something he hadn't had before—a scrap of self-esteem—and Angel'd been fighting to hold on to that scrap since the day he'd first grabbed a hold of it and it took him for a ride.

"No regrets, Harris." Angel raised his coffee cup in a mock salute toward the shore. "Even if you fucked things up afterwards."

"Who you talking to?" Rather than sit down next to Angel, Roman launched himself at the couch, and Angel held his cup up to avoid getting splashed with hot coffee. "Oh crap, sorry. I didn't see the cup."

"Yeah, it's a ninja cup." Putting the mug on the low table next to the couch was harder than usual with Rome's feet in the way, but Angel managed. His back popped when he overstretched, and for a brief moment there were stars in his eyes and his collarbone went numb. "Okay. Back just crackled. Not sure if it's a good thing or a bad thing, so I guess you'll have to stay up for a few minutes to make sure I'm okay."

"I can do that." Roman flipped over, gouging his bony hip into Angel's leg. "Oh, and I got a note from the principal for you."

Eyeing his brother, he asked, "Is this a bad note or a good note?"

"He says I can't sell candy anymore out of my locker. 'Cause he's a dick." Squinting, Roman studied Angel's face.

There were too many questions flying around in Angel's head, so he plucked out the first one that came to rest. "*Why* are you selling candy out of your locker?"

"Because they took the candy out of the vending machines this year. There's only rice cakes, nuts, dried fruit, and some other crap," Roman explained with a huff. "People want their stuff, Angel. So I brought some things in."

"Where'd you get the money?" His mind was in full scramble. Roman's allowance sure as hell didn't cover a candy operation, and besides, his brother didn't come with impulse control installed. If he had a quarter, he'd spend a dollar. "Okay, kiddo, cough it all up. What the hell have you been doing?"

"I used to sell some of the day-olds for a buck, but they're hard to carry around—"

"Wait, so you took cupcakes from the bakery?"

"No, just muffins." Roman shook his head, his face mottled with disgust. "Don't be stupid. The cupcakes have frosting on them. That'll get all over the place."

"Jesus, okay. You know we're supposed to sell that stuff. It's kind of what a bakery does." Angel grabbed a hold of his brain and steeled himself for the rest of Rome's story.

"I only took the ones you guys were going to give away. Nothing fresh." He snorted at Angel's muffled grumble. "It was only like fifteen or so. Maybe. Total. You were giving it away anyway."

"To charity! Not so you could fund some massive underground snack ring." The coffee now seemed tame, and Angel tried to remember if he had any whiskey left from the bottle he'd bought for Christmas. "Fuck, you bet your ass the principal is going to shut you down—"

"Yeah, Principal Carpenter didn't know about the muffins. It was the *candy*."

"How'd you get candy?"

"From selling the muffins. Sheesh, I thought you were supposed to be smart." Roman rolled his eyes. "So now he doesn't want me selling candy on school property. He sent a note to tell you I can't do that anymore because they want everything to be healthy and crap."

"Jesus, Rome, what the hell were you thinking?" It was definitely going to be a shot of booze night, even if he had to go borrow some ouzo from Violet. "You can't just *sell* candy at school. It's got to be illegal or something. And why the hell didn't you tell me this on the phone?"

"Justin said to wait until you were home. Because he didn't think it was a big deal." His brother shrugged off Angel's concerned hiss. "It's not a big deal. I'll just do it on the bus and hand stuff out later. No biggie."

"Rome, you can't… just stop selling candy, okay? Or chips. Or anything." Angel poked at his brother's stomach. "Just stop."

"Then how am I going to make some cash?" He cocked his head, eyes wide and serious. "Because you don't got any. Everything goes back into the bakery and shit."

"Don't say shit," Angel corrected automatically. "No more candy. Got it?"

He didn't hear a response from his brother, and short of forcing Roman to answer him, Angel knew it was a lost cause. Taking a deep breath, he tried again.

"You don't need to make money, kiddo. I've got stuff covered." He tugged on Roman's arm until his brother sat up against him. "We're okay. Really. There's plenty of money."

"Suppose something happens? And I need a stash? Then what? This way, I've got me covered… and maybe some of you too."

Angel's eyes burned with tears and regret. Nothing he'd done or said made a damned bit of difference; Rome was still living in the world their father'd made for them, scrambling and hustling to make every penny count and burning bridges behind them without a second thought. Sad didn't cover it. Unfortunately, he understood exactly what drove Roman to find a need he could fill, because Angel would have done the exact same thing when he was Rome's age.

"Look, I'll spot you a couple extra dollars a day or something if you help with closing down in the afternoon. Maybe take the trash out. How much are you pulling down a day?" It couldn't have been much. He didn't think a lot of kids had cash to toss around. "I can maybe make it worth your while."

"About twenty bucks a day, but then half of it goes back into buy more candy." Roman's eyes grew unfocused, his lips moving as he counted. "Chocolate's an easy seller, but it gets warm, so it goes fast. Hard candies are better, but people don't like them as much, so I'm kind of stuck."

"You're more than stuck," Angel told him. "You're now officially out of business. Tomorrow Frank's bringing the new oven in, so you can help get the front ready for customers. Jesus. Candy."

They sat in silence for a few minutes, and Roman's breathing slowed until his eyes drooped. Angel was about to scoop him up and carry him to bed when his brother murmured, "I just didn't want you to worry about me. I wanted you to know I'm okay. That I'd be okay. Even if you've gotta leave."

"Yeah, I'm not leaving you, kid." He lifted Rome up, cradling his brother against him. Roman felt so small, too delicate for the weight he'd picked up over the years. "You and me, remember? No matter what happens, you've got me right with you. You gotta trust me, Rome. Okay? Do we have a deal?"

"Deal." Roman nodded slowly. Angel waited a heartbeat, then smiled when his brother mumbled, "How about gum? You think I can sell gum?"

Seven

DUSK KISSED the sky, blushing the clouds in pinks and purples. The streets were lazy, filled with children on bicycles chasing the setting sun to get home before dark. Couples strolled along the walks, conversations punctuated by laughter and soft kisses. Main Street slowly dressed itself for the early evening, pearling its lines and buildings with soft yellow and white lights.

A gaudily painted taqueria sat at an angle on a street corner, a café window set on its long wall left open for customers to see inside. A plump-cheeked Latina watched the traffic, her hands quickly slapping at a flour ball, flattening and thinning it as she worked at it. A flat-faced man with silver-shot black hair worked beside her, his thick white mustache curled up with his broad smile, chatting as they began their evening.

Somewhere nearby, someone was cooking a heavily spiced meal, an aromatic tendril weaving through the air to entice and delight an empty stomach. The light turned green and the corner rolled away, leaving behind the older Latino couple, their tortillas, and the two young boys playing basketball in a side alley next to a florist shop.

As delightful a scene as the slow trawl through downtown Half Moon Bay was, West was ready for it to stop. He had a particular stop in mind—a certain shiplap and tin roof shack sitting on the outskirts of a large parking lot.

"Marzo, I'm serious," West grumbled at his driver through the open window between them. "Pull over."

"I don't know, boss."

Marzo hunched over and peered out of the sedan's windshield. He'd made mumbling sounds about rain and a storm, but as far as West could see, the sky was crystal clear with the faintest hint of stars beginning to spangle along the top of the eastern mountains.

"You sure this is a good idea? Your lawyers said you shouldn't talk to this guy."

"Let's not forget who is working for whom." West caught Marzo's scathing glance in the rearview mirror. "The lawyers. Not you. Look, just pull over and let me out. Then go get lost or something."

"You think I'm leaving you here by yourself? You almost died a couple of times this week." His brow slumped forward, a ripple of worry forming rolls over his forehead. "I don't think that's a good idea."

"I'm fine... just... right there! Marzo, pull over!" He liked Marzo, perhaps even loved him in a way much like he loved Lang, but at that exact moment, West experienced an overwhelmingly familiar sensation—the incredible longing to be an only child. "I'll walk the rest of the way."

"You're banged up, remember? Doc said no walking long distances."

"The doctor said I wasn't supposed to run any marathons," West corrected. "And when was the *first* time I ever ran a marathon? So either pull up in front of the bakery and let me out or.... God, this would be so much easier if I had a driver's license. Tell Agnes to arrange for an instructor for me."

"The last two... no... three instructors fired *you*, boss," Marzo reminded him. "I'd offer to teach you, but that's not how I want to die."

"I didn't kill anyone." He shrugged, remembering the look of horror on the woman's face when he finally got the car to stop during his previous driving attempt.

"You broke her leg."

"She shouldn't have opened the car door to jump out," West countered. "I was trying to find the brake."

"You were heading to the pier. Like right *off* the pier." His driver scratched at the side of his head. "I'll tell Agnes, but don't be surprised if it ends up the same way it always does."

"And what way is that, Marzo?" West sniffed.

"You paying out a hell of a lot of money because someone's in the hospital and there's a car in a tree or under the water." He glanced at West in the rearview mirror. "I'll drop you off, but... I'm going to be nearby."

"I don't need a babysitter," he replied sharply.

"You need *something*, boss," Marzo snapped back. "Because I've never met anyone who's almost died as many times as you. You're a *fricking* suit, for God's sake, not a private eye or something. You shouldn't have people shooting at you or T-boning your car. The most trouble you should be around is a bunch of hippies squatting in front of your office building because you wear leather shoes and eat rare steaks."

"I'll keep that in mind. But I'd like to point out, this last time wasn't about me. The lamp died, not me." West tapped at Marzo's shoulder. "There. Park there. Behind the… whatever the hell that thing is."

"That's a VW van. Probably a delivery van because it's got bakery stuff painted all over it." Marzo sighed. "Sometimes, boss, it's like you *just* landed on this planet. West, be… careful, okay?"

"I'll be fine. No marathons, not even a quick hobble. Nice and slow," West muttered as he got out of the car. His ankle was a bit tender but better than it'd been two days ago when Angel'd tackled him in his foyer. Leaning on the cane Marzo insisted he use, he carefully picked his way over a stretch of uneven asphalt. "Just… don't come back until I call you. *If* I call you."

"I don't hear from you in two hours, I'm coming in," Marzo warned. "I don't want to see you get hurt."

"I'm going to go talk to him," West assured. "How hurt can I get simply by talking?"

Marzo leaned on the sedan's window to watch West make his way to the bakery's back door. "Sometimes, boss, talking hurts the most."

WEST DIDN'T knock. The handle of the black-screened metal security door turned easily, and a moment later he was out of the cool, sea-tinged breeze and engulfed in an ocean of sharp, bright scents strong enough to drown in.

And in the middle of the glut of sound and spices stood Angel Daniels, oblivious to the world around him as he slowly worked a bucket of tangerine batter with what appeared to be a drill. There was an ease to his movements, a power in his shoulders as he moved the tool up and down. The clatter of the drill's motor covered West's sharp intake of breath, his heart pounding foolishly quick under his ribs. The sight of a man shouldn't have left him stunned, with the air knocked out of him, but Angel did exactly that.

It was incredibly stupid, this clutch of tightness in his chest and the twist in his gut when Angel glanced up, his marled gray eyes sharp with intelligence and wariness, and there was no other way to react to the simmering heat stoked in West's belly and balls. Angel's eyes narrowed, and he lifted his chin, a silent challenge or acceptance at finding West standing at the edge of his territory.

West knew he didn't put the tension and caution in Angel's probing gaze, but he certainly had added to it. If there was one regret West had in his life, it was deepening the shadows in Angel's already battered soul.

Angel shut the drill off, and the silence hanging between them grew thick with unsaid apologies and accusations.

"What are you doing here?" Angel pulled the drill up, then used a spatula to scrape batter off its odd attachment.

"I was about to ask you that exact same thing." Nodding toward the power tool in Angel's hand, he said, "You've got to admit, that's kind of odd."

"No, odd's you walking in through my back door after two days of cops giving me shit and hassling me about a gun I don't own." He put the drill on the stainless-steel counter next to him, then pounded a lid down on the bucket with a few taps from the heel of his hand. "This is called working."

"I told the cops you had nothing to do with the lamp's death—"

"You think this is funny, Harris?" Angel's chin was back up, and his shoulders were thrown back. Canting his head, he stared West down, a mixture of anger and exhaustion stamped on his face. "Cops hammering at me means I can't work. I don't keep this bakery going, then I'm dead in the water. And when that happens, CPS will come knocking on my door, and Rome's going to find himself in some goddamned foster home where he can't get his meds and they could give a shit if he's doing okay in school. So you've got to fucking excuse me if I don't find this *fucking* funny."

Angel's bitter, sharp rage slapped West hard, and he took a step back, his ankle twisting under him. The pain was brief and stabbing, nothing like the entrenched anguish in Angel's hot words. The cane's handle dug into his palm, and West gripped it tightly, refusing to buckle to the temper he felt rising in him.

He took a quick spice-scented breath, then said, "I'm sorry. I was trying to… I'm trying to find some common ground here."

"You're standing on it." Angel gestured to a pile of papers on a table near a swinging door. "One of your asshole lawyers served me with papers. Apparently I conned your grandmother into letting me buy this place, so you're suing me. Civil court because, you know, criminal—"

"I instructed *no one* to file charges against you," West protested. His cell phone was in the car, keeping Marzo company as he circled Half Moon Bay. "Let me see those."

"Yeah, you know where I'd like to put those for you?" Angel exhaled, somehow folding in on himself. He blinked, fighting the shimmer in his eyes. "I don't need this, West. I can't fight you. I don't have the money to fight you. And I'm too busy trying to figure out who the hell is trying to fuck me over, and the only name I'm coming up with is yours. So yeah, I kind of would like to know what the hell you're doing here because you're the last person I want to see right now."

"I can make this go away, Ange." West swore, his mind racing. He had no idea what Angel was talking about, but a few phone calls—reaching out to a couple key people—and he could change *everything* for Angel. "Just give me some time. Half an hour, tops, and I can fix so much of this."

"I don't know if I trust you, Harris." Angel wiped at his face with his sleeve. The tears were more evident now, heavy on his lashes, but not yet fallen. He wiped again, catching them this time. "*Fuck.*"

It hurt to see the pain in Angel's eyes. The anguish dug its claws into West's throat, and he reached out to touch Angel, to hold him, to do something to fix every broken thing in his life, maybe even Angel himself. West's fingers barely brushed the other's shoulder when Angel jerked back, putting some distance between them.

"*Don't.*"

It sounded more like a prayer than a curse, needy but strong, but Angel's strangled plea broke West apart, shattering him with a single hot shot to his heart.

"Finish up here and let me use your phone." West leaned heavily on his cane, silently cursing the doubt in Angel's face. "Trust me. By the time you come up for air, I'll have everything fixed."

ANGEL WORKED his last batch of batter, a cinnamon-and-nutmeg-spiced acorn-squash muffin he'd planned for his baker to fill with caramel and mascarpone. He'd already written out the instructions for the morning crew and was trying not to listen to West's soft baritone through the kitchen door. Stalling wasn't going to do him any good. Running away never solved anything. He knew that. If he hadn't learned that from watching his father burn every bridge behind them, he certainly understood once he'd taken Roman in.

A final swipe of a wet towel on the counter, a locked back door, and Angel was ready to face the demons waiting for him in the front of the bakery.

One demon, to be exact. A blue-eyed, sharp-featured wickedness he could still taste on his tongue, even after two days of anger and soured feelings.

"Fucking asshole," Angel spat, throwing the towel into the sink. "And fuck you for showing up here. Easier being pissed off at you if I can't see you. *Asshole.*"

With the soft lights from the dining room's chandeliers dimmed and the rolling shades stretched down across the storefront windows, the space went from a cheery place to have a cup of coffee to something more… intimate.

He did *not* need intimate. What he needed was a pot of coffee, maybe some actual food, and to kick West Harris's ass.

But he'd settle for the coffee.

"You want some?" Angel held a cup up for West to see, but the man was elsewhere, lost in a sea of buzzwords and low rumblings.

One arm slung over the back of the velvet couch and his button-up gray shirt undone to his chest, West looked more like an ad to sell fine imported whiskey than the boy he'd made laugh hard enough to squirt orange soda out his nose. The West Harris he'd known back then never wore jeans, didn't own a T-shirt, and had never eaten a hot dog slathered with mustard while sitting on the beach. By the end of the summer, Angel'd lost half of his wardrobe to the lanky young man he'd fallen for and all of his heart.

He'd gotten back most of his T-shirts, but his heart seemed lost forever.

"Harris, you're such a dick," Angel muttered at the banged-up French press he'd pulled out from under the countertop. "I don't even know if he drinks coffee. Probably needs to be the kind you pick out of cat shit."

It'd been a little over an hour since West took the bakery's phone over, hardly enough time to do anything, or so Angel thought. Tomorrow morning would be the first time they'd fire up the oven, and he'd promised to be at the back door if his baking crew needed him, but there'd been little sleep over the past couple of days, and he didn't think he'd last until Roman came home from the movies, much less wake up at 3:00 a.m.

Extra strong coffee seemed like his best bet, and a shot of sweetened condensed milk wasn't going to hurt either.

"I don't think you quite understand what I am telling you." Tucking the phone into the crook of his neck, West took the cup Angel offered him with a tight smile and a nod at the seat next to him, as if giving Angel permission to sit down. Grimacing when Angel flipped him off, he listened for a moment to the person on the line, then sighed heavily. "Let me explain this to you. If that lawsuit hasn't been pulled by the time I wake up tomorrow morning, someone else's name is going to be on your office door. I'm going to set my alarm for 8:00 a.m., and I'll be on the phone with you at… let's say eight-oh-five so I have time to brush my teeth. Do we understand one another?"

West took a sip of the coffee, then gagged, shooting Angel a filthy look. "What is this, Daniels? Satan's breast milk? No… no… I'm not talking to you. Just get this taken care of and make sure you get back to me about the weapon. Or better yet, if you can't get a hold of me, talk to Marzo. Just get someone on it. I'll touch base with you in the morning."

"Can't handle the coffee?" Angel said as West shoved the phone at him, then headed behind the counter with his cup. "Need to water it down?"

"This isn't coffee. It's… dear God, it's on my tongue. I can't get it off." West poured some of the coffee down the sink, then eyed the industrial coffee machine on the counter. "Does this hot water spigot work?"

"Yes." Angel shook his head, then took a sip. "Wimp."

The brew was potent, syrupy, and despite the creamy milk he'd added, much darker than he normally made it. The zing hit a second later, and he sighed, slouching down into the couch. West came back around the counter, stepped over Angel's outstretched legs, then settled back into his seat. He had the decency to wait until Angel was a quarter way through his coffee before he cleared his throat.

"The suit's going to be pulled—"

"Yeah, I heard you threatening that guy." Angel's stomach rumbled, a sour mess of tension. "You can't threaten people who work for you. Makes you kind of an asshole, and they're just doing what they've been told to do. The question is, who told them to sue me?"

"That is a question I have no answer for, but I have an idea." West put his cup down on a table. "You and I… we need to talk."

"About a whole bunch of shit," he agreed. "I just don't know if I want to. Or even where to start."

"Do you want to talk about now?" West's sharp inhale startled Angel. "Or then?"

"Now would be quicker." Angel looked into his cup. "I don't know if there's enough coffee in the world for then."

"Now is pretty easy," West said, leaning forward until he filled Angel's view. "I'm getting the lawsuit dropped. *That* I can do now. I have to look into the plans for the motel. I've been letting Derry drive that development because… you and I? We're complicated. I can't have complications between me and business."

"Seems like that's a common thing with you." Angel was surprised at how the bitterness in him drowned out the bite of coffee lingering on his tongue. "That's what I was to you? Back then? Just another complication?"

He could still hear the cold in West's young voice when he'd been tossed aside, his lifeline to a normal existence snapped away with a careless thrust of words and disdain. He'd been waiting for that moment when he could reach out and grab West's hand, *needing* so desperately for West to yank him back to Half Moon Bay. It'd been the only thing he'd ever dreamed of asking someone, the only time he'd trusted someone to save him.

The one instance in his entire life when Angel'd placed his heart and soul into someone else's hands, only to find himself swinging in the wind, his neck ripped to shreds by a noose of his own making.

"You want to start that, then?" The overhead lights caught the blue in West's inky hair, doing strange things to his hawkish face. "Because we can, if you want. I can hold off on everything about the cops and that damned gun they think belongs to you and just start that discussion we should have had back at the house before some asshole shot up my front porch."

"Yeah, let's do that, then." Angel hoped he didn't throw up every drop of coffee he'd pounded down that day or if he did, at least aim for West's custom-tailored pants. "Why don't we start with you telling me to fuck off? Right when I needed you the most. Because after you hung up on me and walked away from *us*, my father fucked me up so bad, it took five months before I even remembered you existed."

Eight

OUTSIDE, NIGHT tapped at the bakery's windows, her dark veil settling a lacework of shadows and blues over the front room. The dark was comforting, muting the glare of light probing through Angel's heart. He didn't want to breach the fractures he'd spackled over. It was going to hurt. There never seemed to be enough time to heal, to dig out the rot inside of him and let his ravaged soul scar over.

Damn West Harris for opening that door, on a night when he'd not been ready to lose his mind over a pair of blue eyes and a wicked mouth he used to love teasing smiles out of. That mouth looked rusted over, bereft of kisses and joys, and strangely, Angel was more afraid of wanting those lips to curve up, of needing to taste West every morning and each evening until the night no longer slithered off the horizon and both of them turned into ash.

It was the high end of stupid to want a man just because they'd loved as boys. It was a stupid Angel couldn't afford, not with Roman, and certainly not with his frantic, parched life, but Angel knew he'd embrace whatever shit storm came his way if West gave him even the slightest of nods.

"Talk to me, Angel," West whispered. "What happened? Between us. Because of us. *Something* happened."

It was like the years between them never happened and they were once again on the sands, staring out at a glassy sea and murmuring secret dreams neither ever whispered softly to themselves, frightened to death of the overwhelming hunger they had inside of them. Despite their past, Angel's heart opened, and the sewage he'd mucked in came pouring out, drowning him in the stink of faded pain and torn time.

"He broke me… my dad." His whisper slammed into the silence, pounding at its flatness until it shattered under the bleakness in his voice. "He tried to beat me to death that night. Or close to it. Right after you hung up on me. I think… he would have killed me… if his friends hadn't stopped him."

The velvet under Angel's clenched fists rubbed at his knuckles, rasping at his skin. His heart broke a little with each beat, his body aching with the memory of the beating he'd gotten that day. He could still hear the crack of his jaw as it gave way under his father's fists, the crinkle of his hand when he'd thrown it up to shield his face, only for his father to grab his wrist, hold his arm against the filthy, cheap motel carpet, then stomp on it with his heavy boot.

The beating came at him during the oddest of times. The crackle of a plastic tub echoed the breaking of his collarbone, and his body would jerk, recalling the shock of bright, sharp pain along his chest. Swallowing the thick glut of his own blood for seemingly endless hours made it difficult to taste the batters, the smooth texture a mocking parody of the bitter metal taint he'd had on his tongue for months afterward. The violence was nothing new, but that night—that singular night—the occasional slap or punch to his face or ribs became a horrifying storm of startling, brutal anguish.

"My dad was angry because…." It was hard to find the words from that maelstrom so many years ago. So many things were shouted, hateful and hurtful spits of rage nearly as damaging as the fists tearing him open. "Hell, West, I can't even—I was crying so damned hard. I hurt so much, and when I turned around, it was like he had to make my body feel what I felt inside of me."

"Did he know you were gay?" West ventured. "Before then? I can't stand that he hurt you, Angel. I can't. God…."

Angel couldn't look at him. There was something raw in West's voice, something trembling on a razor's edge, and if he was going to get through what he needed to be said, Angel *knew* he couldn't look at West. Not if he was going to hold himself together. The lump in his throat didn't get any smaller when Angel swallowed.

"No, not before then. Maybe? He sure as hell knew then." It was a fog of pain and memory brambles, too many confusing lines to follow out of the labyrinth of his father's rage. He'd been hit before he could figure out what his father'd been shouting at him. In the end, the why of the pain didn't matter. He'd only wanted it to stop. "Dad didn't give a shit who fucked what. Shit, he'd been trying to hook me up with… *anyone…* before you. Said I was old enough to party with them. A couple of guys, a few women. Fresh meat, he'd say like it was a joke when they were all drinking, but you could tell, some of them were serious. He was serious. Like he'd make a score if I slept with someone."

"You were a *kid*." Horror and shock did a quick battle in West's expression before indignation wiped it all away. "You were a goddamned kid. And *his* kid. You were innocent, damn it. We didn't even *do* anything."

"It wasn't like I was a virgin when we met, you know? I did some things, West, things I don't want to do again, but I knew what I was getting into. Not everyone can say that."

It was too hard to talk. There were too many things he'd simply done because he had to, too many people and lies Angel tried to bury. Roman standing on his doorstep with bruises on his face and shadows in his eyes brought it all back to life.

And West feeling remorse oddly wasn't helping Angel hold himself together.

"So they pulled him off of you?" West moved closer, chasing away the numb coldness seeping into Angel's limbs. "Why did he do it? Did he tell you that? If he didn't care about you liking guys, why did he hurt you?"

"Dad—he needed me back then. Needed me for his cons, for his deals. Some things are easier to work if there's two people. Better if it's a kid because no one thinks a kid's going to rip them off. There was no chance in hell he was going to let me go. I knew that, but… I needed to get out of there." Angel stretched his legs out, feeling the hitch in his hip where it hurt sometimes if it was cold. "He was pissed off I fell in love. Maybe scared because I was planning on leaving. I don't think he gave a shit if you had a dick or not. I was trying to get out. I needed to get out because he was getting pretty bad. I just didn't know how bad he was going to get."

"No one should have to go through that," West growled. "Shit. Angel, I'm… sorry."

"I woke up angry, you know?" Angel felt… small… again. Folded up inside of himself and broken, the spark of pain he'd tried to extinguish since he'd woken up still tasting his blood and the powdery grit of bone on his tongue. "In that hospital bed. No fricking clue where I was or how I got there, but I was *angry*.

"It took me a few months—five, maybe—to finally remember who I was so mad at." He sucked in the room's spiced air, a far cry from the icy wind he'd been standing in the day he recalled West's hard young voice clipping the thread connecting them. "It wasn't like I didn't remember everything. More like I was in a fog. Then I'd blink, and it'd be a few weeks later. Everything moved weird, but the one thing I knew for sure, it hurt to remember you. I kept seeing your face, and I knew I loved you. Then one day I heard a click and everything came back to me. The call. How I felt. Everything."

"Your father…." West's anger sparked, a hot outrage flaring to life in his eyes. It caught along his body, stiffening his bones and muscles until he thrummed, a rigid statue of cold beauty and searing rage. "Angel, I didn't—"

"You wanted to know, West, then you've got to listen." He cocked his head, warning West off when he reached to hold Angel's hand. "If I feel you on me, I'm going to break apart, so… *don't*. Because that's what you've done to me. I'm… thin… like sugar or glass. So just… for right now, okay?"

His words hung between them, flightless lead balloons tossed up in the hopes a zephyr would pick them up and make them fly. Angel knew they'd plummet to the ground and shatter. Like he'd done, like he still was doing, but this time West caught them up and held his words—held him—with a soft smile and a graceful nod.

"Okay." West nodded, holding his hands up. "But where did you go? Why didn't you try to call me again? What did the cops do?"

"What do you mean where? I went back to my dad. Where else was I going to go?" Angel canted his head, studying West's expression. The cluelessness in his ocean-blue eyes was nearly as funny as the question he'd asked. The space between them, how they'd grown up and who they'd become, stretched out, the deep gap becoming a chasm. "There were no cops, dude. There was no one to take me somewhere else. It was an ER, an IV, and a story my dad wove about how I'd been jumped outside of a bar looking for a guy to fuck me.

"Only reason he took me in was because he could score some pills out of the deal—don't look at me like that. It's a pretty common con. A couple of punches to my face and a trip to Urgent Care usually could score about two hundred bucks in drugs." Angel's side ached, reminding him he needed to stretch out a bit. "What he did to me? He scored off of that for months."

"That's—"

"Wrong? Sick? Fucked-up?" Angel completed for him, shrugging off West's disgusted grimace. "Up until I met you, I really didn't think there was anything else but that. People were something to bleed out.

Hell, the first time I walked into your grandma's house, all I could see was the stuff I could pick up and shove in my pockets.

"I'm not going to lie to you. It's still like that sometimes. I go piss at a restaurant or something, and it's close to their back room, there's this part of me screaming to grab rolls of toilet paper, forks, or hell, anything really." It was harder than he thought to look back at who he'd been. Harder still peeling himself open for West to take a good look at what he had inside of him. "It's what you do, and you don't even think about it. And I knew it was wrong, even back then when I was a little kid, but how else were we going to get this stuff?"

"You didn't steal from my grandmother, right?" West asked quietly, his expressive face going suddenly still. "Please tell me you didn't."

"Didn't take one damned thing from her. Promise," he replied. "And it's not to say my hands didn't itch. Because they did. I ran from my dad and eventually ended up back here. One of the first people I ran into was your grandma, and she helped me out. No way was I going to break that trust. She was kooky and elegant. Kind of like you."

"She was… odd. Kind of like Lang-odd." He smiled at Angel, a quirk of his mouth touched with fondness and melancholy. "He was her favorite. Don't bother denying it. It's okay. She loved me, but Lang, she needed to rescue him. Mostly from our father, but Grandma liked to rescue things, people. Hell, those damned cats of Lang's are hers, remember?"

"Yeah, the damned orange one bit my leg the first time I came over to mow her lawn."

"You mowed her lawn?"

"Someone had to. The gardening guys she'd hired kept running over her flowers. Pissed her off. Then I started cooking sometimes because… Lang was kind of checked out, and the housekeeper kept leaving this foo-foo crap she didn't want to eat." Angel sighed. "I never told her about us. I mean, she knew we'd been hanging out together, but I didn't tell her how we were. I didn't know if you wanted people to find out. Actually, I kind of felt like you wanted to… forget you ever knew me. Your grandmother was just… she was nice to me, and I needed the money. She helped me get my shit together. It about killed me when she died. It wasn't like I was family or anything, but I really liked her."

"I didn't find out you were in Half Moon until… the motel. If I'd known you were close, I would have made sure you were at her funeral."

"Lang said that too, afterwards. He really was out of it back then. He didn't know we were close until the will was read. Then he felt shitty because she left me some money to help with the bakery." It'd been a long day at the bakery, and he'd come home to find West's twin on his doorstep with the keys to his future and a face he could never get used to Lang wearing. "I think he was kind of pissed off I hadn't said anything to him about going, but... not my place, you know?"

"You wouldn't have liked it anyway. Lots of brittle people pretending they knew her. Brittle, drunk, unhappy people." West chuckled. "My family... you used to say you wished you had a family like mine, but Angel, I've got to be honest, if I'd known then what I know now, I would have taken everything I had, and we could have both left. God, I wish I'd stood up to that fucking bastard. Both those bastards. My dad and yours.

"I didn't hang up on you because I didn't want you." He exhaled, hard, then rubbed at his face. Years of worry surfaced in his weary expression, his mouth turning down as he spoke, softly as if he didn't want to disturb the shadows lying between them. "Please believe me. I never, ever wanted to hurt you. If I could take back anything I've ever done, it was that phone call, *those* words."

"I was stupid, West. We were kids." This time Angel was the one who reached out, his fingers ghosting over West's arm. "Hell, I was an idiot to think you could help me out of that kind of shit. It's one of those stupid wish-on-a-star things you do when you're a kid, and you somehow convince yourself that it's going to happen.

"Teenagers are idiots. I've got an almost teen, and he does some stupid, asshole things. And when I ask him why, the best he can come up with is *I don't know*." Clasping West's hand, Angel was relieved to feel West return the squeeze. "I hurt myself believing you had that kind of power. I know that. Even as pissed off as I am about you walking away from me, I get it. I do."

"If I could have saved you from that, I would have. If I'd known—I could have done *something*, Angel. A couple of hours before you called, my father overheard me telling Lang about... falling in love with a guy. I never told him who. I don't think you two even met that summer, not really, but my father heard us, and... things were difficult. He wasn't... pleased. Nothing like how your father reacted, but... he made it clear he wasn't going to... he had plans for me, and me falling in love with you wasn't *acceptable*.

"I could have done something, Angel." West's eyes glistened, his mouth tightened down into a thin, dark line. "Like I should have done something sooner about… this stupid project with the motel. How the hell did I get *here*? Like this? There was nothing stopping me from coming to see you, just my damned pride. I was hurt when you didn't call back because I never got a chance to explain. I never wanted you to get into your father's van that day. I could have come up with something to have kept you safe back then—"

"Did you miss the part where it wasn't your job to save me, Harris?" Angel poked through West's recriminations. "Not about back then. Now, I could use a little saving because you've sort of fucked up my life. We've got to come to an understanding about this crap about the bakery and the motel. I'm not handing it over. I can't, West. You coming back here, showing up in my life to fuck me over with this plan you've got for the motel. I know you say it's this guy Derry driving this, but tell me you didn't know it was me here. Can you say that?"

"No, I can't. I didn't want to. I shoved it all—and you—into a box and let Derry handle it because I didn't think I could take seeing you again." His raspy confession rubbed glass into Angel's torn heart. "I kept telling myself it was business. The land—the opportunity here—is a hell of a lot bigger than what's here now. Or at least on paper. That's how I was looking at it. The *money*—it would take care of you. Because as we both know, I sure as hell haven't."

"I've done some shitty things, dude. I'll admit to them. Have already, really." Angel sighed when West looked away. Pride clotted the air in the dining room, unsaid angry words and hurt feelings laying out a minefield Angel didn't know if he could—much less wanted to—negotiate. "But I've never sold out. What you… and your guy, Derry… what you wanted me to do is hold my hand out and tell you it was okay to tear this place down. See, and I can't.

"Because you're telling me to tear down the only four walls of home I've ever had. Yeah, this place might be crap to you, but it's fucking everything to me." Angel looked away, hating himself for slapping at West, but the sour in him bubbled, needing release. "As soon as I found out it was you trying to get me out of here, it was like you hanging up on me all over again, cutting me off from the one thing—the one place—I feel safe in. I can't let you do that to me. Not again."

"I don't want to hurt you. Shit, I wish I could blame everything on Derry, but I can't. I own this mess, Ange. No one else."

West reached for him, and this time Angel let himself be pulled in.

"I need you to trust me again. I can't go back. We can't go back, but I can make this right. Just... let me make this right. Give me that chance."

West's mouth brushed over his, a delicate frosting of warm flesh and tentative need. Angel sucked in as West breathed out, pulling the taste of coffee, desire, and man. He closed his eyes, afraid of drowning in the temptation West was offering him, but Angel knew as soon as West's fingers dappled a pattern over his jaw, he was lost.

The angry clash of their bodies in the deep cold of a sea-kissed breeze was only a memory. This time their kiss was a banked flight, streaking toward the horizon in the hopes of finding somewhere safe to land. Angel couldn't stop the tears in him from falling. They were too old, too ripe of a pain. The first splash of hot water flavored their kiss, salt and anguish stealing away the sweet of the moment.

Angel shifted, breaking their contact for a brief instant. Then West's fingers fisted into his hair, and he found himself pulled back in, opening up for West's searching kiss. West shifted, swinging his leg over Angel's until he straddled Angel's hips, their tongues dipping in and out of the moist warmth of their joined mouths. West's hair brushed over his face, a crow's feather kiss of satin on his skin.

He couldn't fill his hands with enough of West's body, didn't have enough of West pressed into his, and Angel growled with growing frustration at the press of desire unspooling from his belly. Every inch of him was on fire, his cock tingling and growing heavy, milking at the soft heat of West's ass pushing into him through his jeans.

His breath stolen and his heart beating fast enough to become a steady thrum in his ears, Angel came up for air, mewling with the need for the man sitting across his lap. He knew better than to fall into West's kiss. Every sane thought he had... might have had... became vapor under the intensity of West's heat. He needed more than air. He needed space, time to think. Time to absorb how much he needed West and to figure out some way to shake off the addiction he had to the man's kiss, his touch.

Even as Angel's mind scrambled, frantic for a way to escape the flame flickering in front of him, luring him in, he knew there would be no running away, not this time. This time he would cheerfully fly straight into the blaze, and he would dance as his wings caught fire, his world burning away around him as he gave in to the temptation of the man he'd always wanted to love.

"West—"

"Whatever you're going to say, Angel, please just listen to me. *Please*." West cupped Angel's face and whispered into shadows lingering in the scant space between them. His husky, smooth voice as broken and jagged as his breathing, West pleaded softly, "Don't… leave me alone. Give me another chance. Because I don't think I could survive losing you. Not when you've made me feel again. Not… when I need you more than I've needed anyone before. Just… please, Angel. *Please*."

Nine

"ANGEL!" A young boy's voice blasted from the kitchen. Even with the door shut between the two spaces, West could clearly make out a stomping rush of feet on the floor and the scramble of bodies running toward the front of the bakery. "Where are you?"

"We'll… talk, okay? I'm not… we…." Angel whispered as West tried to pull away. His hands were fisted into West's shirt, his arms barely straining to hold him still. It was like trying to break free from being chained to a rock, his liver and heart eaten away by ravenous birds, and he hadn't even stolen fire from the Gods to deserve his punishment. Angel gripped him tighter, then forced West around to look him straight in the eye. "Do not walk away from this… from us. Just later. We *can't* just… leave it like this. I don't want to leave *you* like this."

He'd bled out onto Angel's hands, his heart pouring out through their kiss and his tears. When Angel released him, West pushed himself off the couch, needing to put distance between them. He couldn't breathe right, his lungs were origami cranes under his still bruised ribs, and every heave of air into his body crackled with a bristle of razors and heartache. Angel grabbed at his wrist, his fingers nearly white at the knuckles as he tightened his hand to hold on to West.

"I can't *talk* anymore, Angel," West ground out, yanking himself loose. "What more do you want from me? What else can we take from each other? What you do with that… with me—"

West was still close enough to feel Angel's warmth, smell the man's tanned skin, and his mouth watered at the thought of licking the stretch of his throat where his pulse beat frantically near a tiny flat white scar. His face hurt from the tightness of keeping his emotions in check long enough to get his words out, and his palms burned with the memory of Angel's cheekbones pressed into them.

The door closing off the front from the kitchen boomed when it hit the wall, rattling the room and throwing the artwork askew. What emerged from the warm kitchen was a squalid whirl of dark hair, flashing gray eyes, and a hydra of flailing limbs. His clothes were comfortably worn in, a size too big for his lanky frame, and his feet sported a pair of formerly gray sneakers mottled with mud splatters and something pink. He looked so much like the man at West's side, the boy could have been Angel's.

Especially since they shared suspicious looks and hooded resentment shone out of the kid's face, a wariness he'd only seen in Angel's expressions.

"Angel?" The kid jutted his chin out, amusingly aggressive considering he was a little more than a foot shorter than West. "Wait, you're Lang's brother, right? What's he doing here?"

"How'd you get home? That's the bigger question," Angel countered, getting up and edging around the table. "Where's Justin? You guys were supposed to call me so I could come get you."

As if there were any question of the universe laughing its ass off at the pranks it pulled on West, his gut twisted into a Gordian knot when he heard Lang shouting at Zig to slow down. His hellspawn niece must have taken the door at a full run because it swung out in a quick whoosh, narrowly missing smacking the boy across his back. He jumped forward, jostling a counter display, and other than a soft hey of alarm, his attention remained fixed on West.

"Hey, Uncle West!" Zig came around a glass case and coiled up, ready to launch herself at him, but a quick shake of his head and a jiggle of the cane stopped the young girl in her tracks. "Sh... *crap*. Sorry."

"It's okay, brat." His face throbbed, eyes prickly with the heat of his tears, and West tasted an ocean of salt in his throat and mouth. "I take it Thing One and Two are around somewhere?"

"One's outside in the car. Dad Two didn't come with. He's working the store so Margie could bring Xiah to the movies with us."

She grinned up at him. Then West watched as her lips slowly drooped into a thin, judgmental line.

His niece wasn't stupid. She'd spent a good part of her early childhood surviving the tempers and mercurial shifts in mood in the people around her. Zig could spot tension a mile away, and no matter how hard West reined in his emotions, she dug through him with a cunning ease quick enough to frighten him.

Her expression went sharp, and Zig tilted her head, staring up at him as he ducked down to grab at the phone he'd left on the table. "You okay, dude?"

"I'm fine. Tired, but you know how that is when you've been rolled around in a car. I didn't know you… all of you knew Angel and his brother." Unless there was another reason for the boy to have Angel's eyes, he was going to go with sibling over son. West smoothed over his awkwardness with a brief nod, then handed Zig the phone. "Please do me a favor, brat. Would you hang that up on the wall over there, please? My leg's not bending very well right now, and this table is a bit hard to get around."

"I can move it," Angel's brother offered. "Zig and I—"

"Rome, focus more on me and less on Zig. What the hell happened to Justin?" Angel tapped his brother on the shoulder, but the boy barely shifted his attention. "How'd you get home?"

"We caught a ride with Zig 'cause her dad asked if we wanted a ride home, so he took us."

Roman's chin rose up farther, and he sniffed dramatically, flaring his nostrils at West. He'd have laughed at the tiny bantam of a boy if West hadn't heard the heartbreak in Angel's words a few minutes before. Whatever their father'd done to Angel, West would have laid bets Roman suffered an equal or greater anguish.

"Justin gave me the key so he could go grab a book for Deke from his place."

"Would it have killed you guys to call and let me know? Shit, suppose something happened?" Angel paced around the table until he was in front of his brother, towering over Roman. The boy broke and took a step back. "The back door was locked. How'd you get in?"

"You weren't at home and the lights were on, so he told me to come look in here for you. Zig came inside because—"

"Cupcakes." She beamed at Angel, a blast of charisma and trouble bright enough to blind a sightless mole. "Rome said maybe you had some leftovers. And I could have some. Cupcakes."

"Which you shouldn't beg for, baby girl. And not calling's on me. Sorry," Deacon growled from the doorway. "Hey, Ange. Didn't know you knew the Evil One."

"It's good to see you too, Deacon." West didn't have the energy to snipe back. His brain hurt along the curve of his skull, a flat gray spike of pain cutting across to jab at his temples. "I hope you all had a good time at the movies."

"You okay, West?" Deacon straightened, a frown forming across his face. "Want me to drop you off at the Hellmouth? Or is Charon circling his boat somewhere?"

"Perfectly fine." He steadied himself, refusing to give in to the tremors working through him. As hard as it was to talk, it was harder still to be standing near Angel and pretending as if they hadn't scraped open the scabs on their souls a few moments before. "I was just leaving, so no, no need to take me anywhere. I'll get Marzo to swing by shortly."

"If you say so," Deacon replied slowly. "Okay, pack it up, Zig. Time to head out. Say good-bye to Rome so we can head home."

"Hey, Rome's promised cupcakes, so take some with you before you go." Angel cut off the kids' whine before it could reach its peak. "Kid, grab a small box and pack some for them. I've got to finish up with West, and then we can close."

The smaller, darker-haired Angel clone didn't look persuaded to do anything but glare at West. "But why's—"

"Now, Rome."

They stared at one another for a moment longer. Then the boy's shoulders lifted up in a careless shrug.

"Only thing I want to hear out of you is *yes* and *thank you, Deacon.* Quit picking at West, and grab Zig something to take home."

"Sure, okay. And I already told Deacon thank you. Come on, Zig," he mumbled at the girl. "I can get eight in a box. You can choose what you want. I'll make 'em fit."

As sharp as Zig was, her uncle was much keener, and Deacon kept his eyes on West as the kids filed past him. After a quick glance over his shoulder, Deacon jerked his chin toward Angel. "You sure you guys are okay, West?"

The question shocked West, more for the consideration than anything else. From what he could gather, Angel and Deacon were at least acquainted and probably on a heck of a lot better terms than West was with his brother-in-law. A quick nod sent Deacon on his way, but not before the two men exchanged a perplexingly assessing stare.

"We've got about ten minutes before they tear back in here," Angel said softly after Deacon closed the door behind him. "Rome has school tomorrow—well, art classes. So he'll be gone in the afternoon—"

"I don't know, Angel." West leaned on the cane, thankful for its support. His knees were weak, and his ankle ached more than he'd care to admit. The sprain's throb nearly matched the pounding in his chest. "I don't know if I'm strong enough to—"

The door swung open again, and Angel threw his hands up in disgust. "What?"

"Hey now, I just came in to offer up some space," Deacon rumbled from the door, breaking the tension West nurtured in his belly. "You guys look like you need to get some shit worked out. Ange, what do you say I take Roman over to our place and you come grab him when you guys are done?"

"Just let me know when he graduates high school so I can drag myself to the ceremony," Angel shot back. "No, you know what? I haven't eaten dinner, and West can just join us for whatever I can find in the fridge."

"I already fed Rome," Deacon countered. "He had half a medium pizza, a hot dog, and some fries."

"That's like a predinner. He's an eleven-year-old boy off his meds. Swarming locusts aspire to eat what he can when he's finally hungry." Angel shook his head. "You grab whatever he's packing up for Zig, and I'll cut you guys loose. I think you've already suffered enough with him."

"He's a good kid. Just… a little rough around the edges." Deacon laughed. "Oh, and before you ask, yeah, those books he dumped on the table are his. Stopped by at the store before we came over here, and Lang made them take the trash out for him in exchange for books. I'm thinking Lang got the short end of the deal. Kid must have taken him for about sixty bucks worth. Most expensive trash dump ever."

"That's my brother." He let out an exasperated hiss. "Take whatever you can out of someone even if you don't need it. A Daniels to the bone. Tell Lang I'll pay him for—"

"No, you shouldn't," West interjected. Deacon and Angel looked at him like he had grown a second head between his shoulder blades. "A deal's a deal. It's something he agreed to with my brother. If he negotiated the price and Lang agreed to it, it should stand." They continued to stare, and West added, "Not that I have children or anything, but it's something my father—"

"Perhaps not the best role model for my con artist little brother," Angel suggested. "Deke, we'll figure something out. Maybe it'll be something as simple as telling Lang to stop giving away the damned store every time Roman hits him up for something. What'd he con out of him now?"

"Dragonriders. First six books, I think. Weyrs and bards." Deacon shrugged at Angel's hiss. "Paperbacks, but he also scored one of the *People Of* in hardback Lang had in the back collecting dust. Comprehension level might be a bit out of his reach, but I wasn't going to say anything because what the hell do I know about what he's reading at?"

"Nah, that's fine. He's read the first two from the library but couldn't get the first bard one. He's been wanting to finish that out for a while. We'll do something." A loud burst of giggles from the kitchen jerked Angel's attention away from the conversation, and his eyes narrowed when the kids suddenly dropped to a low hushed whisper. "Can you go keep an eye on them? Just for a little bit so West and I can hammer something out?"

"Yeah. Tell you what, you two lock up here, and we'll be over at your place," Deacon offered. "Your living room looks like Roman threw everything he had in his backpack across every flat surface he could find. I'll get him started on picking it up. Head over when you're done. Want me to grab anything out of the freezer?"

"No, I'm good. I'll grab some eggs from here and toss something together. Thanks, though." Angel waited until Deacon was through the door, then crossed his arms over his chest. "So what do you say, West? Want to come over to my place for dinner?"

"I DON'T see why spinach has to go into a perfectly good omelet." West poked at the folded-over egg dish in front of him. There were bits and pieces of things he couldn't identify, and other than a mushroom peeking out as if to reassure him of its normalcy, West doubted the edible nature of whatever it was Angel slid onto the plate and put down on the table.

"It's either that or pizza rolls." Angel sat down next to him, their elbows jostling together.

"I don't even know what those are," West said softly.

"Kind of like microwave pizza wontons," he replied, shaking hot sauce over his eggs. "You'd hate them."

"They sound disgusting."

"Yeah well, sometimes food's a battle I don't pick to fight." He shrugged. "There's some weeks where all Rome wants is mac and cheese, pizza rolls, and beef jerky. On the weekends he decides he wants to skip his meds, he'd eat me out of house and home if I let him. The pills they've got him on make him lose his appetite, not something he can afford right now."

"But microwave pizza wontons?"

"Just eat your damned eggs, because no one else is going to."

Roman's pissiness lasted about fifteen seconds after Angel walked through the front door and asked how Rome's day was. Once off and running, the boy's mouth seemed to struggle to keep up with his brain, and the torrent of information, ideas, and sounds pouring out of him was almost too much to bear, but Angel seemed to take it in stride. Any resentment or disgruntlement over finding West in the bakery seemed to have been replaced by an awestruck wonder at West being in the backseat of a car as it rolled over. Unable to defend himself from the tidal wave of questions Roman threw at him, West thanked every star he'd ever wished on when Angel declared it was time for Rome to grab a bath, then go to bed.

The negotiations between the brothers over an extra slot of time following the bath to play a video game was like sitting at one of his own board meetings. The give and take was one-sided, with all the power in Angel's hands, but compromise and Rome's happiness were definitely factored in. The shower wasn't on the table to be discussed, and the video game seemed to be a point of contention, mainly to do with time. A brief skirmish of cajoling on Rome's part, and contemplation on Angel's, then the brothers agreed Roman could read for half an hour before the lights were turned off.

The kid was out and snoring before the five-minute mark, and Angel'd closed the door to let his brother sleep, then told West to sit down at the old dining room table set up near the motel room's kitchenette.

And as the brothers argued good-naturedly, West wandered about the room to take in the bits of their lives together.

According to a report card on the fridge, West deduced the boy was smart, keenly smart if the notes from one Mrs. La Costa were to be believed, but he lacked interest in many of the subjects and was unwilling to pace himself with the class. His grades were up and down, but several tests with high marks were tacked to a corkboard, and a pencil sketch of a too familiar-looking pair of cats was hung on the wall next to the television. The drawing was eerily well done, loose lines and scribbles on a piece of cream parchment, but there was no mistaking the signature on the bottom. Roman Q. Daniels certainly excelled at capturing the likenesses of cats.

There were other signs of their days. A backpack with patches sewn onto its canvas flaps, odd detritus of games West didn't know. Cookbooks took up a lot of space on one bookshelf, while fantasy and science fiction dominated the other two in the room. The motel apartment's dreary walls were clean, brightened up a bit by a slap of paint, but the cinder-block front wall remained concrete blocks, and the rough hollow-core doors leading to the bathroom and tiny bedroom were pitted from years of hands and knees.

It all seemed a bit fatigued around the edges, drooping in on itself, and West found himself lit up with envy over the life the two brothers shared. No one'd ever hung his report card anywhere, and he could count on one hand the times either of his parents spent fifteen minutes letting him ramble on about a movie featuring anthropomorphic animals and the monsters they fought. Listening to Roman, West's heart hurt for Angel, knowing he'd burdened him with the weight of losing the home he'd built.

At least it had until Angel slopped cooked spinach in front of him. Then any sympathy was tossed aside like yesterday's filmed-over coffee.

"Want some Tapatío?" Angel waggled the bottle at him.

"No… it's just… spinach."

"Eat it, and you'll get a cupcake. There's chili-hot chocolate, salted caramel, and brown-sugar-cinnamon curry." Cutting into West's omelet, Angel scooped out a layer of wilted green leaves and moved them over to his own plate. "Buttercream frosting. Might even be an ice cream sandwich in the freezer with your name on it if Rome hasn't shoveled them all down his throat."

The hot sauce looked deadly, a brilliant orange-red West'd only seen used to warn people away from cliff edges or alligator ponds. He shook out a drop onto the paper plate, then dipped a tine into it to taste. The barest whisper of sauce on his tongue set his lungs on fire, and West gasped, dropping his fork to reach for his water glass.

"God, are you trying to kill me?" he choked out past the fumes rising up from his throat. "That's… horrific."

"Barely hot enough to wet the eyes," Angel replied smoothly. "Now eat your damned food so you can have a cupcake and we can talk."

"Is that how you parent your brother? Very stick, stick and carrot." The water did little to quench the fire in his mouth, only spreading the heat around his gums. Another mouthful and he swallowed, finally rinsing away enough of the hot sauce. The eggs weren't bad. Despite the iron clench of spinach, the rest of the fillings were nice, a layer of mushrooms and cheese mingled in with minced applewood bacon. "I think I'd rather talk than have the cupcake because that curry one... kind of scares me."

"The hot sauce scared you."

"At least I'm honest about how I feel with you. Now." Their food was getting cold, and through the motel's crappy interior doors, West heard Rome snoring in his room. "Let me eat this... salad you've put in my eggs. Then... I don't know."

They ate in silence until Angel pushed his plate away and leaned back in his chair. The shadows marbling the skin under his eyes were a dusky purple, but his gaze was as keen as ever. West finished a minute later, and when Angel reached over to grab his plate, West grabbed his hand.

"Don't. Just... let it sit for a bit." He stroked at the scars across Angel's knuckles. "Talk to me, Ange. Tell me... something... anything about what I've told you back in the bakery. Tell me you understand what happened and why I am so damned sorry for what happened."

Angel took his hand out of West's, plunging a cold white shot of pain into West's heart. It skipped and stuttered in the moments it took Angel to rub his knuckles over West's lower lip.

"I know you're sorry. I'm sorry too. For being pissed off at you... hell, for still being pissed off, but I don't know what to do here, man. We've not seen each other for... hell, long enough for me to get a baby brother that's almost old enough to date, and you... you actually went out and became some kind of mogul. We're further apart than we've ever been... and maybe that summer, we were just... I don't know... some kind of freak happy thing."

"I've fucking missed you, Angel," West admitted softly. "I've tried to forget you. Hell, I've gone through entire clubs of gay men looking for someone who got me like you did. I even contemplated sleeping with my college roommate because he's your exact opposite, then hired him instead because, well, he's straight, and while Derry looks good on paper, he's not you. He's not Angel *fucking* Daniels."

"Derry's that asshole trying to fuck us over with the motel, right? That one?"

"Can we focus on what I'm saying… the gist of it and not get too caught up in the sideshow?" West wrapped his fingers into Angel's hair, gently pulling the man closer to him. "I'm asking you to give us a chance, Angel. To let us see if we'll be good together. Like we'd been before. Because God knows, I still want you. And I know you still want me."

"Rome—"

"I'll do right by Rome. Even if we… don't work, I'm not going to build up a relationship with him and just disappear. You ask Lang, I don't throw away a broken kid. That's not me, Angel." He whispered a kiss across Angel's lips, silently begging him to part them so West could taste the heat lingering there. "Just… one chance, Daniels. *One*."

A klaxon screamed outside, its shrill, terrified shriek tearing through the murmuring pleas West'd built up. Not more than a second later, someone was pounding on Angel's door, heavy thumping blasts of a fist beating through the shaky wood. Startled, Angel got to his feet, yelling for Roman to wake up. Then he headed for the front door. The scent of burning plastic and wood hit West as soon as Angel jerked the door open, and the wild-eyed, lanky redhead stood on the stoop, naked except for a pair of sweats and perspiration on his forehead.

Smoke whispered in, and the redhead gasped, his fingers moving quickly over his cell phone despite the tremors in his hands. West heard someone on the line ask what the emergency was, but the redhead didn't answer. Instead he glanced back at the parking lot and grabbed Angel's shirt, yanking him out of the apartment.

"Justin, what?" Angel snatched the phone when it tumbled from the redhead's grasp. "What's going on?"

"The bakery, Ange," Justin cried out, trying to pull Angel with him. "Come on! It's on *fire*!"

Ten

SMOKE BILLOWED from the front of the bakery, settling over the parking lot in an oily black sheet. The wind twisted around the buildings, catching licks of fire at the Shack's engulfed porch and whipping the flames around the overhang's supporting posts. A macramé planter hanging from a hook on the far corner of the porch twisted when the fire worked through its plaits, curling into a blackened coil while its plastic planter melted and cracked in the heat.

The macramé had been a gift, a little something Violet wove together to celebrate the bakery's opening. It wouldn't survive the fire, but if they didn't get the flames under control, neither would the bakery.

"Boss, over here!" The large Italian bruiser who'd shown up nearly the moment Angel's bare feet hit the parking lot slammed a pickaxe into the side of the porch, breaking part of the patio covering away from the main structure. "Does the hose reach?"

In his tailored clothes, leather shoes, and expensive haircut, West Harris wasn't someone Angel would expect to wade into a burning fire armed only with a bright yellow garden hose and a watering spigot, but there West was, shoulder to shoulder with them. Soot smeared a mockery of war paint over his sharp cheekbones, and a drop of something dark dappled his lip, probably blood from where he'd bitten it trying to break the glass enclosure surrounding an old barrel fire extinguisher in the motel's infrequently manned front office.

While the extinguisher was regularly serviced, getting it out of its glass prison proved to be enough of a problem, Angel abandoned West and Justin to it and attacked the fire with a stretched-taut garden hose attached to a spigot near the long-empty, fenced in pool. A gorilla of a man pulled up in a sleek black car, panicking Angel. The man's arrival was too much like the night of the shooting, and he'd screamed for Roman to get the hell back inside of their room and call the cops.

He'd acted on instinct and punched the muscled, dark-suited man square in the face, then stood over him long enough to take a good look at the size of the man he'd floored, wondering if Justin was prepared to raise Roman by himself after the broken-nosed thug got up and took Angel apart.

"Marzo! Get up off your ass!" West yelled at the hulking man sprawled out on the pavement. "Grab something and help get the fire out! There's a shed over there. See if the gardeners left something."

Mumbling a brief apology, Angel surrendered his hose to Violet, leaving the nozzle on jet, then ducked the stream of water shooting from a hose West apparently found hooked up near the Shack's left wall. Vaguely recalling a charity car wash he'd let happen in the parking lot a month or so before, Angel caught a mouthful of stale-tasting water, grabbed the heavy shovel West's employee handed him, then proceeded to beat at the flames before they destroyed everything he'd worked for since he returned to Half Moon Bay.

"Beat a line into the ground. Keep it from spreading." West turned the water stream toward the bakery's entrance.

"Gonna see if we can get the porch off," Marzo shouted back as he bashed at the railing. "Keep the fire off the main building."

The porch attack seemed reasonable to Angel, or at least it felt like something he could do. He and Frank threw it up one afternoon after a torrential storm, and he'd been more concerned about keeping his customers dry than anything elaborate.

He hadn't planned on Frank's diligence and the sheer stubbornness of bolted-in wood.

"Aim for the wall!" Angel made room for Justin to get in beside him so the redhead could hit the flames with retardant from the fire extinguisher. "Cover anything you can reach."

His throat hurt, crackled from the smoke, and when he swallowed, trying to wet his gullet, it felt as if he'd swallowed handfuls of glass. One of the heavy planks connecting the porch to the bakery gave under Angel's shovel. Digging the tool's tip under the crack, Angel strained to break it. It cracked, and his shoulders ached from the effort. His hands were torn open, leaving bloody streaks on the shovel's sunbaked wooden handle.

Sirens circled in the air, piercing audibles dipping and rising in the night. Angel couldn't tell if the klaxons were cops or firemen. He didn't care who arrived, so long as they brought help. He was caught on a dual edge, his body worn down from a long day and stress, but his nerves jangled, flushing the metallic taint of panicked energy through his blood.

Another swing of the shovel, and the sky lit up with flashing lights, a macabre disco promising salvation as it painted the roiling dark smoke with blue and red swathes. The roar of heavy vehicles hit the tight street, and a long blast of a deep horn sent cars scrambling to let the long trucks through.

The air was ashy, a filmy veil of sticky white flakes soft enough to feather over Angel's face with a touch more tender and delicate than any lover he'd ever had. He'd tried wiping it away, smearing it into his chin, and his sweat turned the gray dust into paste, caking over his skin. He took a second to breathe, then went back in. They were still fighting to drag the porch from its moorings when the fire trucks arrived, smashing at the rails and hooking the garden tools into the slats to yank the overhang down.

Someone was shouting directions from the parking truck. Its brakes squealed, and the rig rocked as the fire crew poured out. The wave of voices nearly drowned out the crackle of the fire, and Angel dug in again, bumping his elbow into a stern-faced man who'd come across the street to help them. He couldn't see West, but Angel could hear his rolling authoritative voice urging Justin to coat the side of the building with water.

"Back up, back up!" A fireman Angel didn't recognize shouted at them as he hooked a wrench on the cap of a hydrant a few feet away from the bakery. Dragging a hose around the squat steel fixture, he worked fast, keeping one eye on the fire behind him. "I'll be needing all of you to clear out."

"Give me an all clear!" Someone from the truck—a woman— yelled through the din. "And get everyone else back. We're going to go at this!"

It seemed like forever and a day before the steely-eyed firefighter with a slather of Irish tapped through the hydrant. Then the world bent around a gush of pressurized water and prayers. Someone'd pulled Angel back, strong arms wrapped around his waist and dragging him from the bakery's front wall. He didn't fight the embrace, but his feet were reluctant to move. There was a niggling kernel of alarm digging into Angel's thoughts, and he resisted being dragged away. He saw something dark moving behind a curtain in the front room, a shadow or a trick of the light from the lamps lining the historic walk, but in the consuming flames, Angel's heart skipped and stalled when he thought he saw a face in the smoke.

"God, Rome!" A fear—a stupid, irrational fear—took over his brain, seizing up every last dreg of energy he had in him and ramping it up until it burned like lightning through his blood. "Where's Rome! He's not inside there, right? Is someone in there? Is someone inside?"

"Marzo's got him, Ange," West murmured into his ear, barely audible in the slush of noises surrounding him. "He's okay. This is going to be okay. There's no one inside."

"I just saw…." He twisted about in West's arms, refusing to be led away. "God, I don't know what I'm going to do. We're… fuck, we're going to lose *everything*."

"It's just the front of the bakery—"

"They're going to shut me down." Angel's terror settled, and a cold, hard bite of reality took its place. "They're going to have to. Everything inside… I can't serve it. Even if they save the Shack, I can't fucking use the damned building. Fucking *everything*—"

"I'll handle this. *We* can handle this, Angel." West turned him around, and Angel stared into West's determined, handsome face. "We'll figure something out and deal with it, but this is *not* going to take you out, okay? I've fought worse things than a damned fire. You are not going to lose this."

"I can't lose it. I lose the bakery and I've got—nothing again. They shut me down and I'm done, West."

The tears came, long, sudden, jagged, too heavy for Angel to hold back. He didn't have a name for the emotional stew drowning him. It ran the gamut from terror to resignation, with everything else in between. It wasn't going to end well for them. He'd lived through too many failed hustles and broken dreams to think it would turn out any better than any other time he'd failed.

"They're not going to shut you down," West assured him, dragging Angel into cooler air. "You're going to be okay."

"I can't keep my… family together…. Roman… if I fall." Angel couldn't stop crying. His chest shook with every draw of air, but Angel couldn't seem to catch his breath. "They're going to take Rome from me, and I *cannot* lose him. Haven't I already lost so *fucking* much? How much more do I have to give before something goes *right*?"

He sagged.

Deep inside of where Angel kept every single one of his doubts and trepidations, the walls he'd been shoring up to hold himself together finally gave way, and he tumbled forward, dragged down by the weight of everything resting on him. West caught him, a stile he'd forgotten he'd buried in the tall grasses of his unkempt life.

The cacophony faded, and Angel closed his eyes, wishing for a peace he could never seem to see much less grasp. Tears were the least of his worries. The hot slag of salty water stinging his lashes couldn't compete against the crumbling ruins of his life. He'd dumped everything he had into the bakery, learned everything he could to make it a success, and stretched every dollar until it bled, and still they'd been beaten into the ground.

For a single moment, Angel wanted the luxury of being able to sit down in the middle of the road and simply stop moving, to not hustle and steal bits of time from every day to manage every thread of life being cast off of the Fates' chaotic spindle.

"Fuck it. I'll just take Roman and we'll run," Angel gasped, searching for any lick of fresh air in the smoke choking him. "Not like we don't know how to do that."

Running seemed like his only option—the only viable one—especially since the paint was bubbling off the Shack's outer walls and the burly Irish fireman was now joined by what looked like a sea of men and women in heavy gear, their feet digging into the asphalt and smoking grass to hold on to the massive hoses pouring foamy water everywhere.

The van he'd leave for Justin, since the SUV was better suited for long hauls. He'd have to hide Rome someplace safe, deep in the folds of Seattle or somewhere else he could get his hands on his brother's medication. They weren't leaving much. He'd never succumbed to Rome's begging for a dog or a cat. They'd have to tighten in, closing in on each other until Rome was old enough, adult enough to be safe from CPS's intrusive reach.

A brush of a mouth on his and Angel's plans shattered, a glass pane made of panic and dread crushed under a whisper of hope, a slender beat of a stitched-together heart too tired of bleeding out, its mewling throbs begging for the touch of the man pulling Angel free of the fire's harsh smoke.

"I'm not going to let you run, Daniels." West drew Angel in close. "Not when I've got you back. Not when you haven't given me my second chance to piss you off and love you. I'll be fucking *damned* if I let you run out on me now, love."

His arms were steel, locking Angel into an embrace he wasn't sure he ever wanted to break out of. It was so tempting to simply give in, to fold himself into West's control and let the blue-eyed devil who'd haunted his dreams take over.

No one's going to take care of you, Angel, his damaged brain reminded him. *West wants—*

Angel slammed his thoughts down, burying them under years of anger and betrayal. The whispering digs in his mind were mines placed in a field his father'd sowed. There were people he'd come to depend on, people he loved and in turn, felt love from. Justin was as close to a brother as he could get, and they'd both embraced Roman into the fucked-up little family living at the Moonrise Motel.

He'd spent long evenings cooking holiday dinners on burners in five different rooms to eat at an off-kilter picnic table set up in the parking lot. From stringing garlands over the road-exhaust suffocated palms planted around the dead swimming pool to hiding plastic Easter eggs in the stairwells for everyone to find after the pancake drive at the church down the street, Angel'd *found* the place he needed to be.

He'd made himself a spot, a patchwork oasis of misfits and glitches, and he'd regret giving it up. More than he regretted giving up on West. Or at least damned close to it.

"Whatever happens, Angel…." West's whisper tickled his ear. "We'll fix it. Okay?"

It took everything for Angel to find his voice. It was buried under ash, terror, and life-honed razor blades. The wind no longer played with his hair, and the rush of water no longer battered the bakery. There were still yellow-jacketed firemen crawling over the building, and he'd lost track of the blue-eyed Irish man who'd first doused the shack, but the fire with its terrible, hungry flames smoldered across the rubble of the detached overhang, its crumpled sides spread out over the sidewalk to be picked through for embers.

"Go find Rome, love." West's arms loosened, letting Angel go. Wiping at the wet on Angel's cheeks with his thumbs, West laughed. "God, I'm making a mess here."

"I'm always a mess," he replied softly. A hiccup caught Angel unaware, and he ducked his head, attempting to force the bubble of air in his stomach out. "Fuck, aren't I always a mess? You sure you want to take this on? There's a lot of… crap in my life. A lot of shitty, shitty things."

"I've already taken on flying bullets and now a fire for you," he said, shrugging. "Bring it on. Go check on Rome. Then we'll see what the firemen say. They'll probably want to talk to you. After that, it's time I got you home."

"I live across the parking lot, Harris." Angel smirked. "Not a far walk."

"Yeah, you're only going to be there long enough to pack some clothes." West kissed the corner of his mouth. "Stray bullet notwithstanding, the safest place I can think of is my house… especially since Marzo's going to take up residence in the guest quarters. I'm not going to be able to sleep unless I know you're okay. So go grab some things and your little brother, Daniels, so we can go home."

THE HOT shower felt good. Almost as good as the numbness of the painkiller kicking in nearly as soon as West collapsed onto the couch in his living room. Armed with an icepack for his knee and a glass of iced tea, he stared out into the night, catching the barest hint of his own reflection cast back at him in the living room's enormous windows.

Marzo'd taken the apartment over the garage as his home base, accessible through a flight of stairs off the kitchen, and the bodyguard did a circuit of the property before heading to bed. Perched on a rise in the cliff, the house was approachable from the front and sides, which were apparently too many options for Marzo's liking. Grumbling about a lack of electric fences, guard dogs, and gun turrets, he hadn't been too pleased with West pointing out none of those could have stopped the bullet shot through the open front door.

His intense scowl was enough to tickle West's humor long past the time Marzo stomped outside to do recon.

There'd been laughter upstairs as the two brothers playfully fought about baths, pajamas, and school attendance. Listening to the Danielses chatter, West found a small ache in his chest pulse, deepening with each guffaw and mocking outrageous accusation. He'd never had that kind of relationship with Lang. Their childhood was a fleeting blur of grayness, lessons, and rigid coldness. He couldn't recall a single time he'd laughed with Lang. Not with the unfettered glee Roman belted out with his older brother.

"Grandmother's house. Those summers," West murmured to himself, shifting the pack over his slightly swollen knee. "When we were at her house. Did we laugh, Lang? Did we do *anything* together?"

They laughed now. A bit. Teased and jabbed in a way West felt was almost comfortable, but the awkwardness remained, his driving, controlling personality butting up against his twin's easygoing nature. At some point, West became their father's echo, and as he contemplated the ruins of his life, he didn't like what he saw.

"Going to have to rebuild, Harris." Toasting himself in the glass, West chuckled. "And this time, you're going to have to get it right."

"What are you planning on getting right?" Angel appeared behind him in the window, his vivid coloring muted to grays and browns with a hint of red from the shirt he'd pulled on over his hewn chest.

West drank him in, stared at the window and let himself enjoy the sight of Angel standing behind him, then leaned his head back to see Angel smiling down at him.

"You, love," he whispered softly. "Well, us, really. I'm hoping that this time, I can get us right."

Eleven

"GOT YOUR brother all settled?" West kept his tone as casual as he could, but his body thrummed in response to Angel's light touch on his shoulder.

"Yeah, Rome passed out before I turned the light off. Pablo's going to be at Joey's in the morning to bake up those batters they cleared for use. I should go down there and help him—"

"You're going to run yourself into the ground, Daniels." West shook his head. "If Pablo can do it by himself, let him. Take it from someone who has to control everything, you need to let some things go."

"And you shouldn't have jumped in to fight the fire, but that didn't stop you." Angel slipped around the end of the couch, then eased onto the cushion beside West. "You've screwed up your knee again. Shit, between the car, bullets, and firefighting, you're going to be dead before the end of next week."

"The knee was because I slipped badly off the asphalt... *again*. I'd injured my ankle in the car accident." He shifted to give Angel room, leaning against him once they got settled. "I'm trying to take preventative measures to keep the bruising down. Or at least that's what I'm going to tell the doctor."

"Somehow I don't think that helps you out there, Harris. You've got to stop trying to die on me."

"Wasn't planning on it. Not unless we fuck each other to death." West shifted the ice pack around. The burning sensation on his skin grew intolerable, and his rolled-up sweatpants were getting damp. "Because really, that's how I'm planning on dying. In bed, a smile on my face, and possibly a few shots of good whiskey in my belly. And bacon. There should have been mass consumption of bacon."

"And we go straight into talking about fucking?"

"*That* I planned on. Or at least hoped for. Maybe not tonight but... at some point." He studied Angel's expression, wanting to dig past the wariness he saw there. "Not originally. Certainly not with Marzo and Roman sitting in the car with us, but afterwards, in the shower... I had *thoughts*."

"Interesting." Angel's eyes stormed, roiling thunderous gray behind his long lashes. "So you didn't say something to Justin?"

"Like what?" He tilted his head, fascinated by the heat in Angel's glance. "Mostly pointing out hot spots to him, but other than that I might have said good job or something afterwards. Why?"

"He threw clothes into a bag for me while I was getting Rome's stuff, and for some reason, he felt I needed a couple of handfuls of condoms and a large tube of something called Ease-In. Scented and self-heating, of course, for someone's pleasure."

"As you do when you're packing a friend's bag." West chuckled. "I honestly debated having Marzo grab some on the way to the bakery but thought he'd kill me for it. There's only so much you can ask a man to do."

"You, Harris, have got to start participating in your own goddamned life." Angel twisted around, pushing on West's shoulder to lean him forward. Pulling his knee up, Angel ordered, "Move so we can sit sideways."

They'd sat chest to back at least hundreds of times when they were younger, but that'd been before... everything, and West eyed Angel skeptically, then shifted over. After a too-long day of emotional savaging, then an exhausting fight to save Angel's livelihood, he should be dropping off to sleep. Instead, Angel's beautiful long body left him... energized, his skin aching to be touched.

Dipping his shoulders down, West moved back, sliding into a spot he hadn't lain in years. He couldn't remember the last time he'd leaned against Angel's chest, and he regretted not having that moment to hold onto. It was easy to recall the first time. They'd been mostly drunk on a bottle of cheap wine and sitting on the cold sand, watching the stars push their light through the stretch of cobalt-black night sky.

Their bodies seemed to remember the planes and dips of the other, because when West leaned back into Angel, it was like... coming *home*.

The feeling of Angel around him was both familiar and strange. West knew the scent of the man against him, and his skin warmed with the touch of Angel's hands on his arms. Their legs remained almost the same length, Angel's thighs and calves thicker than West's, but his feet were still smaller, his right pinky toe scarred from the fishing hook West accidentally lodged into it. It was odd finding their adult bodies fit into one another. Odder still when West slid down a bit against Angel's chest and leaned his head back, the ridge at the back of his skull once again nestling in the crook of Angel's neck as if they'd once been a single stone split in two and cast far apart, only finding one another on the same shore because of a mercurial tide.

There were small whispers between their bodies, intimate, sibilant slithers of fabric and skin. Angel chased away the chilly spot between West's shoulder blades, his toned, hard stomach a welcome warmth to ease away the aches in West's bruised bones. Their touching resonated, striking hidden wells buried deep inside West's soul, the comfort of Angel's breath on the back of his neck soothing away the prickles dug into his troubled mind. Angel's strange, steady wildness calmed him, an unexpected heart-pounding rapid rush of a ride until a corner turned and he found the serenity in the middle of the storm. West closed his eyes, took a deep breath, and engraved the moment Angel wrapped his arms around his chest into his heart to keep for the rest of his life.

"I wish I'd forgotten how good this feels," he murmured.

West felt Angel's soft chuckle resonate up out of him, burying his laughter into West's spine. Laying his hand on West's belly, he said, "I'm not sure how to take that."

"If I'd forgotten," he explained, shifting his hips to lodge himself tighter into the V between Angel's parted legs, "I would be able to discover it all over again. How magical that would be. To feel that all over again."

"I think those painkillers of yours are working. You're turning all sweet on me." Angel bent his head down, brushing his lips across West's cheek. His breath was minty, the tip of his tongue a hot daub on the corner of West's lips. "So should I yell at Justin or thank him with some cookies?"

"Fuck the cookies." West craned back, savoring Angel's deep kiss. "I'm going to buy him a damned car. Maybe a damned pony."

WEST'S SHIRT didn't survive the twenty steps it took for them to get to the bed. It tore, snagged around Angel's fingers, and the thin, silky fabric gave in easily to the tension of being fisted, then pulled. It was understandable. West had every intention of giving in to Angel's hands, mouth, and everything else offered up to him.

And he wanted to give as good as he got in return.

His ankle complained about the scramble across the polished wood floor, then the sudden grip of the plush area rug around his bed. Not far behind, West's knee twisted and moaned, but he shoved aside the twinges and pain. It'd been forever since he'd tasted Angel in his mouth, a slap of a kiss in the middle of his foyer and his soul creaked open, shaking off the rusted iron bands he'd forged around it.

"God, you taste so fucking good."

Angel's mutter was low, poured hot sugar over West's tight nerves. His voice, rich and velvety, stroked at West's balls, cupping them as Angel's laugh slid down West's throat. His stomach caught the flutter of Angel's smooth, silken baritone, ripples of sound feathering down the length of West's torso, then spreading over his thighs.

Angel's dark hair ran damp near his skull, leaving wet slathers on West's fingers when he dug them through Angel's mane. They fought to kiss, struggling to shed their clothes, but not break apart, a violent dance of fractured symmetry disjointed enough to frustrate, but West soldiered on. He needed to have Angel against him—in him—and the weight of his desire frightened him more than the fire eating through Angel's bakery or the bullet flying through his foyer.

He'd never given himself to another man. He'd never offered his body up for anything other than his own pleasure. Sure, he'd returned blow jobs and jerked his casual lovers off, but the pleasure he'd gotten from sinking into another man's body was not anything he'd ever imagined, much less actually contemplated doing.

With Angel—his Angel—West knew he was safe. The enormity of his fear numbed his limbs, seeping into his face, and he bled white, the sensation in his cheeks going dull. Blinking, he stared hard at the man he'd never wanted to lose but lost anyway.

"Do you know I've never...." West exhaled. "I've never had anyone inside of me. I've always been...."

"Tab A?" Angel teased. Then his eyes shone silver, a contemplative mirror West feared to find himself in. "I'm good either way, West. Hell, I don't care if we rub up against each other like we're getting splinters off a pair of chopsticks, so long as I'm doing *something* with you."

"Hear me out, please. See, I like sex. Don't get me wrong."

It was little more of a naughty whisper, but his words made Angel smile.

"But I've never loved sex. It's always been... something I need to get done because I needed it. Like eating a sandwich because I needed food, but not really tasting anything. Just enough to keep my body going so I could get on with my life. It was never on the table. Like I was giving too much of myself. It's not that I didn't want it. I just—"

"And now?" Angel ventured softly. "With me?"

"I want you so fucking bad, I can taste it." He shifted in Angel's arms, their bare stomachs slightly slick from the heat of their touching skin. "I want you inside of me. And I want to be inside of *you*. See, I just figured out I've been afraid this whole time.

"It was easier to keep what I wanted in a box. Hell, I didn't need my father to shove me into a closet. I built one around me." Caught in Angel's arms, West pulled his lover in close, curving Angel against him. "I've trusted *no one*. Let *no one* in… and none of them were… you. God, I've been a shit to a lot of guys because I've never given them anything *except* sex. This? You and me? It's different. It feels different. I've spent my whole life holding my breath, waiting for *us* to happen, and I'm so very sorry it took me this long to find you again."

"How about if we take our time and see where we end up?" Angel's dimple flashed in his cheek.

"I've got a better idea." West swallowed the lump in his throat. "I like having a goal, something to work towards. Helps me keep focused, and I like knowing where I'm going, so how about if we take our time and you fuck me so I work on my trust issues with the only man I feel safe with?"

"Well, then," Angel murmured, dipping his head down for another kiss. "That sounds like a hell of a great plan."

THERE WAS a taste to a man. It was hard to describe, a sweet musk tickled with an elusive erotic note meant to seduce and entice. Angel loved the scent of men, savoring the uniqueness of every one he'd been with.

Being with West was… different. As he licked up the inside of West's thigh, the dapple of masculine essence left him needing more, aching for the glide of another inch of skin on his tongue. West's tang filled him, quenching a desire he'd buried deep inside of him. Naked and laid bare to the stars glimmering through the bedroom's massive windows, Angel sculpted his tongue around West's velvety cock head and suckled off the slick fluid pearling at its slit.

It was the first true taste of West's body, and Angel held the drop up against the roof of his mouth, reveling in the salt-bitters of his lover's spend. He gripped West's hips, digging into his lover's soft skin, then went in for more.

"Angel," West moaned, writhing under Angel. "God… *damn it*."

Angel was torn, desperate to envelop himself in West's heat and longing to explore every inch of the man's long, strong body. There was a sleek power to West's length. Hidden beneath the pressed button-up shirts and cuffed linen slacks was a study of planes and ridges, sloping muscles stretched taut over a graceful form. His pale skin flushed pink across his belly when Angel ran the tip of his tongue around West's navel, the blush chasing up West's chest to stain his cheeks.

West's fingers dug into his hair, then his shoulders, brief sunbursts of burred pain and want. His body trembled under Angel's mouth and fingers, his firm cock pressing into the dip in Angel's tongue. Angel swallowed around him, then lightly dragged his teeth down West's shaft, drawing out another shaky, rasping sigh from West's kiss-swollen lips.

"Not… *shit*." West's nails sliced into Angel's skin, his back bowing into a tight arch. Shuddering in Angel's mouth, he twisted to get loose. "Damn it… *Angel*. Not…."

"Want me to stop?" Angel pulled free, catching West's sensitive cock ridge with the barest nip of his teeth. "Or—"

"Swear to God, if you don't fuck me—"

"That's all I was waiting for," he promised. "I just needed to hear you wanted me."

"What do you think I've been saying since we started this?" West lifted his head, scowling down the length of his body at Angel.

Angel sat back on his haunches and grinned at his lover, his sharp features turned saturnine from the pools of shadows, the faint golden light gilding the edges of his deep blue eyes. With his shock of inky hair rumpled around his face, West looked younger than his years, an echo of the innocent, soul-injured teen Angel'd met on the carnival's thoroughfare.

"God, I love looking at you," he whispered, crawling up West's body.

He didn't dare delve deeper than that for how he felt about West. Already trembling inside by having West naked under him, Angel couldn't risk any more of himself, not when things were too nebulous, too fragile between them. As much as West talked of second chances and destinies, they were sitting in the ashes of their past, stoking the fires of the now between them. Angel wasn't sure if he would survive the night, much less rise from the sear of their heat with everything still intact.

But West was worth the risk. He knew it in his gut. No, after what happened between them, he'd hold on to the night he shared with West and treasure it to his grave.

The mattress dimpled under his outstretched hands when Angel straddled West's hips, his kiss stealing the air from West's chest. They fought through the touch of their lips, delving in deep until they had to break apart, lungs tender from the strain of holding a single breath between them.

West brushed his fingers over Angel's cheek, a feathering, soft caress tracing over the bone, then skimming over a small triangular scar near his right eye. Angel's lashes caught on West's thumb, flicking over the plump flesh's ridges.

"I am so sorry about this. You know that?"

His smile was bashful, white and perfect against his faintly golden skin. Angel loved that smile, with West's eyes crinkling at the edges. It was a face he could watch grow older, mellowing with age.

"I can't believe how many scars I gave you in just a few months."

"Felt like we were together forever, didn't it?" Angel whispered against West's palm. "All these years... and I didn't regret one single second we had. Although, maybe less fish hooks and bottle cap duels in the future."

"God, we were stupid kids."

"Can't say we're much smarter now," he admitted slyly. "But we can certainly find something better to do on a cold, crisp night than see who can fling a beer top into the fire."

It was a slow dance, one filled with quiet laughter, bobbled lube splotches, and heated kisses. The condom was an exercise in patience, and Angel caught the tip of his tongue between his teeth when West slid it down Angel's shaft. A few kisses later, Angel chuckled against West's belly when the skin-warmed lube slid around on his fingers instead of slicking West's body, and West teased him about taking his damned sweet time, then sucked in his breath when Angel rolled his balls around, making them draw up into the hollow between his thighs. Stroking his knuckles against West's taint, Angel worked the lube into the tight ring below.

The hiss he drew out from West made him smile, as did the muttering threat he was given as he slid his fingers into West's clenched hole. Angel lightly bit at West's hip bone, drawing a bit of his attention away from the press against his rim. West was tight, nearly too tight, and Angel took his time, sliding and teasing West's entrance.

"Angel—"

"Right here, West," he murmured.

His lover's body held his fingers tight, his oil-wet ring giving easily when teased apart. After coating his latex-covered cock with a handful of lube, Angel pressed against West's rim and gently pushed in. West's eyes were nearly black, and he caught his lower lip in between his teeth, huffing once when Angel guided his head past West's ring and into the clenching heat beyond.

"Relax, babe," Angel cautioned. "If it's too much—"

"It's not enough," West ground out. Raising his hips, he grabbed at Angel's side, skimming his hand over Angel's hip. "Fuck, I need more of you. *Please*."

There weren't words for how delicious West felt around his body. He was a delectable wrap of warmth and velvet, engulfing Angel's length, but it was the shuddering of pleasure West did when Angel worked in deep that drove Angel wild. Pulling out, he paused for a moment, then went back in, drawing another shaking response from the man under him.

With West's legs hooked over his hips, Angel fell into a rhythm, and West rose to meet him, their bodies slowly moving to touch, then drawing away. The window near the bed fogged up, the silken dew from their joined heat masking their reflection, but the other panes left them open to the sky and its dark drape of sparkling cobalt.

Digging his knees into the mattress, Angel held West's weight up and snapped his hips, driving harder into his lover's body. They were quickly losing the beat they'd found between them, a tingling building as Angel's balls roiled and danced. His cock throbbed, its head almost painfully tight from the stimulation of West's tightening hold. Twisting his hips, Angel drove in deeper, harder than before, and a drop of sweat fell from his chest, splashing down on West's sleek, bare belly.

Bending over, he laved at West's plum-hued nipples, drawing the nubs up into tight buttons with his teeth. He bit, perhaps too hard, because West arched up, his stomach pressed into Angel's, and his hard cock wept, trapped between them. Balancing carefully, Angel shoved his hand down to grasp West, then pulled up, falling into a counterbeat. West's fingers covered his palm, and he murmured at Angel, urging him to help him finish.

Angel knew the moment West reached his peak. His face lost all its guard, and West simply sighed, opening his expression until he was peeled apart, his vulnerable and bruised nature breaking free of the chrysalis West'd built up around himself. The hot stream of cum from West's cock was all Angel needed. The aromatic sting of West's scent filled Angel's senses, and he growled, his own release breaking free and gushing into the tight envelope around his shaft.

It became too much for Angel to bear. Thrown off-balance from their bodies' spasms, Angel fell forward, resting his shoulder against West's chest as they emptied themselves. Heart pounding through a roar in his ears, Angel panted, body slick with sweat and West's spend. His lover's neck was wet, and Angel licked at a spot beneath West's earlobe, then bit at the sweat-dewed skin he found there.

"I've missed you so fucking much, Angel," West whispered. "I've missed you since the day you left me."

"I've missed you too." Angel eased out of West as he stretched over his lover's still trembling body. "I've missed the friend I had in you. And as much of an asshole as you are at times, you're one of the best people I know. And I've kind of missed that too."

"Stay with me." West's plea was soft, but Angel heard the frantic, hard desperation hidden in his rich tones. "Let me wake up with you. At least… just tomorrow morning."

"I'll be here, West." He kissed West lightly. Their bodies were sticky with release and sweat, but Angel nuzzled in closer, feeling West's need to be touched and reassured. "Tomorrow morning and any morning you might need me, okay? For as long as you want me, I will be here. I promise."

Twelve

ANGEL WOKE up alone and in the dark. He was comfortable, oddly so. Nothing poked up into his back, and his feet seemed to be on the mattress. A soft mattress, firm enough to support his body, and when he stretched, he didn't hit his head on a couch cushion or snag his toes into a minefield of exposed coiled springs.

The heady scent of sex and West slithered into his brain, and Angel blinked, his tumultuous thoughts settling down long enough for him to remember the yesterday he'd endured and the glorious hours he'd spent with West before sleep finally claimed them.

"Okay, being alone is okay," he told himself. "West owns a huge company. Probably has to go do mogul things at—" Angel checked the clock. "—five in the morning. Totally normal. And… oh shit, Rome. Okay, get up, Daniels. Your baby brother can't find you in—"

It wasn't as if Roman didn't know Angel preferred men, but Angel's dating pretty much dried up long before his brother moved in. Between taking care of Rome, covering the motel's infrequent issues, and the bakery, his life was a tumble of work and sleep set on a rinse-and-repeat cycle. A niggle of guilt at leaving Pablo to take care of the morning baking load slipped down to a dull roar when he reminded himself the scrawny older man was not only competent but hated when Angel needlessly hovered.

"Less hovering," Pablo would say, shaking a spatula at Angel's nose. "You need to live more. You do the batters, and I bake. Now is baking time. So get out of my kitchen."

"Okay, so right now it's Joey's kitchen. Again." Angel took a quick peek at his phone, but Pablo hadn't reached out for help. "Do what the man tells you. He does this all the time. Years now. Just… let everyone do their job… and take a shower so Rome doesn't find you naked and raunchy."

His shoulders and arms hurt, stings of prickling pain sharp enough to remind him of working the heavy shovel to fight the fire, and places along his neck throbbed, bruised from West's lust-driven bites. He was marbled in black and blue along his chest, purpling welts scattered across his skin in a trail from his nipple to his upper arm.

"Okay, you need to eat more food if you're going to stick around, Harris," Angel muttered to himself as he scrubbed their night off his body. The shower spray was a battering of needles along his back, and even accounting for the strain along his shoulders from fighting the fire, there were too many sore spots along his spine for him to count. Twisting around, he frowned at a pinked bite mark on the back of his left thigh. "Really? Even there? Dude."

Dried off and with a damp towel wrapped around his waist, Angel padded out to the hallway and froze at the soft murmur of voices coming from downstairs. Clutching the towel tightly, he peeked into the bedroom he'd left Roman in only to find it empty, the bed linens a pile at the end of the bed.

"No worries. He's... *fuck*." There were a million reasons for Roman to be awake, innocent little scenarios for him to be up before dawn and wandering around a strange house, but his brain refused to seize onto any one of them. Instead, he had visions of cops, missing rediscovered lovers, and lost baby brothers.

His bare feet hit the stairs midlanding, and Angel heard Roman's raucous, boisterous laugh slam into the house's soft quiet, shattering it with a hearty bray. Skidding to a stop in the middle of the living room, Angel stared at West and Roman sitting at a long pale oak dining table set in a space at the far end of the house, their dark-haired heads nearly touching as they studied an enormous laptop's screen.

They looked nothing alike except for the dark hair, but their body language was alarmingly mirrored on their faces. There was a cunning air about them, their attention focused tight on what they were doing. Angel was too far away to see what was on the screen, but he had his suspicions, especially when West tapped a few buttons to pull up a candy distributor's website.

"So, do you see? Markup has to vary," West explained. "Yes, you do need a few lower-cost, high-profit items interspersed with your high-ticket candies, but what you want to do is keep your eye on flash deals. Something goes on sale, grab it and do a limited run. Don't keep it at the same cost you normally have it at, but don't make the markup so low people wait for you to have sales to buy."

"What about the lollipops? I can get those big ones for a buck a bunch. I think I want to sell them at a quarter each because kids always have a quarter. *And* I don't want to make change."

Roman tapped a few buttons on the keyboard, and Angel saw a spreadsheet fill the screen.

"I don't make a lot of money, but I think it helps to keep people coming, you know? And when they've got more money, they'll buy from *me*. I'm worried some guy's going to come in and try to shove me out. The older kids, you know? Maybe I need a Marzo."

"Never ever get muscle for anything other than protection. Besides, you'd have to pay him," West commented softly. "But if you do, make sure it's a friend. Marzo's not only my bodyguard, but he's also a good friend. Even if he didn't work for me, I'd want to make sure he did okay."

"I thought we agreed you wouldn't be selling candy at school?"

Angel padded up behind them. West's surprise flitted across his face before dissolving into a disciplined smirk.

"I'm not selling it at school." Rome's attention flicked over to West, then returned to Angel. "I'm taking orders the day before and handing stuff out in the morning. On the sidewalk. Before school."

Angel rubbed at his face, then tightened his grip on the towel knotted at his waist. "Jesus. Rome—"

"Shouldn't you put some clothes on?" Roman asked. "And *then* you can bitch me out?"

"You should ask him why he wasn't sleeping in his own room."

West's faux whisper into Roman's ear brought a grin to his brother's face.

"Not going to work, Harris." Angel quelled Roman's question with a hard look as soon as the boy opened his mouth. "I ask a question and it stays on topic until I'm happy with the answer. House rules. But yeah, I'm going to go put some clothes on. If you're going to stay up, you're going to bathe and brush your teeth. Then we're going to talk about this, dude. You keep this up and you're going to get suspended. And you know what happens when you're suspended."

"I end up working in the bakery." Rome made a face. "Without pay. Hey wait, it burned down! So I don't have to—"

"Porch burned down. Bakery's fine. Guy from the fire marshal's office said we'll probably going to be cleared to go in today. Just in time for you to peel tangerines and separate the flesh out," Angel clarified.

"You guys going to kiss? That's why you're sending me upstairs?" Rome's challenge was light, a flicking tease. "'Cause you guys are boyfriends now? I could be scarred for life."

"Boyfriends, huh?" Angel shot West a look. The man stared right back with an innocence so fake Angel could taste it. "Yeah, that's something West and I are going to talk about. But so you know, I'm going to kiss who I want, when I want, whether you're around or not, brat. So get your ass upstairs, Rome. And Harris… you and I need to get a couple things straight. Right after I go find me some pants."

WEST LEANED against the doorframe and watched Angel button up his jeans. He'd gotten there almost too late but soon enough to see Angel tug his pants up over his tight rear. As tender as his own ass was, watching Angel's guileless sensual dressing set off more than a few fires in West's belly and balls, with his cock chiming in for another go at the man he'd pulled back into his life.

He *liked* the slender nipping marks he'd left on Angel. It wasn't a civilized thing to discover about himself. If anything, it was brutish and primal, a declaration of ownership no sane and mature person would be proud of. It was stupid and childish. No question about it. But damned if he didn't feel proud to have dappled Angel's golden skin.

"What are you grinning at, Harris?" Angel looked up through his sun-streaked mane. The caramel strands were a dull bronze in the scant light, but they shimmered through the umber silk framing Angel's strong face. "Rome done brushing his teeth and showering?"

West shook his head and chuckled. "He actually didn't make it that far. I stuck my head in and he was facedown on the bed, snoring."

"You sure about that?" His lashes dipped down, shadowing his eyes briefly. "That's a pretty common scam, pretending you're asleep so you don't get a talking-to."

"I tugged the blankets out from under him, got flailed at like he was going a few rounds with Ali, then he started drooling." West pushed off the doorframe, crossing the room toward the bed. Its mattress was firmer than his own, not uncomfortably so but still more than he liked. "If he's acting, he'd have stopped pretending as soon as he saw it was me. I'm not the one he's avoiding."

The con artist West first met still lurked in Angel. He'd turned it into something else, something purer than a scrabble of fast words and sleight of hand, but that hard, sharp intelligence still shone out of his warm quicksilver eyes. An intelligence honed to a point and piercing through West's words, digging through them for any hint of a lie.

"*Huh*," Angel grunted at him, reaching for a T-shirt on the bed. "So, that means you and I can talk… about Rome. You know he's been warned about selling candy at school, right?"

"He told me the long, sordid story. About how he's being oppressed and fighting against the Man."

"He's not being oppressed. He's breaking the rules. School doesn't want junk food on campus, and he's dealing sugar bombs out of his locker," Angel spat back. "I can't risk him getting kicked out of school. He doesn't seem to get it. And for what? Candy?"

"It isn't about the candy, Ange," West said, leaning back on his hands. "Or the money."

"No?" Angel shoved his head through the shirt's larger opening, tugging it down over his hard torso. "Then what? Because it sure as hell isn't about getting better math grades. That asshole's been chewing his way to Ds and Cs ever since I got him, so if I thought hawking Hershey's Kisses to a bunch of classmates would do him any good, I'd drive him to the store myself."

"Can you actually call a kid an asshole?" He smirked up at Angel, stretching his legs out. "I mean, are you allowed to? Sure, you're pretty much his parent, but I don't think you can."

"You're not supposed to, but let's face it, sometimes kids are assholes." Angel dragged a wooden chair out from under a desk by the window, then planted it in front of West. Straddling it, he rested his arms on its back and said, "He knows it. Like I know I'm an asshole sometimes too. He's my brother, West. I'm doing the best I can, so I'm going to ask you this one more time… stop giving him ideas on how to break the rules. Because if it's not about the money or pissing in his principal's mouth, what is it about?"

"It's about the game. Getting around those rules." West toed the back of the chair with his bare foot, dislodging Angel's arms. "Come over here. You've got that chair in between us like a wall."

"Maybe I need a wall. Did you ever think about that?" Angel pursed his lips in mock anger, then sighed when West patted the bed. He stood, then swung the chair out of the way. Climbing onto the bed, he warned, "No fucking around. We need to hammer some shit out."

"Promise." He shifted over, giving Angel some room to stretch out. Leaning against the headboard, West waited until Angel's shoulder nudged his before nodding his chin toward the bank of windows. "Sun's behind us, but we can watch the sunrise hit the ocean."

"Feels weird to do this and not be on the beach," Angel murmured, shoving a pillow behind the small of his back. "But I don't miss the damned sand. Okay. I'm here. Talk. Give me one good reason I shouldn't shut down Roman's candy thing."

"I'm not saying you shouldn't shut it down. What I'm saying is that he's bored. School bores him." That earned him a sidelong glance. He deserved it. After spending half an hour with the younger Daniels, West'd come to appreciate the odd blend of love and animosity the brothers shared. "He's good at math, as he is art. Hell, he's already got a good grasp on supply, demand, and pipeline strategies, but what he doesn't have is a way to channel that brain of his. So the candy thing? It's a challenge."

The tired and worry resurfaced in Angel's eyes, extinguishing the light West put there. Leaning over, West brushed a light kiss over Angel's mouth, then wrapped his fingers through Angel's, holding his hand tightly. The horizon silvered, reflecting the light coming from the sun still hidden behind the mountains. Waves rippled through the metallic sheen, picking up shadows and brights from the sky. They sat there for a few minutes, silent but for their breathing. Then Angel sighed.

"I'm really doing the best I can, West. You know that?" Angel's head became a weight on West's shoulder, and he firmed his spine, giving Angel a solid place to rest. "Jesus. I don't know what to do anymore. And I've got another seven years to screw him up?"

"You're not going to screw him up. You're not screwing him up *now*."

"You just tagged me for calling him an asshole," he pointed out. "We call each other asshole and dickhead all the time. How is that not screwing things up? Shit, every time I watch Deacon with Zig I think I'm the world's shittiest parent and how I've got to do better. Then I fuck it all up again."

"For one thing, Deacon and Zig aren't you and Roman," West replied softly. "Did you remember his medications?"

"Yeah. I've got to." Angel frowned. "Sure, he can skip on the weekends if he wants, but that's just so he knows he's got control over it. School days are a no-miss unless I fuck up and forget. Then I'm sending cupcakes the next day to say sorry to all his teachers if he's had a bad day."

"And you talk about how it'll get easier for him to deal with this imbalance when he's older, right?" West grinned at Angel's humph. "I was up at four, Ange. Rome came downstairs about ten minutes after I got my first cup of coffee. And he'd already brushed his teeth or rinsed his mouth out because he smelled like mint. As soon as he sat down, all he talked about was you. You're a *god* to him. His biggest fear is that one day you'll be sick of him and kick him out or give him back to your dad."

"I'll fucking die before that asshole ever gets near Rome," Angel growled. "Swear to God, West. I'd run him over if I see him crossing the street."

"You ever tell Roman that?"

"Who do you think's going to be riding shotgun?" There was a brief skip of time. Then Angel muttered in his low, silken voice, "*No*. He doesn't need to hear that kind of shit from me."

"Sit up," West ordered. Angel leaned forward and let West pull him in close. Nested into the curve of West's arm, Angel sighed contentedly. Kissing the back of his lover's head got West another sweet murmur and a mouthful of citrus-smelling hair. After he spat the strands off his tongue, West murmured, "Look, you're a good mostly-parent. You're raising a damned smart kid into a pretty solid adult. Most people don't give their own kids half the effort over their lifetime that you put in during a single day."

"If I'm doing such a damned fine fucking job, why can't I get him to flush the fricking toilet?" Angel tilted his head back and stared up at West. "He's eleven years old and really likes microwave bean-and-cheese burritos. It's like chemical warfare in there sometimes."

"Okay, that's a battle you can't stop fighting." West shuddered. "Really? I can't…. God… just no. I can't even imagine what would have happened if we'd left a dirty toilet behind after we were done using the bathroom. I think my parents' heads would have exploded."

"Some days, the battles I pick are the big ones, like getting to school and doing the work." Angel shrugged. "Other days, it's eating vegetables and scrubbing down the bathtub. I just don't know how the hell to tell if I'm doing okay, because I look at everyone else, and all I can think is fuck, I'm screwing this up. He's wearing two fucking different *shoes*."

"Do the shoes matter?" West prodded softly. "In the long run, does that matter as much as the vegetables or helping with the bakery?"

"Sometimes the shoes matter," he replied. "I don't want to tear him down, you know? If he's wearing one orange shoe and one green shoe because that's his thing for that day, then I'm all for it. But if he's got to do something serious or professional, then Rome needs to know that orange and green combination isn't going to work.

"It's crap like shoes and speaking properly that he's got to know. It's all shit I never knew, and when I got… free… cut loose from my dad, it was like everyone knew all these secret rules. I want to make sure he knows all of that before he steps out my front door prepared for whatever he's going to do." Angel bit his lower lip. "I don't want him to feel stupid like I did. I never, ever want Roman to feel like he's stupid. I want him to know he can do anything he wants to… if he works hard enough and does right by people."

"Then you're giving him a hell of a lot better head start than I got from my father, Ange," West confessed softly. The rigid image of his father's stern scowl flashed through West's memories of the man. He'd rarely seen his father smile, and when he had, it'd been a thin, smug line, stretched over his hard features because he'd driven someone or something to the ground. "I was taught people were things to be used. Friendships were stepping-stones, connections to be maintained in case you needed them later. Lang… hell, Lang broke away first, pretty much telling my father to fuck off by not responding to the old man's tirades and pushing. Back then, I thought Lang was an idiot."

"And now?"

"Now, I know better." The knot in West's stomach was hard but loosening as he spoke. "Maybe six months ago I looked at my life and said, *West Harris, you are a shitty person.*"

"Sounds more like Marzo." Angel laughed.

"He had a lot to do with it." He patted Angel's chest, then laid his hand flat, feeling the man's heart beat under his palm. "Marzo's helped me put a lot of things in perspective. Kicking and screaming out of my tar pit but still… perspective. He wants a lot of things in life… things that were never on *my* radar, but we talk… especially when we're stuck in traffic, and I learned a lot of things about him… and me… while stuck on the bridges.

"Things like… wanting more than an apartment in San Francisco and working a hundred hours a week," West ventured gently. "And rediscovering a lover who now has a younger brother and a slightly overdone bakery in Half Moon Bay. Maybe learning how to drive, but I think the whole relationship thing is front and center."

"I want to make this work." Angel's breath tickled West's forearm. "I just don't know how we're going to do that. A part of me thinks we're moving too fast—"

"We took how many years to get back together?" He wrapped both arms around his lover, not minding the dig of Angel's shoulder blades into his chest. "This is me not letting you go. I'm not perfect, and much like your brother, I'm probably going to be an asshole more times than I care to admit, but probably for different reasons. That being said, we *like* each other, Ange. I hear your voice and the prickly thin-razor parts of my soul settle down. You bury my demons because you make me laugh. You remind me I'm human, and as stupid as it sounds, I've lived more in these past few days with you than I have in the time we had apart. I can't lose you, Angel, and in a lot of ways, you can't lose me."

"Let's take a good, hard look at this, West." Angel shifted, pulling himself free of West's arms. Turning so he sat cross-legged, he shook off West's reproachful grumble. "Listen to me. Money-wise, there's a huge gap between us. *Huge* gap—and the last thing I want is you thinking I'm using you. Hell, I don't want Roman to think he *can* use you, because I've seen some of the shit you give Zig. That's not going to happen. It *can't* happen, babe. I can't have Roman think you're going to bail him out of shit, and I can't have you doing—"

"I know." West sat up, tucking his legs under him. "I get that now."

He'd woken up thinking of all the reasons Angel could push him away, and most of them had dollar signs attached to them. Some were personal. He knew he wasn't the best of people. On his best days, he could be arrogant and demanding. On his worst days, he was impossible to please and deal with. He just had to convince Angel he was worth it.

"I want to fix things. The hardest thing I'm going to have to do in my life is not to fix everything that goes wrong in yours. I'm not saying we should move everyone into this house and live happily ever after. It's been less than a week since we've gotten to see each other again. Yeah, it's too soon, but for me, it's almost too late." He blinked as the sky brightened suddenly, catching the sun's rays in its pale haze. "I want to see where we go, and yeah, that means working hard not to overdo things with Rome. But at the same time, I want you to know I'm here for you to reach out to. You don't have to do everything by yourself. Yes, I can help you financially, and if you let me, then great, but it'll be as an investment or loan. Can we agree on that?"

"You okay with dumping the plans for the motel? Or are we going to fight about it? I know you said… before—"

"Is the motel a condition? Something I've got to give up to have you?"

"No, because that would be fucked. I don't do emotional terrorism." Angel shoved his hair out of his face. "But I'd try to convince you to find somewhere else to build. I'm not giving up the bakery. It's a crappy shack on the edge of a parking lot, but it's my crappy shack."

"And I'm with you on that. I can always find someplace else to build, and the bakery's as much of your baby as Rome, so yeah, the condos are off the table," West whispered. "I won't be able to find another you. So… you and me? Is there going to be an us?"

"Yeah, there's going to be an us." Angel leaned in, capturing his mouth.

If he died dipped in starlight and gold, West would already know what it felt like. Angel's kisses gilded his insides, pouring a soft warmth threaded with shivering chills into his body. He heard bells, or at least the echo of them, and West swallowed, taking in as much of Angel as he could. His body still ached from their lovemaking, and if he hadn't promised Angel, he'd already have his lover stretched out onto the bed so he could explore and taste whatever he'd missed the night before. He'd just fisted his hands into Angel's long hair when West heard someone clearing his throat at the open door.

"Go away," West grumbled, then glanced at the window, groaning at Marzo's reflection in the panes. "Damn. What now? What the hell else can happen?"

Reluctantly letting go, West stroked at Angel's face, unable to stop from grinning at the blush pinking his cheek. A muttered "Fucker" was all he got from his lover. Then Angel climbed off the bed. Tugging his shirt down, West stretched his legs out, wincing when his ankle and knee throbbed from being overstrained.

"I'm sorry to bother you guys, boss," Marzo rumbled, and he didn't move when Angel padded to the door. "That detective is downstairs… Montague."

"Swear to God, that man's like a stalker," West ground out. "What's he want now?"

"Probably thinks I tried to burn down the bakery for insurance money or something," Angel interjected. "Guy's got it out for me."

"No, he's here for something else. The cops were investigating a shot-up SUV in a warehouse down the street from the motel and found a dead body inside." The Italian's eyes grew troubled, and his face softened with deep sympathy. "Boss, you've got to go down and talk to him. He says the guy they found is Derry, and they're calling it murder."

Thirteen

"I WAS angry the last time I talked to him." West's coffee cup trembled, and his brain glitched, wondering if there was an earthquake rolling through the coast. Then his mind caught on to his hands shaking, creating waves in the creamy brown liquid. "Argued, really. I wanted to talk to him face-to-face, but he was up in the city and didn't want to make the trip down. And now you're telling me you found him here? In Half Moon? Dead? I can't…."

He'd taken the coffee when Angel shoved it at him, needing something… wanting something… and since he couldn't drag Angel up to the bedroom and hide under a mound of warm blankets, the coffee seemed like his only choice.

It was good coffee. Perfectly fine coffee. A smooth, silky punch of roasted beans right to the back of his throat, its bitter ridge softened with heavy cream and a whisper of sugar. It tasted great. Even through the raw, salty taint of his swallowed grief, the coffee was great.

It'd have tasted even better if there'd been a dollop of whiskey in it.

Hell, it'd have tasted great if it'd been mostly whiskey with a dollop of coffee in it.

Or, his thoughts mocked, it would be fucking fantastic if it were *all* whiskey and sipped under that Angel-warmed blanket fort where nothing in the world could touch them and Derry was still alive, slowly tearing apart West's world with his over-the-top ideas and fast-paced deals.

There was movement around him, too quick for his eye to follow, or maybe his brain was simply too mired in sludge to respond. Marzo was being interviewed by another detective in the living room after Montague'd taken over the study. Justin had come in, hot on the heels of Angel's phone call, to help keep Rome squirreled away. The redhead looked like he was bursting with questions, but a quick slap of whispers between he and Angel and he hustled Roman upstairs with a promise of early-morning video games and waffles once the cops were gone.

"I'll have questions for you later, Daniels," Montague said when Angel settled on the couch beside West.

"No, I'd like him to be here." West blinked, clearing some of the haze in front of him. "It's… this is insane."

After a brief flurry of people, noise, and shock, Montague sat across of West, a rumpled hulk of a man with old-school movie-star looks and cop-sharp eyes, waiting patiently for West's answers to his questions. The detective's hands were massive, making the pen he held look like an ink-spewing toothpick as he made notes in a tiny brown notebook. Angel was next to him, nursing his own cup of coffee, the black brew as dark and bottomless as the hole West felt in his soul.

Montague was a skilled interviewer, affable despite his breadth, someone who was casual enough in his body language to make another person feel safe, but West'd heard the steel hidden in the man's velvet depths. The cop and Angel'd come to a tenuous détente of sorts, soldered together by a mumbled apology over a gun Angel never owned, much less purchased in a town he'd never been in. It all could have been another manipulation, but West didn't have the brain cells to pick it all apart.

Derry was dead—slaughtered and left alone in a warehouse while West was being made love to.

Swallowing a gulp of coffee did little to fend off the rush of sick gurgling in West's belly, but he clamped down on the feeling. He refused to lose his stomach in front of the cop and Angel, but damned if he didn't have to fight to keep himself in check. Angel's hand on the small of his back helped, and West took another sip, finding comfort in the other man's touch.

"What did the two of you fight about?" Montague pried gently. "And when was the last time you spoke to him?"

"Yesterday… around noon, I think." West combed through his memories. "Crap, the fire… that was yesterday. There's just been so much going on, I'm having a hard time separating out the days. Yesterday, we spoke about the motel. He was resisting closing down the project. He does that sometimes.

"I'd brought it up to him and wanted to see how we could shift it elsewhere without incurring a lot of costs. That was… before I'd spoken to Kathleen in Acquisitions later in the afternoon." He'd been irritated, but Derry dragged his feet more than a few times on projects he didn't want to change, and West was used to shoving him along before Derry shifted his course. "I was pissed off because Derry hadn't contacted them or legal about shifting the project. I'd left a message for him to call, but he never got back to me. I was going to follow up with him later this morning. Maybe have Marzo drive me into the city to meet up with him. As far as I knew, he was in San Francisco."

"Did he normally refuse to change something the company was working on?" Montague looked up from his notes. "Even after you spoke to him about it directly?"

"Derry's known for it." West barked a short laugh at the pointless odd struggles he'd had with his friend. "We argue about it. Then after a couple of days, he'll make the changes I've asked for. Derry has...."

It hit West that he'd never argue with Derry over the stupid little things in a project ever again, and he swallowed at the growing lump in his throat. He must have made a noise or some sort of sign, because Angel's hand squeezed around his, anchoring him in the conversation.

"Shit... had. Derry had a problem letting go of things he wanted. He'll... he'd have a vision of how something should be and go after it, pushing until it was how he saw it," West explained. "It's why I brought him into the company, why I put him in charge of new project development. I knew he would get the job done right and on time."

"But he worked for you, right?" Montague pressed. "You own the company. Inherited it from your father. Why didn't he act immediately when you ordered him to do something?"

"That's not how I work. People put in charge of projects have a large sense of autonomy. Ultimately, they answer to me, and everything goes under review and adjustments are made, but sometimes a project will be tapped to close, and the person in charge comes back at it with a different perspective." He shrugged, fatigue creeping through him. "I might have given Derry a lot more leeway because we were friends, but if I said something was final, he gave in. At the end of the day, it *is* my name on the building and my signature on their paychecks. Derry just likes... liked to push things a bit further sometimes."

The cop, it seemed, wasn't quite done. "Were you lovers? Is that why you let him push things?"

The shift in questioning took West by surprise, and he felt a gasp burst up from his chest. Shifting on the couch, he leaned forward to put the cup down and glared at the cop. "Are you fucking kidding me?"

"That is bullshit, Montague," Angel snapped. "Where the hell did you get that?"

"Remember, Daniels, you're here because you agreed to sit tight and be quiet. And to your point, it's a standard question, Mr. Harris," Montague replied, his voice low and even. "One I have to ask considering his previously antagonistic dealings with Mr. Daniels and your recently developed relationship. If Mr. Washington harbored feelings for you and came down here to—"

"Montague, you're way off base. Derry was my friend. We never… *shit*. It was never like that between us. And I shouldn't have to explain that to anyone, especially not to you." West fought to keep his tears back. Gutted and confused, he shoved away, holding on to Angel's hand to ground himself. "You going to tell me why I'm sitting here with you as you take my friend apart? Why are you here asking me questions instead of looking for his killer?"

"Because your friend Derry Washington was found dead next to a vehicle we found in the warehouse." Montague met West's gaze, flaying away West's anger with a dismissive snort. "A warehouse owned by Harris Investments. Did you know he was here in Half Moon Bay?"

"I just told you I didn't." West rocked back, catching his breath. "I didn't even know about the warehouse. It's not something HI would normally purchase. We usually only buy properties or land to develop, then sell. We do hold title to a few office buildings, but a management company takes care of the day to day."

"What about the Moonrise? The motel next to Mr. Daniels's property?" Montague asked. "Wasn't Mr. Washington attempting to get Mr. Daniels to sell so you could develop it?"

"The motel is a fluke, and the development project for that property was terminated. It's what Derry and I have been arguing about for a while." Shifting on the couch, West hit his ankle against the table, sending a shock wave of pain through the joint. Hissing, he leaned over to rub at it. "I don't know why the warehouse was purchased, but I can find out."

"And he'd have purchased this warehouse using company funds?"

"He'd have to go through Acquisitions, but yes, he would have, if he'd been the one to buy it." West frowned, trying to recall any conversation he had with Derry about property purchases. The wind was knocked right out of him, stolen in the emotional upheaval. He'd gone from grief to rage to confusion, and it was getting too much to take in. "I don't know what he was doing there. He should have been back in the city, ignoring my texts. He shouldn't have been in Half Moon. Are you quite certain he was murdered?"

"Mr. Harris, Derry Washington was found with two bullets in his head, lying next to a shot-up SUV that, judging by the damage on its rear quarter panels, was used in a fatal shooting at Mr. Daniels's bakery." Montague's words were gentle, but the stark imagery of Derry's death slapped West out of his fugue. "The gun was left at the scene, and we have every reason to think it was used on both your friend and the SUV."

"I can't... this is... why would someone kill Derry?" West spread his hands, helpless under the barrage of information. "He never carried a lot of money on him. Maybe someone killed him because they tried to rob him and he had nothing on him."

"See, all of this leaves me with a lot of questions." Montague's handsome face turned stony as he flipped a page in his notebook. "There was someone else in the warehouse and possibly using the location to hide the SUV, which, oddly enough, is also owned by Harris Investments. Would you know about that purchase?"

"HI owns several vehicles. Most of which are driven by our executives," West explained. "It's a company perk. Derry owned his own car—some sports thing he raved about for months before getting it. That's what he'd have driven down here. I don't know what it was, but Agnes, my assistant, can get you information, along with HI's vehicles."

"And you don't drive?"

"As it's been pointed out to me time and time again, it's safer for mankind that I not have a license." West snorted, recalling every disastrous attempt he'd had behind the wheel. "That's one of Marzo's main duties, getting me to where I need to go."

"You had a benefit dinner the night of the shooting at the bakery. Did your driver take you there?" The detective poised his pen over the empty page. "And what time did he drop you off?"

Angel opened his mouth, probably to protest where Montague was leading the conversation, but West put his hand on Angel's thigh and said, "Marzo's also my bodyguard. He comes with me to events. I've had... incidents when people who are angry about one thing or another try to hurt me. So before you can ask, he was there. I think he had the fish, a bold choice at a benefit. Let me ask you this, Detective. What makes you think I had anything to do with Derry's death? Because that's what you're inferring, isn't it?"

"*Someone* shot him, Harris, someone he knew and trusted enough to shoot him up close. So I'm willing to entertain any and all reasons about who else was there," Montague replied. "You were here, have a bodyguard who has a sketchy past with the law, and if Washington was getting in the way of your relationship with Daniels, I can see how an argument could go wrong. So let's go over this again, starting with where were you yesterday, before you showed up at Daniels's bakery."

"SO THE cops think West's best friend tried to kill you? Then West had him killed?" Justin gaped at Angel from across the kitchen's long steel table. "Holy shit. That's crazy! Like telenovela crazy."

"Not as crazy as I'm going to get if you don't stir those raspberries," Angel warned over the hammering coming from the front of the bakery. "We can't sell cupcakes and muffins out of the back of the van forever, so as soon as Frank and his crew are done with the new porch, I've got to have stuff for the cases. And I need those raspberries broken down, Just."

"You, Ange, have no appreciation for gossip," his friend grumbled, but he picked up the wooden spoon and stirred the simmering pot. "Seriously, what the hell is going on with your life? Your place gets shot up, someone dies in the kitchen, then the bakery catches on fire, and your secret millionaire lover's best friend is murdered."

"Really? Secret millionaire lover?"

"Look, you're shacked up with a multimillionaire and you don't talk about it. That's about as secret as it gets. It's been what? Almost two weeks since the fire? Rome's driven to school every day in a limo by some guy who looks like he works for the mob, and you go home to the fortress of solitude when you're done working here." Justin's nostrils flared, a sure sign he was gearing up to lecture Angel. "And why the hell *are* you working at the bakery? You should be jetting off to Paris or something to have your armpits waxed by snippy women in tall black stilettos."

"I *own* the Shack, Just. I'm not just working here. I *own* it." His shoulders hurt a bit from sleeping sideways next to Rome after his brother's nightmares the night before, and there was a throbbing crick in his neck every time he turned left. A handful of ibuprofen did little to make the pain go away, and combined with the gallon of tea he drank that morning, his stomach felt like he'd run it through a shredder. "I'm not looking for a handout from West. Not now. Not ever. And I'm not doing anything with my armpits."

"But he's not closing the motel down, right? So you guys definitely have something going on." Justin sniffed. "I need material here, Ange. I've got an evening shift at Yvonne's, and if I don't come back with some juicy gossip, she's going to make me clean out the storeroom or something."

"You've never cleaned out a storeroom in your life," Angel scoffed. "And we're... shit, I don't know what we are, but that cop sure as hell tried to work West over. Bad enough that dick Derry was killed. Now he's got to deal with the cops trying to say he did it?"

"Are you supposed to call a guy names after he's dead? I thought that all the crappy stuff got wiped out." Swinging the pot off of the burner, Justin set it down on the long counter where Angel placed a pot and strainer. "My grandmother used to say everyone's a saint after they've kicked the bucket."

"Your grandmother also kicked you out of the house when she found out you liked boys," Angel reminded him. Justin's eyes narrowed, but he only sniffed again, a brief note of disgruntled annoyance. "Look, the reason I haven't talked to you about West is because it's kind of new... ish. We fit into each other, and that's kind of scary. Dude, we haven't been around each other in almost ten years, but it's like... I can't explain it. I *know* him. I don't know how to explain it."

"Tale as old—"

"You start breaking out into show tunes and I'm going to waterboard you with the raspberries," Angel threatened. "It's easy to be with him. Even when he pisses me off, I still want to be there to work things out. It's just... fast. And then I've got Rome to think about."

"Yeah, because college is paid for," Justin snorted.

"Doesn't work like that, Just."

"It does if you let it." He rolled his eyes at Angel's exasperation. "Look, I grew up in a trailer park where the best entertainment we had was tying traps to the top of the fence and betting which side the canal rats would fall when they got caught. You bet your fucking ass I'd be sitting in that house, eating bonbons, and ordering everything I wanted off of the shopping network."

"You'd be bored out of your skull," Angel replied. "You work two jobs and take classes in everything from basket weaving to Russian folk dance. You'd last one day. Then you'd be climbing the walls."

"Doesn't mean I wouldn't like to try," Justin muttered. "Besides, you told me he and Rome get along really well. Why shouldn't you grab at that brass ring? Okay, in this case, a platinum ring. But you should grab it."

"Because suppose it doesn't last? Forget jerking Roman around, how the hell am I going to deal with losing him again?" Angel leaned against the counter, picking away at the scabs in his soul. "Yeah, we were kids and we had some shitty things happen to us to keep us apart, but when it's all said and done, what do we really have in common?"

"Other than hot sex—angry or otherwise—and both of you really needing one another?" Justin shrugged, then lifted the pot up. "Nothing at all. Hold the strainer so I don't get this all over the place."

Angel gripped the container and sieve. "Look, it's not that I don't want… okay, I don't know what I want. Maybe I just want him and the rest of the crap between us can take a flying fuck for all I care."

"So then do that, let it take a flying fuck, Ange." Justin put the pot back down on the counter. Tears glimmered in the redhead's enormous eyes, and a soft smile touched his lips. "If anyone deserves to fall in love, it's you, baby. Say to hell with the world and let yourself fall in love with this guy."

Angel reached over the counter and wiped at a teardrop at the corner of Justin's eye. Sighing, his voice broke when he let go of what he'd been holding inside of him since he'd first seen a blue-eyed, black-haired lanky teenaged boy biting his lip in the middle of a carnival's thoroughfare.

"What makes you think I'm not already in love, Just?" Angel whispered. "Because I've been in love with him before I even knew his damned name."

"YOU DOING okay, boss?" Marzo's familiar gruff bark jerked West back to the present.

He was done crying, a painful wringing of emotion, and moved on to a numbness he couldn't seem to shake. The days following Montague's interrogation were filled with more interviews, mostly fielding calls from other businesses and one-on-ones with employees who'd worked with Derry. The shock of Derry's death faded, scrubbed away under the overwhelming press of responsibilities and sidestepping questions he had no answers for.

"I'm fine," he answered, shaking his head. "Why?"

"Because you're wearing Angel's clothes." Marzo jerked his chin toward West's chest. "And I've never, in the time I've known you, seen you willingly put on a T-shirt, much less one advertising a tattoo shop."

West stared down at the T-shirt he'd put on after his afternoon shower, startled to discover it was slightly too large, nearly threadbare, and definitely Angel's. There was a faint hint of cinnamon clinging to the fabric, and West couldn't recall when he'd seen Angel wear the faded gray shirt or if it was even clean. He sniffed at it, hoping Marzo didn't notice, but the pressure in his chest faded when he realized he had a bit of Angel wrapped around him.

"I don't even know what this means," he confessed. "A tattoo shop? Are you sure?"

"Four-One-Five Ink? Yeah, that's up in San Francisco. Got my koi there." Marzo began to unbutton his trousers, then laughed when West paled. "I'm joking. It's on my back. I just wanted to see your face."

"Glad I am here for your amusement," West drawled. "Thank you for your concern."

"Ah, we're back to the guy I met in the club." Marzo eased into the chair next to West, letting out a long contented sigh. "Gotta admit, I like Angel's West a hell of a lot better."

"Yeah well, let's see if Angel sticks around through this shit storm." He picked at the edge of a cushion, half hoping it would fray so he would have something solid to be angry about.

"Have you talked to him? About Derry?"

"No." It was time for a haircut because the front fell forward into his eyes. Brushing the strands out of his lashes, he shook his head. "What am I going to tell him? Hey, I miss the guy I sent to kick you out of your house so I could make the place into condos? Not exactly snuggling conversation."

"I don't think you give the guy enough credit. Sure, Washington was an asshole to everyone who met him, but he was your friend," Marzo pointed out. "Your only friend until I came along. Now you're up to at least four… five if you count your brother."

"Is that counting Zig?" West lifted his eyebrow.

"I don't count your niece. She's a parasite wrapped up in a cute package. Her sole reason for existence right now is to bleed you dry and help you piss off your brother. We'll see how she is when she hits puberty."

"Chances are looking good that's not going to change," he replied. "I will lodge a complaint about the word parasite. She's more of an... opportunist. Less so than Roman or maybe just with a stealthier method of manipulating the situation."

"Yeah, I say that about my nieces and nephews too. Con artists, all of them." Marzo watched West through hooded eyes, then said, "You've got a nice thing here with Angel. He's a good guy and doesn't put up with your shit. That's what you need in your life. What you need in your heart. I know this thing with Derry hurts, but the two of you weren't on the best of terms for the past—what?—two years? I'm not saying what happened to him didn't suck, but closing up on yourself isn't the way to go."

"I just don't know how to...." West dug the heels of his hands into his eyes, rubbing at the grit he found there. "I'm not good at relationships, Marzo. You know that. Hell, how many times have you seen me crash and burn with other men?"

"You didn't give a shit about any guy you dated. They were something to fuck until one of you got bored." Marzo inched up to the edge of the chair. "This is different, West. This guy is real. He makes you smile, and if you can look at me and tell me you haven't been holding your breath waiting for him to come back to you, then I'm going to punch you in the face and call you a liar."

"God, wasn't that first punch enough?" West smirked, then chuckled when Marzo shook a ham-sized fist under his nose.

"I don't even know why I give a shit about you."

"Because Derry wasn't my only friend." He jabbed Marzo's chest with a stiff finger. "I'm insulted you didn't count yourself in that pile."

"Two... three if you count Agnes... isn't a pile," he replied. West's phone chirped, and Marzo grabbed at it, making a face as he read the screen. "Speak the devil's name and she shall come a'calling. Here, it's Aggie herself."

"Thanks. And yeah, I'll... talk to him," West promised. Flicking the call on, he said, "Hello, Aggie. How are—"

What she told him stole the breath out of him, his wind knocked clear away. A sticky mire closed in around West, and he choked on the words he couldn't quite seem to get out. Marzo reached for him, but West shook his friend's hand off, willing himself to listen to every single syllable Agnes said over the line. Drowning in another wave of grief, West closed his eyes, unable to stop Derry from breaking his heart all over again.

Fourteen

WEST HURT.

Only a rock wouldn't be able to see it, but Angel didn't know how to fix it. There was no taking back Derry's death. Or the fallout of his murder. The calls kept coming. Rolling in and slamming West down with every ring, every layer of betrayal Derry heaped on West's shoulders until Angel thought West couldn't take any more. The weeks after Montague shoveled dirt over Derry's name were difficult, made harder by West's refusal to talk to anyone, including Angel.

Instead, West closed in on himself, shutting down and dealing with everything in a cold, clipped manner Angel soon learned to hate. He'd debated packing Rome up and getting out, leaving the house on the cliff behind with maybe a note to say he'd left, but the glimmer of pain in West's strained face was enough of a reality check.

They'd had a tense meal that night, the four of them sitting around a dining room table eating a white-sauce lasagna Angel picked up on his way back from the bakery. Well, everyone except Rome, who chattered away about someone letting loose a fart in his class. Marzo's deep laughter boomed across the table, shattering the glassine fragility between them. It was the first time Angel'd seen a smile ghost across West's mouth, and when he met Angel's gaze, he'd winked.

They'd not spoken—not really—since the cops left, but Angel held on to that wink and every touch they'd had for dear life, reassuring himself things would be okay between them.

"Got to be," he muttered to himself as he scrubbed a plate clean. The water was scalding, but its heat felt good on his skin. Frothing the dish soap bubbles up with one hand, he dunked a glass into the foamy water. "He fucking needs someone in his life, and it might as well be me."

"It can only be you." West slid up against Angel, reaching across his arms to shut the kitchen faucet off. His shadow fell over Angel's arm, stealing away the light. "There's a dishwasher. Dishes go in. You press a button. And walk away."

"Sometimes, washing dishes helps me think." Angel debated turning the water back on but decided it was too childish. Shaking the frothy soap from his arms, he nodded at a towel on the counter. West handed it over, tugging at its corner, then letting go when Angel grabbed it to wipe himself dry. "Dick. And I don't like walking away. Sure, I think about it. Damn, I think about it all the time, but—"

"Too much like your dad," his lover finished.

"Exactly," he agreed. "I kind of want to be an asshole to you right now. Not going to lie. It's been a shitty couple of days, and I—"

"I came in to tell you I'm sorry. For… being me. I'm not good at dealing with shit like this. With Derry…." As simple as that, West deflated Angel's anger, pricking through it as neatly as a pin through an overinflated balloon. "I'm just so goddamned pissed off right now. And I am horrible about sharing those kinds of things… those emotions. It's just so much… *crap*."

"He died. Someone killed him." The water stayed off, and Angel turned around, leaning against the counter. "I'm mad at Montague for tearing him down. I know he was doing his job, but shit, he could have been a bit more sensitive about it. Derry was—"

"Bastard was stealing from me," West murmured softly. His voice cracked, breaking on something hard inside of him. "Derry—my best friend—was stealing from me. I got a call from Agnes this afternoon. Someone in Finance verified Derry'd been siphoning money off of projects he'd been put in charge of."

"How long have you known?" Angel asked. "About the money?"

"Suspicions cropped up a few days ago, but today… shit… it all started to come together. I don't know how much. Not yet. What I do know is I've been a dick to you, and if I could take back every single dickish moment I had over the past few days, I would. I don't know how to say this other than I'm sorry."

The knot in Angel's belly loosened, letting the poison he'd built up inside him dissipate. Hooking his hands on the counter, he then leveraged himself up to sit on the cool, hard surface. Knowing where West hurt made things easier. Harder to fix but easier to understand. Tugging on West's shirt, he pulled him over, bracketing West between his legs.

"Fucking hell." It was all Angel could find in himself to say. Holding West close, he gritted out a prayer for a hot fire to toast Derry's balls once the devil got a hold of him. Pressing his mouth against West's temple, he asked, "Are you sure? About him ripping you off?"

"Oh God, yes." West laughed bitterly, leaning away from Angel's shoulders. "We're pretty fucking sure."

"Did he... fuck... I don't even... I mean it's not something I'd expect a guy like Derry to do. He was rich. How much money does one guy need?" Angel caught West's slightly disgusted look. "Okay, yeah. I get it. Some guys can never have too much money, but... dude, he was your friend."

"It apparently was a one-way relationship," he grumbled. "Much as I've been with you. I just... I feel like I'm digging myself out of a hole and just dumping more sand on top of me. I should have talked about this with you as soon as I found out, but... I think I just needed time to process all of it."

"Okay, I get that. I do. We're just going to have to lay a few ground rules." Angel rested his forearms on West's shoulders. "If we're going to do this, you and I have to talk our shit out."

"I might need some time. Bad behaviors are hard to break, and I've had a lifetime of them," West explained. "I'm used to chewing on things a bit. I don't mean to be an asshole. I don't, and I can't say I'm going to be great at communicating, but I sure as hell can try."

"You get hurt and you clam up. I can deal with that. What I can't deal with is getting shoved out." He hooked his fingers together behind West's neck. "Look, I get just as pissy as you do. Right now, it's rough. And I'm kind of angry at Derry right now for you. I'd like to kick the fucker in the ass for what he did to you."

"I'd like to help you. It'd be easier if we knew everything he did, but all I have is just some nebulous maybes and a bunch of money he'd skimmed off." West sighed, leaning into Angel's chest. "It's a stupid, amateur skim. I can't believe he... it's just crappy because... fuck... I trusted him with everything I owned. Then he went and did this."

"Is it for real? I mean, you've got proof?" Their hearts slowed, beating in sync. Angel's twisting nerves calmed, and he stroked at West's shoulder blades, shifting forward as West's arms came up to hug his waist. "Real proof?"

"Yeah. Standard procedure calls for shutting down someone's accounts and a quick audit to make sure everything is captured on the books. A few red flags went up, and Finance began to dig deeper, but they don't know exactly what they're looking for." West tightened his hold, straightening until they were eye to eye. "Might be months before we know what actually happened. Meanwhile, I've got people going over all of his projects with a fine-toothed comb. We've got to find out where he padded and hope to God it wasn't anything structural."

"I am so fucking sorry." Cupping West's face, Angel gave him a gentle kiss on the mouth, grimacing when West stuck his tongue out quickly to part their lips. Pulling back, he wiped the slobber West left behind and laughed. "God, you are such an asshat sometimes."

"Not denying it." He studied Angel for a moment, then said, "I never tell you thank you, and I should. I shove you around, moved you in here under the excuse that you need to be safe from whoever is trying to pick apart your life, but that's a damned lie. I want you here because I need you. It's not been even a month, and I can't imagine not having you with me."

"Yeah, we should probably talk about that too." Reluctantly, Angel let West go, pushing at his chest until they were a few inches apart. "I've got to go home, Harris. I can't… squat here with my brother and play house with you. It's too confusing for him—and for me—but at the same time, I don't want you to be alone. This is kind of fucking me up, and I don't want it to screw *you* up in the long run."

"Don't take this wrong, but you kind of live in a shit hole. *And* I own it. I'm more than a little ashamed it's a shit hole. It shouldn't be, but that can be fixed too," West muttered. "I hate that you don't have your own damned bed to sleep in. Shit, even a bed in a walk-in closet is better than a couch with a gassy eleven-year-old in the next room."

"Yeah, well, rent's free, and the commute's insanely short," Angel pointed out. "I don't want to go back. Hell, I'd love to say we've got everything all worked out between us and we'll have unicorns at our magical wedding, but we both know that's not—"

"Bottom line is, I need you in my life, Ange," West whispered, a single golden thread of words strong enough to bring Angel to a screeching halt. "It's stupid. It's too fast. It's too raw. But in the middle of all of the shit that's been happening to me, I kept looking for you to hold on to, and it scares the crap out of me, but that's just how it is.

"I will do whatever it takes for you to stay in my life."

The sincerity in West's face was too painful to look at, and Angel shifted his gaze, unable to stand seeing himself reflected in his lover's blue eyes.

"The funny thing about this is, I can't do anything other than hope. Because you wouldn't take anything from me to be here. You want the one thing that's the hardest for me to give, Ange, and that's myself. So I'm asking you to stay, just because I need you. Not because it's a big house and there's cool toys but because I'm here... and I need you."

"Rome is beginning to depend on you, West. And I know you say you'll be there for him even if we can't do this thing right, but you're asking a hell of a lot from me. That's a hell of a lot of trust."

"We have to trust each other. I'm not going to say it'll be easy. We're both wary bastards, and we've been bitten too many times to count, but we've both agreed this is worth reaching for." West cupped Angel's chin, drawing him back around to where West could see his face. "I talked to Marzo about you this afternoon, and as much as I hate to admit it, he brought up a good point."

"Marzo usually does," Angel drawled. "What'd he say?"

"That I'd known you were here. In Half Moon. But I was too damned scared to reach out to you."

"Why didn't you?" It was a good question, one he'd pondered a few times when he'd seen West's name on the bottom of a letter sent by Harris Investments. "It would have been a hell of a lot easier for you to get a hold of me than me getting a hold of you. Even if the cops think otherwise."

"Because I'm a coward." West chuckled. "And sadly, Marzo didn't disagree."

"I don't know about coward...."

"No, it was pretty much agreed on. I'm sorry for that too. I can't take it back. I can't change the past, but we can do something about the future," he murmured. "So, how about this for a compromise? We start over, in a way. Sort of."

Angel snorted. "Kind of too late for that, don't you think? We've already had sex."

"Sex is not off the table, but it's not like we've moved into the same room to play house," West pointed out. "What I'm suggesting is we spend time together. Like we've done before. Lay some groundwork for the pretty hot sex I'm sure we'll have in the near future but definitely give ourselves something to build on."

"And I'm supposed to stay here while we do that?"

"Yeah, you should. Because starting this week, the Moonrise Motel is going to be gutted and remodeled. I've got Agnes working on where to put people while the work's being done, but in the meantime, Angel love, it would be easier on my nerves and ulcers if you just stayed here." West sighed. "And when or if you decide to go back to that dump, it's at least going to be decent. I can't have people saying I let my lover live in a shit hole, especially if I'm the one who owns it."

"DERRY.... GOD, if he weren't already dead, I would strangle him." West paced around the study, unable to sit. His ankle injury flared up a warning, a low, steady throb threatening to turn to pain, but he ignored it. Acid growled through his stomach, the stress in his nerves stoking the fires burning in his gut. "I can't believe he'd do something like that. I just… can't. How is Finance doing? Are they able to get into his files?"

The morning light was harsh, stabbing him in the eye as he turned toward the window. Lack of sleep plagued him, but the hours he'd spent talking to Angel were worth every imagined grain of sand in his eyes when he blinked. They'd fallen asleep on top of one another, sprawled out on the couch together for Rome to find when he thundered downstairs in search of food. Angel's quick kiss after they'd been jolted awake made the teasing Rome kept up bearable.

"That kid is going to be the death of me," West muttered.

"Pardon me?" Agnes asked over the phone.

"Sorry, Aggie," he apologized. "I'm a bit distracted. What were you saying? About Finance? And are they cooperating with the cops?"

"Nothing concrete yet from Finance, and yes, everyone's fully onboard. I've got IT partnered with one of the techs from the police department. They're working on getting into his locked-down files. The police wanted his desktop, but everything is kept on the servers, so that would have done them no good. Legal stopped them from confiscating the network machines." Agnes tapped at a keyboard, the *tick-tick* of her fingers hitting the keys coming over the phone line. "I've rescheduled all of your onscreen meetings for this week and dropped all of the hot items to your expedite folder, but there's contracts that you'll need to read and e-sign before the Marbles project can go forward."

"What are we looking at, Aggie?" West stopped in front of the study's window bank, numbly staring out onto the windswept landscape.

The enormity of Derry's betrayal was massive, and if he'd been hurt by the man's murder, he was devastated by the carnage Derry appeared to have left behind. "Do we have a rough number, other than the one we already threw out there? How much? He was the goddamned CFO. He had access to everything. How far does this go?"

If he were in the office, West knew Agnes would be lowering her glasses, perching them on the tip of her pert nose so she could stare at him from across his desk. She'd been his right-hand person seemingly forever, driving his life forward each and every day. Grandmotherly one instant and a shark the next, he'd come to rely on her presence and sharp intelligence to balance out his often blind ambition. She saw things he missed, ferreting out shadows he hadn't seen in the glare of his passions.

And somehow they'd both missed Derry's stealthy bleeding off of Harris Investments.

"I can't give you an exact number. You know that. We've only got that first estimate, but we'd have nothing if it hadn't been for that bounced transaction on Tuesday after we'd locked down his accounts." She spoke to someone in the office, a quiet, forceful directive he'd have given if West was there. "And before you say anything, there's nothing you can do here except fret and drive people crazy. You've got other things to worry about—"

"What things?" he spat.

"Marzo told me about Mr. Daniels, West. I'd say he's more important than anything else. Especially now."

"Agnes, remind me to fire Marzo. Angel isn't a part of this mess. Hell, after dealing with me for the past couple of days, I'm surprised he's even talking to me." West sat down hard on the couch, jostling his back. "What did Marzo tell you? Exactly."

"That you've been running around like a chicken with his head cut off and not taking care of yourself. And that Mr. Daniels was someone you knew a long time ago. Really, you should have told me everything. I'm rather mad at you for trying to build those condos now. You are an idiot, West, and I say that with the utmost respect." She sniffed loud enough for West to feel her disappointment across the miles between them. "Is he still there at your house? With his brother? Daniels. Not Marzo."

"When he's not working. Angel, I mean. The brother goes to school. He's eleven. So yes, Angel is here. So is his brother. Marzo? He might not be after I hang up."

"You'd be more lost without Marzo than you would be without me. Go spend the day doing something other than pacing and working. Well, do nothing but deal with those quick contract fixes and go spend some time with him," she ordered gently. "Or if Mr. Daniels is busy right now, go talk to your brother. You have family there, West. Reach out to them."

"And if I don't?" he teased.

"Then I will skin you alive and roll you in salt." Agnes snorted. "Trust me. You've pissed me off enough times. I have a long list of things I'd like to do with you, and none of them end well for you. I'll call you tonight to check up on you. If something's on fire, I'll let you know."

"If you find out that number—"

"You'll be the first to know it," she promised. "It's not as bad as it could be."

"A few million," West reminded her. "Maybe as high as five, which we can probably recover. It's not like we've been operating with it. It just… pisses me off, Aggie. I *trusted* that fucking bastard. I *mourned* him."

"I am sorry. I know you are hurt, West, but it will get better." Agnes sighed. "For right now, just take care of yourself. Whatever you and Mr. Daniels are doing, keep safe. Today is a day off. I'll handle things."

"I know you will." He cleared his throat, then said, "Thank you for being here, Aggie. I don't know what I'd do without you."

"Probably something stupid." She laughed. "Now, go find someone there to have coffee with you and let me get back to paying the bills. I'll call you later."

West disconnected the call and laid his earpiece on the low table. Turning, he arched an eyebrow at his twin standing in the study's doorway, holding out one of the two mugs he carried in with him. West didn't think he'd ever get used to seeing himself in his brother, the echo of his face living an entirely different life.

"Oh good, coffee," West drawled. "Like I haven't been drinking gallons of that this week."

"You're welcome, jerk." Lang straightened up. "Don't know why I even try to be nice to you."

Lang's casual stance spoke of a man who'd found his place in life, a happy, content place filled with a growling, rough-mannered bookworm husband and a wild-hearted daughter. He'd envy Lang if he had any sense, and maybe he did a little bit, but it wasn't anything he'd ever mention. Not unless he was prepared to hear Lang's *I-told-you-so* for the rest of his life.

You're going to hear it anyway, his heart whispered, *because that's what you want with Angel.*

"How goes the embezzlement?" Having passed off one of the mugs to West, Lang settled on one of the love seats in the middle of the room. "Did Agnes have any updates?"

"Nothing substantial. The cops are trying to shut down the network so they can gain access, but that would turn us into a brick. Legal is working with them. Hopefully, we can keep everything on track while we shake this out." West sipped at the coffee, making a face at its bitterness. "Did you forget the sugar?"

"Sorry, this one's yours. I only take cream." Lang exchanged the cups.

"There is something seriously wrong with you, brother." He sat down across of Lang, thankful to get off his feet.

His ankle twinged, a pointed reminder he'd been abusing it. Rubbing at the elastic bandage wrapped around the strained joint, West hissed when he massaged a tender spot. There were threads of uncertainty winding through him, and the shakiness resonating through his bruised emotions left him off-balance. As always, Lang waited him out, drawing along the seconds with small sips of coffee and probing glances sharp enough to dig out anything West festered inside of him.

After a few minutes, West gave in and sighed. "I feel like… a fool, Lang."

"Because of Derry?" Lang cocked his head. "Because of what he did to your company? Or is it something else?"

"The company… hell, we'll recover from that. It's just… I don't know." He rubbed at his face, then stared at his brother through his hands. "It feels like… I can't even explain how it feels. I'm *angry* at him. For dying. For stealing from me. For… everything. So *fucking* angry."

"He was like a brother to you," Lang said, setting his cup down. "More than I've been, to be honest."

"No, that's not—"

"It's true, West." Lang cut him off, shaking his head. "You and I were always set against each other. It's what Father did to amuse himself. Well, that and sleep with anything with boobs who'd have him. We were raised to be competition to one another. We were at each other's throats before we even had teeth."

"You refused." West smirked. "You checked out of Father's game long before I even knew he was playing one. I used to think I'd won. Took me a while to figure out you did and I was still dancing on his strings. Even after he died, I was still dancing away like the puppet he'd made me."

"You're a better businessman than I am."

Lang's soft protest was buried under West's derisive laugh.

"Don't disparage what you've done with the company. You've taken it places Father never could. I think you stopped playing his game long before you realize, West."

"Still stupid enough to be taken in by Derry." The burn returned to his belly, kicking up a searing flush into his throat. "Right under my nose, Lang. Right under my *fucking* nose. He looked into my face every single day and lied. Every single word he said to me was a lie. And I'm still torn apart because he's dead. Because he... *shit*."

"He *was* your brother, West. He was there for you when I wasn't."

"That's not how it was—"

"It was, and it's okay. He was in my place, as your brother because that's what you needed. I used to resent him... before... but I saw how close you were. Now I'm fucking pissed off because I trusted him to be there for you." Lang's rumble dropped to a whisper. There was a wealth of pain in his voice, a tearing of his smooth growl. "I told myself you didn't need me because you already had a brother. And I'm making this about me... about us... when you've got all this shit you're dealing with, but I wanted you to know that I'm here, West. If you need me."

"Is this where I call you Sir Didy?" West teased, sliding over to the love seat next to his brother. Nudging Lang over, he sat down, pressing into his twin. "You were never *not* my brother. We are finding our way. We're different—"

"You're an asshole, and everyone loves me," Lang interjected.

"There's that," he agreed with a slow smile. The hurt in his heart remained, soiling the memories he had of Derry. "But I count in that everyone. I *do* love you, Lang. This past year... we've worked hard to be better with each other. I've always loved you, idiot. It's just that now, I like you too."

"I love you too. And I like you some of the time." Lang bumped into him. "I was serious, you know. If you need anything...."

"Want to come be my CFO?" West chuckled at Lang's horrified expression. "Okay, so that's a no. What if you just be my brother and we go back to trying to learn what that means?"

"That I can do." The smirk on Lang's face was eerie, a mirror of West's own sardonic grin. "How about if we start with Angel Daniels? I hear you two go back... *way* back."

Fifteen

"I'D RATHER be home with West. Instead you drag both of us out here," Rome snarled, kicking a loose pebble out of the way. "This is going to be boring."

It was getting to be a common complaint, one Rome tossed out a lot over the past month whenever Angel dragged him away from the cliff house to interact with anyone other than West or Marzo. As always, Angel ignored his little brother's sullen grumbles, pushing him forward into the crowd. Rome dug his heel in, then jerked forward, unable to hold his leg rigid when Angel tapped the back of his knee.

"Jerk," Roman muttered, scowling at Angel from under his beanie. "Why do you need everyone to come to the farmers' market with you? It's Saturday!"

"Yeah, shut up," Angel replied casually, smiling broadly at a woman frowning at him as she walked by. "Ma'am, if that's your kid, you might want to stop him… um… her… from eating that."

He'd learned to take criticism about his parenting skills with a grain of salt, especially when given to him by a woman who was handing their free-range toddler a kale smoothie in a plastic bottle while the child picked up a piece of chewed gum off the ground and popped it in their mouths. He eased around the woman, wincing slightly when West elbowed him in the ribs.

"Seriously, a farmers' market?" West echoed behind Rome. "Are we going to have to churn our own butter? Milk the cow for the cream? What's wrong with a grocery store? Food comes in nice, little clear plastic containers, all plump, pretty, and ready to eat."

"You shut up too." Angel glared over his shoulder at West, but it was good to see him smile. He'd been somber since Derry's death, punched in the gut first by the loss of his best friend, then the discovery of his betrayal. Shoving West and Rome out the front door to hunt for ingredients was a good call, and he enjoyed poking at them. "Pick up the pace. You two are my pack mules today. The sooner I get what I need, the sooner you guys can go burn your eyes out playing… I don't even know what you're playing. Something."

"*Katamari*," West supplied. "Old school. You need good hand-eye coordination—"

"And if you go too fast, it gets you sick and you puke," Rome proclaimed proudly. "I hurled on West's foot the first time I played."

"He says that like it's a badge of honor." The man shuddered, lengthening his pace to catch up with Angel. "I will have you know, for relationship purposes, I have a sympathetic vomit response."

"It was awesome." Bouncing on his heels, Rome grinned up at Angel, walking backward through the crowd. "I only threw up Kool-Aid. *He* had *corn*."

"I did *not* have corn. Don't be disgusting." West hooked his arm around Angel's shoulder. "He's trying to gross you out."

"Great. Just… great. Now I've got two disgusting idiots to drag around the market instead of one." Making a face at his brother, Angel twirled his finger in the air. "Turn around before you walk into people. I take it you two slackers let Marzo clean it all up."

"It was either that, or we'd have tossed up our stomachs like starfish and died." West leaned over and whispered, "And since we haven't had any time… *together*… since that night almost a month ago. I thought maybe I would live to see another day."

"Maybe you should grow up and clean up your own puke." He pulled away, playfully giving West a light shove. "You know, like an adult. With his own company."

"*Died*. I would have *died*." West drew out his words. "Really. Believe me. It was horrible, and it's something we should not talk about anymore unless you want a repeat performance. I can't even think about it. Change of subject, why *are* we here? And at eight in the morning on a Saturday?"

"Grabbing stuff for the bakery because I don't need pretty fruit in plastic boxes. What I need is cheap and a lot of it," Angel explained. "I'm going to remind you, you're the one who wanted in on this. And no more stories about any bodily functions from either of you for at least a couple of hours."

"If I don't talk about that kind of stuff, can I get kettle corn?" Roman flashed Angel's own smile back at him, an off-center half smirk loaded with as much charisma as he could muster. "Or cotton candy?"

"Why should I give you shit just because you behave?" Angel asked, returning Rome's smirk. "You get extra stuff for going above and beyond, not for showing up and keeping your face clean."

"'Cause you don't want to be a dick in front of West?" his brother wheedled.

"West knows I can be a dick, especially to you," he replied, pretending not to hear West's muffled snort. "You help out, you get extra stuff. That's how it goes."

"Carrying the bakery stuff counts, right?"

"That it does." Angel jerked his chin toward a stand at the end of the row. "So does looking for stuff I can use, like Johnson's got over there. Find me something cool, and we'll talk about cotton candy."

"Deal." Rome bolted off, then skidded around a few yards away, facing his brother while he half jogged backward. "You're still a dick."

"Nice, asshole," Angel called out, but Rome had already turned around, his long legs eating up the distance to the large stall on the row's corner. "Seriously, what's with you guys? You're just as bad as he is. It's like I've got two little kids now."

Like most California open-air markets, the rows were filled with a wide spectrum of vendors. The stalls ran large to small, filled with a variety of local produce, silk-screened T-shirts, pickled vegetables, and junk people bought in bulk to sell cheap. Some of the faces they passed were familiar ones, sun-worn hawkers Angel saw nearly every time he ventured out to a shuttered bowling alley's grass lot, and he nodded a few hellos, scanning the rows to see which ones he'd go back to once he had a better idea of what people brought in.

Early in the morning was best. Only the most hardcore of market browsers were around, and the air sparkled with a hint of morning dew. The mountains held back most of the sun's glare, and there was a touch of deep-fried bread on the breeze, the promise of powdered sugar and cinnamon leaving a kiss on Angel's senses, and he pondered a spiced apple cobbler muffin, topping it with crumble and a piece of twisted puff pastry.

The rows were wide, the field's packed-down grasses smelling dusty-sweet as people walked from stall to stall. Carla from San Mateo Hot Buns yelled out a hello as she bagged up *torta* rolls for a customer, the small booth's yeasty aroma tickling Angel's nose. A few steps later, the produce stalls were still being set up, crates of sun-ripened vegetables and fruits being laid out on long tables, most gently set in loose for picking through. A bucket of apricots tempted Angel, but he kept walking, wanting to see what everyone had before circling around to buy. Magnus Johnson always had interesting fruits, purchased from Asian fruit farmers along the interior, and from the colorful piles of dragon fruit and rambutan bristling over Johnson's gray bins, he'd hauled in the mother lode of exotics.

He didn't notice West's silence. Not until his lover slowed his pace and quietly remarked, "Rome makes me feel like... a brother."

West whispered so softly under the market noise Angel wasn't sure he'd heard him right, but when he turned to look at West, he found his lover staring down the row at Rome, who was contemplating a bin of sunset-blush loquats.

"It sounds stupid, but... it's kind of... nice," West continued, picking up one of the plump bubble-gum-flavored fruits to study it as if it held all the answers to every question he had. Setting it back, he turned to Angel. "I've never felt like a brother before, you know? Lang and I never... we were never brothers. Not like you two are, and... sometimes it hurts to feel that. Maybe I realized there's a piece of me I'll never ever have, but now I know what I'm missing."

"West—"

He let out a shuddering breath, then interrupted, "Being silly with Rome kind of makes me feel like I'm filling in that hole, Angel. I know it's stupid, but—"

"I was teasing, West." Angel stopped, gently pulling West to the side and out of the way of the crowd. Hooking his fingers through West's, he held them together, tightening his grip when West looked away. "Hey, it's a part of... it's kind of what we do. He gives me shit, I give him shit back. I just kind of rolled you into it. Kind of makes you... one of the family, I guess. I didn't even think about it."

West's cool assessing look lasted for several heartbeats, and then a glimmer of a smile ghosted across his mouth. Dabbing his tongue on his lower lip, he gave a short hum, then said, "Guess now's when I try to con you out of cotton candy."

"You can try," Angel scoffed. "But don't hold your breath. Same deal holds for you like it does Rome. You've gotta work for it."

"I could buy and sell this market twenty times over," West grumbled. "And you're holding me hostage for slave labor."

"Yep, pretty much." He shoved the totes he'd been carrying into West's hands, then peered over his lover's shoulder. Angel couldn't see his brother anywhere, but Johnson had a big booth with tall displays, making it hard to spot a lanky eleven-year-old boy no matter how quickly he seemed to be growing. "Where's Rome?"

"He was right there." West turned around, breaking away. "He's got to be nearby, right?"

"Yeah, he should be. I told him if he can't see me when we're out, then he's in deep shit. Come on."

Angel strode over to the booth at the end of the row, jostling his way through the crowd. His nerves were already on edge, drawn to a fray by everything from the shooting to the fire, and he tried to reason with himself as he hurried through the ever-thickening river of bodies around him. Rome'd been at the market with him at least a hundred times before. His baby brother knew all the regulars, probably even had a better relationship with them than Angel because he hadn't quite gotten to the level of detached wariness Angel layered over himself since leaving their father behind.

A quick scan of Johnson's booth came up empty, and Angel frowned, looking down the next row in the hopes of seeing a dark-haired youth bobbing along the booths. Clearing his throat to get the broad-shouldered, towheaded vendor's attention, he asked, "Hey, Magnus, did you see Rome?"

"He was just here. Asked me to hold a bin of sugar salak." The man ducked to avoid one of the booth's beams from hitting his forehead. "Tasted a bit of the sample I put out and said it would get him a bag of cotton candy."

"Find him?" West trotted up to the booth, favoring his ankle. His brow furrowed when Angel shook his head. "I came from the other side, but I didn't see him."

"Must have gone back to look for me," Angel muttered. "He's trying to sell me snake fruit."

The dread crawling through his thoughts whispered poison into his mind. His breath shortened, pulled in by the fear tightening its chains around his chest and throat. Swallowing didn't help. It only thickened the already viscous saliva coating his tongue. Every gulp of air only seemed to drive a panic-forced slender dagger deeper into his sternum, and his stomach churned, kicking up a froth of sour bilious foam to burn the roof of his mouth.

"He's got to be close by," West reassured him, but Angel could hear the crack in his voice. There was a hint of worry, not enough to blossom into concern but skirting its edge. "We'll find him."

"Rome!" Angel walked back to the row they'd just come down, craning to see over the crowd. Cupping his hands around his mouth, he yelled his brother's name again, but no one turned around, and Roman didn't emerge out of one of the other booths. Giving one last shout down the opposite row, Angel tried to clamp down the icy sweats running through him. "Rome, get your ass over here!"

Nothing.

And panic struck him, gouging out his heart to broil it in a cold fire he couldn't seem to get control over. It raged through him, cauterizing every sensible reason he could come up with about why Roman wasn't there at his side… wasn't hearing him… wasn't coming out to joke about how he'd scared Angel half to death.

Every. Sensible. Reason.

Leaving Angel with only the nightmares of where his little brother could be and what was happening to him.

"It's okay, love. He's around somewhere." West intruded into Angel's rapidly tightening panic. "We'll find him. Let me go back to the car—"

"We need to call the cops." Angel reached for his phone. His mind raced, circling back to all the horrific possibilities lurking within the dark. A flash of sanity punched through, and he grasped at it. "Mag, can you call the security guard? Maybe they can call him on the PA."

"Good idea." Magnus's soft Nordic accent carved odd planes into his words. "They'll find him, Angel. He can't be far."

It seemed like forever until he heard a crackly voice mostly order Roman to high tail it over to Magnus's booth. The world continued to turn. People meandered by, haggling with Magnus over bananas and apples, with a particularly shrill-voiced woman outraged over the price of cherimoyas. West was gone, lost in the market's throng, periodically raising his voice to call out for Angel's brother.

But not a hint of Roman in the crowd.

"You better make that call, Angel." Magnus's voice was rough, tumbled with heartbreaking gravity. "Just in case. Better they be here and we not need them than…."

Angel began to dial his phone, fingers trembling, when he heard a faint scream above the market's low murmur.

The scream came again, familiar but riding high with terror. Tossing the ringing phone at Magnus, Angel shouted for West to follow him and took off running toward what he knew would be his greatest nightmare.

"LET ME go!" Those words froze the blood in Angel's veins. Then heartbreakingly, Roman shouted, "*Angel!*"

His screams were clearer once Angel was out of the market's noisy thrall. The air was crisp, cold in Angel's lungs, keeping him on the razor's edge of collapsing, fueling him along with the adrenaline coursing through him. The bowling alley's cracked bleached-gray asphalt was hard under his All-Stars, the tarry ribbons veining the lot slightly spongy, but not yet sticky from the sun's rising warmth.

Any other time he'd have been walking behind Rome, playing tread on the tar snake on the ground, trying to keep his balance as he kept his feet to the line. It'd been a stupid thing they'd come up with the first time he'd dragged Rome with him to get ingredients, his brother sullen with worry and repressed anger. They hadn't walked the snakes that morning because Rome thought West might think he was a little kid, whispering his fears before they'd left the house. Angel'd planned on introducing West to the snakes when they left, knowing his lover would do anything to make Rome happy.

If only he'd kept as good an eye on his little brother as he had on West.

If only he got a second chance to get sticky black tar all over the bottoms of his high-tops.

If only he'd reach Roman in time.

Angel rounded the building's corner and saw his brother sinking his teeth into a tall man's tanned, beefy arm. He didn't slow his stride. His rage drowned his terrors, its red-hot fingers closing over his squirrely fears and squeezing them tightly until they popped. Every whispering doubt and horrifying thought he'd had while searching for Rome scattered, waxen birds beating their melting wings as Angel lost what little control he had left in him.

His wrath turned the world red, a crimson filter running white at the edges where his temper cracked. Angel was aware of a faint burst of pain down his arm, only briefly noticing he'd punched the man in his already skewed face. He got a flash of a hook nose, already broken far too many times for the bridge to heal and now spurting a river of blood from one nostril.

Another hook into the man's jaw and Angel heard a crack. Pain bloomed over his ribs, a solid hit to his side when Rome's attacker landed a firm punch into him, but it wasn't enough to stem the flow of anger slickening his nerves.

He was briefly aware of screaming at Roman to run back to the market, but he wasn't sure if his brother heard him around the mouthful of blood Angel was forced to spit out in order to breathe. Keeping his panting shallow kept the anguish along his ribs down to a bare minimum, but the ache was intense. Another blow came too close to his face, glancing off his temple, and Angel dodged to the side.

Not a sound reached him. Lost in the tight circle of fear, anger, and blood thirst, Angel was barely aware of Roman scrambling to get away, and when the scowling man lunged after the boy, Angel tackled him to the ground, slamming both of them into the hard-packed dirt.

Gold flashed in the man's smile, a single tooth gleaming amid the blood and yellowed enamel. His lips were fleshy, inches above Angel's face when he rolled them over, pinning Angel to the ground. The man was older, lines digging deep into his cheeks and forehead, dimpled black with dirt. A sour rankness permeated his skin, scraping at the back of Angel's throat with its foulness. His hands were as filthy as his smell, knuckles bloodied and raw, poised over Angel before one thundered into Angel's cheek.

The blow hurt, rattling Angel's brain. It rocked his skull back, slamming it into the ground, and the impact sent stars across Angel's eyes. Grunting, he tasted blood, his tongue swelling along one side where he'd bitten through its edge. Another fist hovered, pulling impossibly back, and the man's ugly face split with a maniacal hyena grin. His arms were thick, fleshy, and beneath a layer of thick fat, probably solid muscle. Another hit would not only hurt, it would do serious damage, and Angel didn't know if Rome was safe. He couldn't risk another strike, not if his brother wasn't out of the man's reach.

His attacker shifted, rising up off of Angel's stomach, gaining leverage for his blow, and Angel jerked his knee, catching the man between his legs and driving straight into the softness of his balls. He didn't have time to take any pleasure in hearing the man's soft *urk*. A shove at the man's chest proved nearly futile, and Angel struggled to get loose, his back aching with the pressure of moving the man's weight. A blow to the man's temple was enough to send his attacker reeling, and Angel suddenly found himself free.

Small stones in the ground dug Angel's hands open, scraping them, and the cold sting of air on his palms was enough to make him hiss. He couldn't breathe out of his right nostril, and his balance seemed off-kilter. The sky tilted, turning fuzzy on its edges, and Angel shook his head, trying to clear away the buzzing in his ears.

"Always was a smartass, boy," the large man muttered, flashing another malevolent grin through his mask of caked blood and dirt. "You always did think you were too good for the likes of us."

Standing toe to toe with the man, Angel combed his memories, trying to place where he'd seen the scraggly-toothed, thin-haired giant before. A glimmer of recognition hit, nothing firm enough for him to grasp, and when he tried to focus, it slithered off, a gelatinous echo of a memory slipping away under a rush of nausea.

"Say nighty-night, bitch." The giant's laugh boomed, his spit spraying over Angel's face. His fists were up, but his stance was relaxed, daring Angel to make a move. "Come and get it."

"Fucker," he growled and clenched his fist, but his punch never landed. As Angel stepped forward to anchor his weight for the blow, his head exploded, a meteor strike of pain blinding him in a flash of fiery white. Someone laughed, a taunting sound. Then he fell, slamming back into the ground, and the sky churned black, taking Angel with it as it lost its light.

Sixteen

THE LIGHTS hurt. No question about it, of every bit of ache along his battered body, Angel hated the blurring burn of the emergency room's harsh lights the most. The slightly off-yellow glow dug into his eyes, scalloping out bits of his brain through his blown-wide pupils.

Blinking only alleviated the stabbing for a brief moment. Then the wash of white pouring past his lashes began the searing all over again. Angel wanted nothing more than to close his eyes against the light and fall back into the soft, warm darkness he'd been pulled out of a few hours before. Or at least he did until he saw Roman's tear-streaked face and West's bloody lower lip, speckled along its plump from where he'd dug his teeth into his own flesh sometime during the time Angel hit the ground, then woke up in the hospital.

Angel'd smiled—he remembered smiling at them—then he'd gone back under, only to wake up alone in a cordoned-off ER stall, shirtless and sporting the largest headache in known history.

Now he was awake and cranky, left to wonder where his brother was and why West wasn't with him.

He hated hospitals. Growing up, he'd been conditioned to avoid authorities, and the only thing screaming authority, badges, and social services more than a hospital was a police station. In this case, Angel was going to have to revise that particular opinion his father'd imparted, because from what he could see from his bed on the ER ward, there were more than enough cops milling about in the outer hall to hire a dispatcher and convert a supply closet to a jail cell.

Then the one cop Angel would have liked to never have seen again walked into the curtained-off space where he'd been placed and pulled up a chair, settling down for what looked like a long talk.

"Swear to God, Montague," Angel ground out as he laid his head back onto the pillow. "I'm going to pay a girl and her little dog to land a house on you pretty soon."

Talking hurt, and Angel half wished he hadn't started the conversation, especially when Montague slid the metal-legged chair across the floor, bringing it closer to the bed in one long ear-shattering shriek. In the last half hour, he'd seen all manner of white-coats and blue-uniforms, enough to last him a lifetime, but no sign of West or Roman.

"You look like shit, Daniels, but the doctors say you'll live. Mild concussion, could have been worse from how the boy tells it," Montague drawled, taking out that damned brown notebook he seemed to carry around like a security blanket. "Mind if I ask you some questions?"

"God, I hate you so hard right now," he grumbled. "What do you want? Haven't I answered enough questions? And where's Rome? I want to see him. *Now*."

"He's with the social worker."

Montague put his hand against Angel's shoulder, pushing him down into the mattress when Angel straightened up to slide off the bed. The IV tube rattled against the metal rail at Angel's side, and he shook the cop off.

"Calm down, Daniels. She's just there to keep him company until you get cut loose. Since you're his only guardian, I'm not willing to hand him off to anyone not legally responsible for him."

Angel took a breath, shoving his worries down deep into his belly. "Where's West?"

"He's in the waiting room… waiting. You were out for the count, remember?" Montague inched the chair closer to the bed. "So CPS was called just to ensure Roman's safety. I need to question him about the attack, but I can't do that without you. He's a minor. If you'd consent, I'd like to talk to him before you get discharged. It's important to get his reactions and answers before his memory fades or he starts to embellish things."

"My brother's not a liar," Angel replied, then grimaced, recalling all the times Rome flat out lied to his face without a shift in expression. "Well, not about the important things."

"I'm not saying he is." Montague's hard face softened a bit, and he leaned over the bed railing, resting his weight on folded arms. "Kids have a difficult time when these kinds of things happen. Their minds try to make sense of things, and that sometimes leads to odd rationalizations. A short man can become someone with dwarfism, or someone with braces suddenly has metal teeth. It's a way for them to cope with what's happened to them, but that makes it difficult to parse out the reality from what they're creating to deal with the trauma."

"Sure." His head hurt too much to do more than grunt, and Montague's answering nod was curt. "How long have I been out? Doctor's not much on the sharing."

"Less than half an hour. Then you were groggy, but from what I understand, your head's pretty hard. Cracked the shovel handle we found lying next to you. It's been taken down to the lab for fingerprinting, but I don't know if we'll get anything from it," Montague replied. "Since you've been conscious and complaining for the past forty-five minutes, the ER doc thought you were well enough to talk to me. Give me five minutes. Then I'll get Rome in here. If you're up to it."

Every part of him wanted to tell Montague to shove off, but his face hurt where he'd been punched, and there was still grit in his hair from the dirt patch he'd been driven into. "Yeah, let's do this. But first, see if they'll let me have some water or something. I feel like I ate a hell of a lot of that ground he tried to punch me into."

"YOU'D NEVER seen him before, then?" Montague prodded Roman. "Are you sure?"

Rome glanced at Angel, his hooded eyes heavy with doubt. His chatterbox of a little brother clammed up nearly as soon as Montague joined them in the small office they'd been left in. Roman clung to him, his arms tight around Angel's bruised side, his dark lashes matted with dried tears. The couch they were sitting on was uncomfortable, and Rome's body was a skinny, bony dig into seemingly every tender spot Angel had on him, but he didn't care.

Holding Roman against him was worth any amount of pain the world could throw at him.

"Angel? How about you?" Montague turned in his chair, a hopeful weariness stamped on his face. He'd already taken Angel's statement, diligently writing down what little description Angel could give him about his attacker. "Maybe if you say something that sticks out to you, Rome might remember something?"

"It's kind of a scary thing. Everything happened kind of quickly." Angel kept his voice calm, a casual banter with the cop, but he could feel the tremble slinking through Rome's body as they spoke. "I wouldn't want to get into trouble if I got something wrong."

"No trouble. I get things wrong all the time," the detective reassured him. "Just tell me what you remember."

It was a touchy game they were playing. Roman hovered at the edge of puberty, a time thick with delicate ego and fragile nerves. Compounded by the inherent distrust he had for authority figures, the conversation could go two ways, help him open up to the cop or shut him down to the point of dead silence.

"He was tall, taller than me. Bigger too," Angel started. "I think he was wearing a red shirt."

"Plaid," Roman whispered into his ear, leaning in close. "It was blue plaid."

"Sorry, blue plaid. Dunno why I said red. I don't know if he was wearing overalls or jeans," he mulled. "He stank, though, didn't he?"

"Bad," Roman muttered. "And he was wearing pants. Not jeans. Dark. Maybe dark blue? And he had a gold tooth, right next to his front one."

"What side?" The cop began writing down Roman's description.

"It's turned around in my head." Roman scowled, then tapped at a tooth. "This one, I think. His hair was greasy, like mine gets if I don't wash it."

"Did you go over to the side of the building and he grabbed you?" Montague asked gently. "Or did he try to drag you over there?"

"He told me he had puppies." His brother made a face, probably disgusted at the scam the man tried to pull on him. "I told him to fuck off."

Montague looked up. "Where were you when this happened?"

"At the end of the row," Rome explained. "I was looking at some comic books. West gave me five bucks before we left, and some guy was selling them for a quarter each. I was going to see if I could bargain him down."

"Same guy who grabbed you or different guy?"

"Different guy." He shook his head, nearly popping Angel in the jaw with his skull. "Comic book guy was kind of young. I was going back around to see what he had on the other side of his tent when the stinky guy grabbed me. That end of the rows is pretty empty. Hardly anyone goes down there because it's all junk."

"And the guy with the comics didn't try to stop him?" The cop's pen stilled, its tip bleeding a bit of ink into the page. "Did he see the stinky guy?"

"Don't think so." Roman pursed his mouth and sighed. "His tent had sides on it. All the way to the ground, and he put tables on either side of the rows. I thought that was stupid because there was only him and he had two tables on opposite sides to watch. Someone's going to rip him off something good that way."

"But not you, right?" Angel prodded.

"Nope, not me," his brother asserted. "I was going to tell him about it, but then the stinky guy grabbed me."

"How did he get to the side of the building?" Montague shifted in his chair.

"He just picked me up and put his hand over my mouth. I couldn't even breathe." Roman snapped his teeth together a few times. "I bit him, but he didn't let go until we were by where Angel found me."

Something shifted in Rome, and his face closed up, building a wall to hide the vulnerability in his eyes. Angel's ribs stabbed through his bruises when Roman's arms tightened around his torso, and he bit back the grunting complaint caught on the tip of his tongue.

"But he found you, right? Your brother?" the cop reminded them. "What else do you remember? Anything will help."

"He was yelling at someone to start the car."

Roman brightened, sitting up quickly. His elbow unerringly gouged into Angel's chest, deep and hard enough for Angel to resign himself to another mark on his already abused body.

"I didn't hear anything, but by that time, Ange got there and punched the guy in the face. Then he told me to run, so I went looking for West."

"Took you long enough to listen to me," Angel teased lightly, smirking when his brother shot him an indignant look.

"I wasn't scared of him," Rome declared, thrusting his chest out. "I did what you told me to do. Except for kick him in the balls. I didn't get a chance to. Then I couldn't find West, but Magnus saw me. So that was cool. He's the one who went after the guy, but he was already gone."

"You did great, Roman," Montague replied.

"He knew my name," the boy said softly. "He called me Roman by the tent. That's what made me stop. Because he looked like someone, you know? But I didn't recognize him."

"Not at all?" the cop asked.

"Nope." He shook his head, then slid back down to rest against Angel's side. "But the first time he called me? I kind of thought he sounded like Angel."

THE NIGHT sky was a sheet of black steel set with a million diamonds, sparkling flares coyly peeking out through a veil of rising evening fog. A cold front edged in along the coast, its brittle caress crisp enough to frost the edges of the cliff house's windows, layering a ghostly lace over the panes. West'd never used the second-floor sitting area off the master suite and even debated tearing down the walls separating it from the main room, but tonight the space provided a bit of comfort, a cozy den dressed in muted earthy reds and soft fabrics, a perfect swaddle for a bruised and shaken lover.

A low-slung couch sat a few feet away from the wall of glass running along the sitting area's west end, and a few blocks of sanded-smooth wood made an obstacle course for West as he came into the room. Maneuvering around one, he carried two mugs of aromatic coffee, fragrant with liberal doses of whiskey, more concerned with accidentally burning himself than ruining the weird puffy dark blue rug the designer chose for the room. He stepped over Angel's legs, murmuring for the man not to move. Then he held out one of the mugs.

"Sit up, love." West was careful not to jostle the block he'd dragged over to rest his feet on. "And careful, that coffee machine is set to brew lava. I'm surprised the cups haven't melted."

Angel stared at the mug for a long moment, then took it from West, sliding upright beneath the duvet mound he'd burrowed under. West held his breath, certain the scalding liquid would end up everywhere, but when nothing happened, he sat down and promptly splashed a teaspoon's worth of coffee into his crotch.

"Fucking hell," West spat out, then looked up when he heard Angel's soft chuckle. "Sure, laugh it up, pretty boy. See how you much you laugh when my dick doesn't work when you need it."

"Pretty sure your dick always works." Angel smothered another chortle. "It's kind of like your mouth, always going whether I need it to or not."

"Is this where I tell you to suck my dick?" West caught himself before he leaned on Angel. Angling his hips, he hooked his left arm over Angel's shoulder. "Come here."

Angel's weight on him felt nice. Even nicer was the lack of hesitation, just Angel's back sliding across him, a shoulder blade resting on his chest, trapping his heartbeat against Angel's warmth. A shuffle of the duvet covered them both, cocooning their legs and bellies in its Angel-scented cotton heaviness. His lover released a soft murmuring sigh, then went boneless in West's loose half embrace.

They sat in companionable silence, the sky turning around over them, a flick of clouds moving in off the water to deepen the fog's grip on the shore. Angel's chest shuddered occasionally, caught in a repressed gulping stutter of pain. West kissed away a tear trembling at the corner of his right eye, cradling his lover in closer when Angel drained his mug, then leaned forward to put it on the block.

"Here, give me that." West took Angel's cup and placed it on the table at his end of the couch. The whiskey had been a smooth kiss of lethargy in the coffee, blunted by heavy cream and soothed over by a couple of sugar cubes. Pressing his lips against Angel's throat, West whispered, "Do you want to talk?"

"About today?" Angel snorted.

"About anything." Stroking the spot he'd kissed, West's heart clenched when he caught sight of the bruises over Angel's jaw. "Today. Tomorrow. Whatever you want to talk about."

"Tomorrow I have to go back to the farmers' market." Angel winced, shifting about on the couch.

"Why?"

"Because I didn't get stuff for the bakery. I need fruit, nuts, and I get my flour from Tony," he explained. "He sells it to me for almost cost, but I've got to pick it up. He's only there on Saturday and Sunday. Then he heads back down to LA."

"Make a list of what you want, and I can have it taken care of, including Tony." West brushed his thumb over Angel's lips as they began to part. "Daniels, do both of us a favor and just take my help."

"I *hate* charity."

"You'll learn to adapt. It's not charity. It's accepting help. This way I'll feel like I'm being a hero, and you get to sleep in tomorrow." West kept his voice light, but the dark circles under Angel's eyes were nearly as dark as the sky outside. "You need the rest. You went a few rounds with some asshole who brought a *kun* to a fistfight."

Angel's groan was enough to lift West's worry from his chest. "Fuck, how long have you been waiting to say that?"

"Years," he admitted sheepishly. "How many other people know Okinawan?"

"You don't even know it. One word! Maybe two," Angel reminded him. "And where was that from? Shit, the sideshow, I had a crush on that guy… the fake martial arts guy they had in for a couple of weeks. Fucking sleazeball, but he was hot."

They'd bonded over the lean, muscular man, jokingly lusting at his sculpted body until it dawned on both of them they were serious. It'd been the first time West admitted he liked to look at men, and Angel hadn't even blinked. A few days later, he'd gotten his first kiss—a real, soul-shaking, ball-trembling kiss—while lying on a blanket with Angel, and since then he hadn't been able to look at a starry sky reflected on an ocean without a rush of nostalgic emotion.

West huffed out his cheeks, caught in a time rich with the ever-present smell of cotton candy and the taste of stolen kisses. "Remember when he found out he'd been sleeping with those twins and he didn't know they weren't the same woman?"

"Remember when *they* found out?"

Angel's low, husky laugh did silly things to West's cock, a suckle of sound digging deep into his mind to pull out every thought he'd had about Angel over the years.

"That place had some crazy people."

"Hey, I was one of those crazy people." His protest was light, just a skim of teasing below his laughter. "And yeah, carnivals draw some pretty insane weirdos, but once you're in with them, you're in for life."

"You're the only person I know who ran away to join the carnival and ended up in a better place than where he'd come from," West confessed. "Okay, to be fair, you're also the only person I've ever known who ran away and joined a carnival."

"I'm glad they hired me for that contract for Half Moon," Angel whispered. "I'm glad I met you. Even if… we fucked it up a little bit, I'm glad it all went down how it did. We're better now, older. Old enough to know what we're doing now."

"Well, I know what I'm doing now," West confessed. "Back then, I was scared to even kiss you. Now all I want to do is roll you into bed and not let you go."

"Yeah, I could use that right now." Angel leaned his head back, resting it on West's shoulder. "Getting rolled into bed. Maybe even getting fucked until I don't know my name anymore."

"Babe, I—" He caught himself, choking at a word he often tossed off casually but not… between them. "You are in no condition to—"

"I almost lost my baby brother today, West." Angel slid on the couch cushion, turning around until he faced West. The duvet slithered to the floor, a rush of cooler air slapping their heated skin, and Angel's nipples peaked under his shirt, his chest straining to hold back something West knew broke when they couldn't find Rome. "I didn't… I wasn't paying attention. I should have… fuck, West. I know what shitty things people do to kids. I can't stop thinking about it, and I'm so fucking scared right now."

"He's here." West cocked his head, trying for a smile, but it died on his lips before it could spread further than a twitch. "Okay, so he's asleep in his bed, and today was *not* your fault. You didn't put him in that asshole's hands. He was taken. From some place he should have been safe to roam around in. And what you're forgetting is in the middle of all the crap happening to him, he kept his head and did what you'd told him to do to get out of that situation."

"He never should have *been* in that situation, West," Angel argued, biting the ends of his words. "Rome shouldn't—"

"I'm not going to fuck you just so you can feel punished for what happened," West growled. "Because that's what it feels like you're asking me to do. You're hurt, Angel. I shouldn't have given you whiskey in your coffee. I shouldn't have dragged you out here where the damned heater doesn't seem to work.

"And I sure as hell am not going to spread you out on my bed and fuck you into the sheets so you can ride that pain to whatever penance you feel like you need to do because of what happened to Rome." He cupped Angel's face, not surprised to find his palm wet with his lover's shed tears. "You can't ask me to hurt you like that. I can't, love. And you shouldn't ask me to."

"I'm not. I promise you I'm not," Angel whispered into West's curved hand. "I'm asking you to make love to me. I need to get today out of my head and get away from all the nightmares I can't seem to shake off. I need to feel safe right now, West, and no one but you ever makes me feel like everything's going to be okay. I need to know it's all going to be okay, or I'm not—"

"That I can do." West folded his arms around Angel's shaking body, rocking him gently as a bank of clouds folded over the cliff, stealing away their stars. He kissed Angel's temple, reveling in the essence of the man he held close. Then as the growing storm broke, shattering the sky in flashes of light and booming thunder, West whispered, "I love you, Angel. I always have. And I always will."

Seventeen

THE STORM was hot and fluid, pouring through the sky in a rush of wind and pounding water. Its furious torrents coursed down the sides of the house, slender rivulets slicking the windows, and the thick glass held back all but a hush of its raging screams. Clouds poured over the beaten sky, their milky plumes quickened with kisses of lightning while the sea convulsed below. Beyond the glass, cradled in a dusky gold glow, the storm could only whisper to the lovers it couldn't reach, its rippling murmurs too low for them to hear above their sighs.

As Nature threw her squalling tantrum against the cliffs, West heard nothing except Angel's sighs after being kissed, and he saw no storm but the deepening silken smoke in his lover's hooded gray eyes. He was bruised, deeply so, uneven purple and black mottles darkening his gleaming golden skin, and traces of the day's—hell, the month's—traumas lingered in Angel's gaze.

"I want to kiss you until you're happy." West rose up from the bed and sat on his haunches. "Or at least content."

He'd kissed nearly every inch of Angel's length, the fragrance of his lover's skin resonating in West's senses. There was a desire for more percolating in him. His cock was heavy, growing taut in response to Angel's naked body, laid out before him. The pain in Angel's eyes held West back. As did the strain lining his handsome face.

"You have no idea how happy I am right now," Angel rasped. Ghosting his fingers over West's nipples, he played with the nubs when they tightened at his touch. "Especially seeing you like this. And with me."

Naked, there was nothing for Angel to grab on to, but he tugged lightly on West's dick, making him gasp at the shocking threads titillating his arousal. A pillow to Angel's stomach was enough to get West loose, but the sensation of Angel's fingers stroking his length remained.

Angel stole his thoughts, a thief whose touch rendered West poor of words and his lungs empty of air. Staring down Angel's body, he consumed every inch of skin and rippling muscle, burning the memory of the night deep into his mind. His dreams would whisper of dark red sheets, a sculpted lean form, and a mink-dark tangle of silken strands tumbling around Angel's strong face.

There were imperfections, to be sure. A life lived as hard and on the edge as Angel lived was going to take its pound of flesh. Tiny healed-over burns marked Angel's sinewy forearms, seared kisses from Angel's love-hate relationship with his ovens. A few nicks on his calf were from one of the carnival games he'd manned, gouges the heavy pull triggers needed to reset the rows of marching ducks almost leechlike in its thirst for blood. There were the blemishes West accidentally put there and a divot in the crease of his hip muscle, a reminder to anyone who knew the story not to taunt a donkey when wearing nothing but a pair of Speedos and a rainbow-spangled squid hat.

The promise of Angel's allure, hinted at during that long-ago season, had emerged, and West's heart twisted in his chest, dumbstruck by the man who oddly wanted him back. There was no accounting for taste. West grinned suddenly, and if he took into account Angel's eclectic palate, maybe he shouldn't have been so surprised.

"Turn over, to your side," West slid his hand under Angel's hip, pushing him slightly. "Please."

Angel shifted, lifting himself up to give West room. Sliding in behind his lover, West guided Angel back, snuggling up against Angel's ass and shoulders. His cock hurt, aching for Angel's skin or touch. Flexing, Angel inched back, nesting West's shaft in his cleft.

Groaning, West rested his forehead against the back of Angel's skull. "You're killing me, love."

"You're not the only one. We need... lube."

Angel hissed, twisting around to lie on his back again. West mourned the catch of his cock against Angel's ass, but Angel's mouth on his was worth it. They lingered over the kiss, taking small sips of air to prolong it, but eventually Angel broke it off, whispered into West's mouth, "I want you. So fucking much it hurts sometimes, but you're worth the pain, West. Just like you're worth the pleasure."

They lost the tube of lubricant when it rolled off the nightstand, only to find it again under the bed after a few laughter-infused seconds. West's tongue dried in his mouth when Angel slid a condom down the length of his cock. He whimpered when Angel enveloped the tip of his shaft in his mouth, Angel's full lips a profane pout around West's glistening head. The lube proved difficult to handle, and West grumbled under his breath about Justin and his choice of sex aids.

"Beggars can't be choosers, Harris," Angel reminded him after he pulled his mouth off of West's cock. "Now fuck me so we can get some sleep."

"I can't believe you don't have a cracked skull," West grumbled. "We're crazy for doing this. Your doctor's going to kill me if you end up back in the hospital."

"Hard head. I'm a Daniels. It's merely a flesh wound." Angel laughed, and West frowned at him. "Yeah, my head hurts, and I got the wind knocked out of my sails, but right now I need to have you inside of me, West. It's stupid, but… I just want to be with you. I want you to make me *feel*."

They moved tenderly, their desire at odds with their battered, healing bodies. There was something affirming in the slide of bruised skin against skin. The aches in West's limbs were a low throb, wicking away under Angel's touch, his desire for the man next to him engulfing his every thought. When Angel dipped his fingers into the lube in West's palm, West chuckled.

When his lover dipped his fingers down between his cleft and slid them around his own rim, West lost all reason and pinned Angel to the bed, kissing him furiously while sliding his own hand down to help Angel slicken his hole.

West had never loved the scents and sounds of sex. It'd been messy and dirty, something to be done to make himself and his fuck-at-the-time feel good. He'd gone out of his way to stay detached, getting involved only with men who'd thought of him as disposable as he viewed them.

Angel—fucking *Angel Daniels*—made West want to immerse himself in everything, to wallow in the sticky slurp of their bodies joined together. He loved the musk of Angel's cum when it welled out of his cock's slit and its tart, salty taste on West's tongue after he smeared a drop on his thumb, then sucked it off.

"Get on your side," West urged. "I don't want to hurt you."

"Trust me, you won't," Angel murmured as he rolled over. "I know you, West. You *won't*."

They lay back to chest, a more intimate press of the countless times they'd leaned against each other before. Angel felt good on him, his shoulders tensing, then relaxing when West eased his cock up to push on

Angel's hole. His own ass twitched, remembering the hot, hard length of his lover holding him open, plunging deep into his core, and West kissed Angel's shoulder, a whisper of lips on sun-gilded skin.

Angel's entrance resisted him, and then his rim flared, suckling at West's tip. Urging West in, Angel bent his head forward and pushed his hips back, sliding most of West's cock head into his tight heat. His breaths went shallow, and his molten sweet murmurs encouraged West to enter him.

"God," West groaned, gently pushing past Angel's tightness. His head broke through, Angel's ass suddenly wrapped around him, and West nearly came from the overwhelming rush of emotions flooding through him. "Shit, you're tight."

"Fuck, come on," Angel urged. "Waiting a long time for this, West. *Please.*"

He moved in slowly, seating himself inch by inch until his balls nested up into Angel's asscheeks. His hips twitched, and Angel gripped him tighter, his muscles undulating slowly, drawing West deeper into him. It was a strain to hold himself back, but from the quiver along Angel's back and thighs, West knew it was worth it. The glide in was a maddening exercise in patience, and he stopped every time he felt Angel take a sharp, quick breath.

Pulling out was even sweeter, especially since West knew he'd be able to go right back in, drawing another quaking response from the lover he held in his arms.

Their lovemaking was as soft as the storm was hard, a gentle rocking of hips and long strokes of West's hand over Angel's flank and belly. Their joining was a delicious waltz, the tension building up slowly, and West ached inside when his body, frustrated at the pace, started to demand more. His hips rocked into Angel's ass, a little harder than he'd done before, and Angel's fingers dug into his thigh. Startled, West nearly pulled free, scared he'd hurt Angel, but his lover shook his head.

"Fuck me, West," Angel whispered, impaling himself fully on West's cock with a shift of his limbs. "Just us. Make me feel just *us.*"

Cupping Angel's balls, West fondled the sac, then stroked his fingers up Angel's hard shaft. "Hold on, then, love."

His cock trembled in Angel's body. Tucked between them, his dick was hidden by Angel's cheeks, but West didn't need to see what his lover was doing to him. He burned each time he pulled back, sliding his cock through Angel's grasp. Through each delicious drag, West's nerves sparked, setting his skin on fire. The tingle started small, a teasing lick of sensation through his body. Then it built up slowly, until West was caught in the tempest he'd brought to life inside of him.

He caught his tongue between his teeth at the first hard slap of their bodies, his balls bouncing up into Angel's curve. Another slap, deadened slightly by the lush sheets bunching up between them, and Angel groaned, his cock twitching in West's hand. His balls brushed the edge of West's palm, rolling up and down, building up Angel's release.

Another stroke and West knew it would soon be over. He couldn't stop plunging up into Angel's body, and his pace broke, their rhythm shattered into a frenzied slam of flesh and bone. His dick begged for release, diving back into Angel's ass in short, hard jabs. His belly clenched, sending a bright, hard tightness punching through his balls, and West gasped as Angel's hand found his. They clenched their fingers over Angel's cock, pulling at his shaft in an odd disjointed fumble.

"Let me," West begged, his voice hoarse and odd in his ears.

The rush of blood in his head made it hard to think, much less speak, but he wanted to feel Angel's climax on his skin, needing to know he'd brought the man to his peak. Angel's hand fell away, landing on the bed. Shoving deeper into Angel's ass, West leaned them forward, driving them both to the edge. Angel's fingers clenched at the sheets, and he gasped, his face hidden by a curtain of burnished umber silk. Using the leverage of their new position, West plunged in harder, tugging at Angel's cock until he felt it throb in his hand.

Angel came first, a gush of fragrant masculinity, hot from his excited body. The scent of his release mingled with the aroma of their sweat and the sweetness of the rain. Unable to stop, West let go, falling into the blanket of sublime, erotic sensation rising up to catch him.

He felt nothing but Angel, knew only the press of Angel around him as his cock emptied into the friction-stoked sear they'd made. His climax was too much to bear, stroking at his face and down his limbs in a numbing wave. Shaking, West convulsed, rocking instinctively into Angel's shuddering body until they both couldn't take any more.

They slowed, a whispering torpor stealing through them, and West found himself sucking in mouthfuls of air, trying to slow the thundering beat of his heart and the slam of blood coursing through his veins. Unable to move, he remained clenched tightly in Angel's grip, his lover panting in his arms.

Dragging his fingers through Angel's sticky release, West murmured, "Are you okay?"

"Yeah," Angel whispered back in his sweet burned-sugar voice. "More than okay. And just so you know, I love you too, Harris. God help me, I love you too."

ANGEL HURT.

He was tired of the constant pain. The past few weeks had been hell on his body and a roller coaster for his heart, but thinking back on how he got the smarting bite on his shoulder and the crick in his neck, he'd do it all over again.

Except for the throbbing in his big toe. That he could have done without. Much like the tub of banana-chocolate-chip bread Rome dropped on his foot half an hour ago, but all things considered, the pangs and prickles were worth it. Especially since his younger brother was doing his damned best to pitch in after a hellish few days.

"Hey, that's cool!" Marveling, Roman reached for one of the peels lying on the bakery's prep table. "It really looks like snake skin."

Angel moved the knife around the piece of sweet salak in his hands and threw his brother a quick, sharp glance. "Aren't you supposed to be peeling tamarind?"

"It's boring." Roman kicked at the table's leg, rocking it under Angel's elbows. "And I mostly finished."

"*Dude,*" he warned. "Holding a knife here. What's the rules?"

"No kicking, and if I'm going to be at the prep table, I've got to have my ass on a stool and my legs tucked under." The stool legs screeched across the floor as Rome dragged it closer to Angel's side of the table. Climbing up, he muttered contritely, "Sorry. Forgot."

"Not many rules back here, kid," Angel scolded softly. "And they're there so no one gets hurt."

"Dude, you've got so many rules—" Rome cut himself off at Angel's filthy look. "Never mind. Okay. I know. Sorry."

"Here, you keep the peels." After shoving the rinds toward his brother, Angel picked up another one of the small blobby fruits Rome'd begged him to buy from Magnus. "Build yourself a dragon."

The sweet snake fruit had been tucked into the box of produce dropped off at the bakery that morning. Nearly a week after the attempt on Rome, Angel'd been glad to see Rome get excited over seeing Magnus, then promising the tall blond a visit to the market the next time Angel planned on going. A brief visit from Montague the day after the attack hadn't been as satisfying. The cops still had nothing about the kidnapper or Derry's murderer. Beyond speculating they were one and the same person, the detective reluctantly admitted they had little to go on.

"It's like this guy disappears into thin air," Montague grumbled in a rare, honest admission. "He clamps his hand over Rome's mouth tight enough to muffle your brother's screams and carries him up to the building without anyone seeing him? It's like he's a ghost or... people don't notice him. He knew his angles. The tent hid him from most of the crowd. He's good at this, very aware of what's going on around him. I'm chasing some leads up in SF, so maybe we'll come up with something. Until then, keep Rome close."

Roman hadn't spent a single moment alone since Montague walked out the bakery door, and Angel wondered if it wouldn't have just been easier to ship his brother off to Upper Siberia. Especially after Rome began to chafe at the constant shadowing.

They'd had a fight about his meds that morning, a full-temper blowout that left Angel shaking when it was all over. He'd been about to give in, too tired to argue any longer, but Rome's pushing back was desperate, nearly frantic. A step away from the tussle and Angel came back at his brother, reminding him the pill, like many things in life, was nonnegotiable during the school week.

"I'm sick of being broken." Rome's soft complaint tore Angel apart, but the boy took the pill from Angel's hand and gulped it down with a mouthful of water. Wiping his mouth with the back of his hand, Rome sighed, then said, "I just want to be *normal*, Ange. Like you."

If his heart hadn't already been shattered by his brother's tears, it would have crumbled under the weight of Rome's wishful longing.

"How much tamarind did you get done?" The fruit's flesh dripped down Angel's wrist, and as tempted as he was to lick it off, he wiped his arm on a damp towel. "At least two pounds?"

"Yeah," Rome grunted, then cocked his head, biting his lower lip. "I got almost four bags done. Then my hands got too sticky."

"You're supposed to wear gloves, kid," Angel reminded him. "So you don't get sticky."

"They squeak when I use them." His brother wrinkled his nose. "Justin doesn't wear gloves. He just said my hands had to be really clean. I washed them like five times before."

"So long as your hands were clean, we're good." Angel pared a bit of the salak off onto his knife and offered it to Rome. "Here. Peel off the membrane. What do you taste?"

It was a game of sorts for them, a question Angel'd asked a thousand times before, but this was the first time Rome was tasting something he hadn't tried first. His brother took the spongy slice, then stripped away the thin skin clinging to the flesh. After popping the fruit into his mouth, he chewed carefully.

"Like… pineapple." Roman made a face. "And lemon, but it's kind of sweet. It's *weird*."

"Yeah, I'm going to make a spread out of it." Angel laughed when Rome stole a whole peeled fruit from the bowl. "Don't eat too much. I don't know if it'll do anything to your guts."

"Kind of looks like garlic, yeah?" He took a bite, then pulled a membrane off his tongue. "It's good, though."

"Yeah, it is. I owe you some cotton candy. Next time we go," Angel promised. "Maybe we can stop by this Saturday and tell Magnus they rocked."

"Cool." Rome sucked on a piece of salak. He leaned over the table, rocking on the stool for a second, then promptly sat it back down before Angel could say anything. "Hey, can I ask you something?"

"Sure." Angel nodded to the damp towel. "Wipe your face and hands when you're done. And not on your clothes."

Rome grabbed the towel, then swabbed his face. Peeking over the edge, he watched Angel peel the last of the fruit. He was choosing his words carefully. Angel recognized the expression from the countless times Rome tried to pull a con on him. His brother had tells—serious tells—and Angel knew every single one of them. The tugging on his hair was a new one, something to watch for in the future.

"Are you and West going to get married?" Rome finally blurted out. His fingers picked at the towel's nap, plucking up the strands.

"I don't know," Angel confessed. "We haven't talked about it. Might be kind of soon. We've been back together for only a month. Maybe a little bit more."

"But you guys knew each other from before, right?"

"Yeah." Angel peeled off another piece of fruit and passed it over to Roman. "Why all the questions?"

"'Cause one of the kids at school said you guys are going to get married, and then I'm going to have to go back to Dad." Rome's lip quivered, and he bit at it, running his teeth over the chapped surface. "I told him to fuck off, but—"

"You're never going back to Dad." Angel put the knife down, letting it clatter on the metal surface.

He eased around the corner of the table and put his hands on Rome's slender shoulders. His brother's striped shirt was snugger than Angel'd have liked, especially since he'd just bought it a few months before. Despite Rome's increasing height and voracious appetite, Angel was struck by how much his brother was still a little boy, with little-boy problems and certainly their fears. Rome grabbed at him, clutching at Angel's T-shirt with his damp, sticky fingers.

Knotting the fabric in his hands, Rome looked everywhere but his brother's face, finally settling on Angel's feet as his focus as he mumbled, "I don't want you to give me away. I want to stay with you."

"Hey, didn't I fight some huge guy in a parking lot for you?" Angel crouched down so he could see his brother's face. "Kiddo, I don't know how many times I have to tell you that you're never going back to him, but I'll say it as many times as you need, okay? I've got your back, dude. No matter what, I've got you."

Rome's eyes were wet and afraid, filled with a terror Angel hadn't seen since the day their father dumped his brother on him. Catching Rome up in his arms, he held his young brother, rocking Rome gently when the boy began to cry. His awkward, lanky body jerked with every sob as Rome broke down.

Shivering, Rome clung, nearly dragging Angel down. Swinging his brother off the stool, Angel stroked at Rome's back. Hunkering down, he cradled Rome, reassuring him as best he could while his brother cried his heart out.

"It'll be okay, kid," Angel promised the shuddering, crying boy in his arms. "Give it another few years or so and you're going to be wanting to punch me in the face when I say you've got to be home by 10:00 p.m."

"Really?" Rome sat up, his weight settling on a lingering bruise on Angel's thigh.

"Yeah, really." He shifted his brother until they were both sitting on the floor. "You're going to be pissed off because I remind you the car needs gas after you take it and that you're going to have to save your money if you want something big because you're eating me out of house and home."

"Well, duh." Rubbing at his eyes, he mumbled, "I meant, really, I get to stay out that late? How come I don't get to stay out until ten now?"

"Yeah, you're fine… asshole," Angel teased, pushing his brother off his lap. "Go wash your hands and come help me finish up the snake jam."

"Oh, yeah." Rome scrambled to his feet. "We can totally call them snake jam muffins. We've got to make a couple for Zig."

"You are a fucking weird little kid, Rome."

The door to the front of the bakery swung behind Roman, its soft wind a familiar sensation across Angel's face. A short day for the dining room, he enjoyed the early evenings alone in the kitchen, a time when he played with the flavors he'd created, sometimes amazed at how something sounding good in his head turned out to be too disgusting for words while the things he tossed together in a desperate attempt to use up what he had ended up being a perennial favorite.

Roman's snake jam muffins were definitely going to be the latter, Angel thought, sucking on a spot of dried salak juice on his thumb. It just was going to need a better name.

The front door's bell clang jerked Angel out of his contemplation of fruit, jams, and batters. Wiping his hands off with one of the damp kitchen towels, he shouldered the partition door open, ready to tell whoever came in that they were closed. It wouldn't have been the first time Justin forgot to lock the front door before he left, and Angel cursed himself for not checking the dining room before they'd shut down for the day.

Rome stood by the door, his face ashen and bloodless. Oddly, West stood next to him, stiff and unyielding. Disheveled, West's button-up shirt was torn, a sleeve hanging slightly off its seam, and spots of blood speckled his chest. His nose dripped, a thin line of crimson smeared above his upper lip, and his blue eyes burned, angry and hot, when the two armed men standing at the front of the bakery shoved West farther in.

He grabbed at Rome as he stumbled in, keeping the young boy shielded with his body, and the man Angel'd jumped at the bowling alley grinned as he kicked at West's retreating back. His boot glanced off West's thigh, throwing him off-balance, and he tumbled over one of the low tables, taking Rome down with him.

The small space smelled of blood, gunpowder, and fear, and Angel took a breath to steady himself, steeling his nerves for what was to come. He didn't care about the man who'd taken Roman. No, he was more interested in the other man, the one with dark gray eyes and deep dimples flashing in his cheeks as he grinned across the bakery at Angel. The man looked haggard, odd considering it hadn't been that long since Angel'd seen him last, but Violet was fond of saying those with the devil in them aged quickly because Hell wanted its own back.

Tossing the towel onto the counter, Angel turned to the man and said, "Now what the fuck do you want, Dad?"

Eighteen

ANGEL WALKED to the middle of the bakery's dining room. They'd tried keeping the floor plan as open as they could, arranging the couches, wing chairs, and low tables into clusters. After the fire, they'd lost a few of the pieces to water damage and smoke smears, but the red velvet low-back davenport survived, earning it a central spot in the middle of the floor. He reached the end of the couch, then bent over to right the table West'd knocked over when he and Rome fell.

His nerves were frayed, snapping thread by thread with each step, but Angel kept his face schooled, a placid mask without a hint of emotion. Keeping his eyes as dead as his expression, he reached West's side, then hooked his hands under his brother's arms, pulling him out from under West.

Sangfroid.

It was a word Ren, West's grandmother, taught him when he'd worked for her. She'd been responsible for much of his vocabulary, reading romance novels out loud to Angel as he took care of her back garden or as he prepared a week's meals for her freezer. Lang'd been a ghost then, skirting the edges of their lives, sallow and wan until one day he'd found his footing and began to practically live at the bookstore. Angel wasn't even certain Lang knew anyone existed, much less paid any attention to the shaggy-haired handyman lurking around his grandmother's house.

The words ended when age finally took the old woman, but many stuck with him. Epaulets, cabriolet, wainscoting, but especially sangfroid. It'd dawned on him back then, detachment and coldness was the best way to deal with his father.

Especially when the asshole was holding a gun.

Angel didn't know the man standing next to his father. *He* didn't matter. No, the only person who mattered was standing right by the door, holding a gun on his two sons.

Cliff Daniels wasn't wearing the last two years very well on his skin. The last time Angel saw his father, he'd been little more than a shadowed outline gruffly shoving Rome out of a faded terracotta beater with bald tires and a folded-over hanger shoved into its antenna mount to catch any signals strong enough for the probably stolen radio to catch.

Before that he'd been standing over Angel, his hands wet with Angel's blood.

It was that man Angel had burned into his memory.

For the longest time, Angel wondered if his mother, a fuzzy ghost of a memory, contributed anything to his gene pool, because he and his father shared the same eyes, hair, and face, their strong features pulled from a mixed bag of indiscriminate ancestors.

A thick-shouldered and robust man, his father loomed in Angel's mind, an oppressive presence Angel once admired but who'd toppled from the pedestal he'd been put on after one too many beatings. As long as Angel could recall, Cliff Daniels was part thug, part snake-oil salesman, with a keen eye for gullible people and a silver tongue he used to cheat people out of every cent he could get. He used his looks and charm to milk a mark dry while his finely tuned paranoia and innate selfishness kept him one step ahead of the authorities and his angry victims.

Most of the time.

From the massive swelling rising up along the right side of his face, Angel guessed his father'd met his match in someone, and after a quick glance at West's torn-up, bleeding knuckles, it didn't take a rocket scientist to figure out who'd given his father a too short beating.

"You okay, kid?" Angel righted Roman, brushing off a bit of dust from his shirt. He couldn't risk showing his father how much he cared for West. Not now. It would give the man leverage, and Angel couldn't risk West being hurt.

Or worse, killed.

Standing as close as he could to West, Angel pressed his leg against his lover's as casually as he could, meeting West's cobalt gaze. There was worry on West's face, lines etched around his pressed-together lips. Then he nodded, turning away to get to his feet, breaking the link they'd briefly shared. West buckled, his hip slamming into the couch's swirled wooden armrest. Grunting, he grabbed at Angel's pants, tugging them down slightly before he got his balance, and Angel leaned over, dragged forward by West's stumble. Pulling Rome to him again, Angel took a few sliding steps to the right, and after a bit of gentle nudging he got them around the end of the couch.

"You and Rome run," Angel muttered into West's ear. "First chance."

He stepped forward before West could respond, then made sure his brother was behind him. They had the couch partially between them and the other men, but Angel knew it wasn't much protection. The padding on the davenport's back was thin, and its wood frame more than likely was a cobbled-together pressboard without enough thickness to it to stop a bullet.

Angel's guts churned, a tempest of fear brewing hot and fierce deep within him. He refused to give his father even the slightest hint of his distress, but it was hard. His tongue stuck to the roof of his mouth, and his gums ached around his teeth, his spit viscous and thick. He wanted to swallow, wicking the sluggish feeling from his mouth and perhaps dislodging the swelling lump in his throat, but those were signs his father was looking for. Signs he'd been taught to watch for when circling a mark.

"I see what you're doing there, boy." His father's idiotic grin widened, and he motioned with his gun for Angel to move aside. "I'm not as stupid as I look. Get out of the way. I'll need a clear shot at the man if you and I don't come to an agreement."

"So you're going to shoot... who? West? Rome?" Angel thrust his chin up, narrowing his eyes. "And for what? To get what?"

"To get what I've worked for these past few months." The older Daniels edged into the room while the man beside him turned, leaning back to scan the street. "This was supposed to be a fast one-time thing. Now Byron and I've got to clean up this whole damned mess—"

"Wait, Byron? Your cousin Byron? That's who this asshole is?" Making a show of studying the man by the door, Angel kept himself between his father and West. Rome's hands were twisted into his shirt, and he silently begged West to get the young boy off of him and ready to bolt if they saw an opening. "I thought he was doing life."

"Life's a shorter sentence when prisons get full up, boy," Byron croaked. His throat worked to move his words out, his Adam's apple bobbing violently when he spoke. "'Sides, that bitch had it coming. Not like she died. Someone up high must have figured that out. Cliff here was kind enough to come pick me up and, well, cut me in on this job."

"And it's not as if his parole officer's going to be able to find us in Cabo." Another wave of the gun, and then Cliff's smile ebbed. "Let me keep this short and simple, boy. My man Washington promised me a cool mil once you and the kid got the hell out of town. I'm here to collect."

"Derry's dead," West said in a flat voice. "And they're going nowhere."

"Dead happens, asshole," Cliff shot back. "And I don't give a shit if they live or die. I was promised some cash to get them out of here, and Washington doing a dirt nap isn't going to change me getting it."

Angel's blood ran cold, and West pushed past him, rushing at Angel's right shoulder to reach Cliff. The couch's legs screamed a protest across the floor when West went by, his furious dash careening it toward the righted table. Left open and vulnerable, Angel grabbed at the taller man, snagging West by the waistband.

If Cliff and Byron weren't already on edge, West's sudden lunge at them honed them to a dangerous sharpness. Their guns came up, the weapons' endless black holes seizing Angel's attention, and he wrenched West back. His arms burned with the effort of keeping West contained, and behind him, Roman's breathing became erratic, a huffing rhythm fueled by stress and panic.

"You didn't have to kill Derry." West twisted around, and Angel's fingers strained from the torque. "Angel, let go."

"West, you're hurting me." The entreaty was quiet, barely loud enough to tickle an ear, but West subsided. The pressure on Angel's fingers let up, and he released West, nudging him with a quick elbow. "Is he right? Did you kill Derry?"

"Like I had a choice," Cliff spat back, prowling closer. "Asshole was selling us out. After all I did for him. He contacted me, convinced me to leave behind a good shakedown gig to come here and kick you in the ass. What does he do instead? Jack the whole thing up and left me holding an empty bag. Whining about cheating you and how sorry he was. Asshole had a sweet setup, and he was going to blow it all because *you* fell in love with my worthless son."

The cracks in his façade were showing, a network of fine lines etched into his face, and his skin sank in under his right eye, the bone underneath too broken to support his cheek. Cliff Daniels had given up. On life. Himself. Everything. And he'd gambled on one final big score—a gamble he not only lost but ended up taking Derry's life as well.

When his father opened his mouth, Angel choked on the sour punch of Cliff's breath. He creaked, oozing with a fetid aroma. It permeated the small dining area, made more potent by Byron's unwashed stench. The two men smelled as if they'd been on a bender on a forgotten mountain, nauseating and filthy. Their clothes were caked with grime, and Cliff's nails were black, his fingers clenching around his gun's stock. Byron was no better, his face speckled with dried blood, and one eye was crimson, blown out from Angel's punch.

The malevolence in Byron's grin reassured Angel he wouldn't be one of the Danielses making it out of the bakery alive.

"All your boy Derry needed to do was agree to make one final push… just one more shot at you and you'd have been gone." Cliff leered at Rome, peeking out from behind Angel. "Well, one more shot at *him* and Angel would have packed up and gone. Instead, the shithead came crawling to us about some sob story, how this dick here wanted to close the motel deal. Bad shit all around, that.

"Says I'm not going to get my money because he's all tapped out." Cliff chuckled. "Yeah, he got tapped out, alright. So now I'm going to do the same thing here to the boy if I don't get what I need."

"Angel—" Rome squeaked.

His heart seized when their father trained the gun on them, then broke when he heard Rome's sobbing gasp. His hand shook when he reached for Rome's shoulder, and his brother felt hot to his chilled fingers. Roman shook free, standing defiant and sullen, staring their father down.

"Go to the kitchen, Rome." Angel cracked, the terror his father placed in his chest chewing its way out. "Dad, let him go. Please, don't do—"

"Kid goes nowhere, boy. You finally come up to scratch, and I can use you for something bigger than dime bag jobs, and you want me to let him go? No, the kid stays," Cliff ground out between yellowed teeth. "What's going to happen is Harris here is going to be taken to the bank while the two of you stay here with Byron. Once I get the money I was promised, I'll drop a call and Byron will take care of things on this end."

He'd grown accustomed to his father's betrayals, but Roman's face was a field of devastated innocence. His brother took a step toward the kitchen door, edging out from behind the couch, an unsure and afraid statue just a little too far to Angel's right than he liked. Rome's eyes were wide, teary, and he frantically glanced back at Angel.

"Right," Angel sneered back. "How stupid do you think *I* am, Dad?"

"As stupid as I've raised you," his father replied, shrugging when he lifted the gun, pointing it at Rome's head. "Guess now's as good of a time as any. Maybe after this, your fuck buddy will take me a bit more seriously."

In the stagnant, fraught silence of the bakery's dining room, the gun's discharge shook the wall, a peal of smoky thunder with an astringent pewter-metallic chaser. West became a blur, putting himself between the brothers and Byron, but Angel knew Byron wasn't the one he had to worry about. There was never, ever any question about where his life and loyalty lay.

Their father intended to kill them. Without hesitation or a single regret, Cliff Daniels planned on wiping his sons off the face of the earth, probably from the moment Derry Washington reached out to him, and Angel had no intention of letting his father kill anymore.

As his father pulled the gun's trigger, he dove onto Rome's trembling, lanky body, shoving his brother down toward the display cases by the dining room's right wall. Rome folded into him, a soft, skittering bag of bones, thin muscles, and fear, and Angel embraced him, rolling himself as tightly around his brother as he could.

When Angel's side caught on fire, his ribs shattering under the bullet's mindless fury, and his blood spurted out of the hole burrowing through him, Angel gasped, riding the pain and the nausea carrying him away. Struggling to breathe around his pounding heart, Angel tightened his arms around his little brother and whispered, "Love you, Rome. Don't forget."

RAGE WAS a marvelous thing. If he'd been by himself, West wondered if he'd be scared, more willing to buckle and fall to his knees in front of the men holding them hostage in Angel's dream. He hoped he'd never have an answer to that question. It was far better to mull that over a shot of whiskey while watching the stars play across the sky.

Angel had to be okay. He scolded himself for thinking his lover would never rise up from the pile of entwined bodies near the velvet couch. There was blood on the couch, a dark crimson splatter quickly being sucked into the fabric's run-down nap. West couldn't look at the blood. He had to keep his sights on taking out the man who'd stolen Rome, then tried to beat Angel into the ground.

"West!" Roman screamed across the room. "Angel's hurt."

"Get out behind me, kiddo," West said out of the side of his mouth. Cliff was on the move, crossing the room toward them.

The display cases were a wall of glass and metal to his right, but a cut through on the left was open. If he could distract Cliff, Rome could at least make it to the kitchen. The key was keeping Cliff and Byron off-balance. "Asshole, once I'm done with your cousin, I'm coming for you next."

"Oh, this is going to be good." Byron grinned through a slick of spittle. "You watch the kid, Cliff. I'm going to deal with this fucker."

West's fingers already hurt. He'd put up a fight when they cornered him in the parking lot. Lying in wait for Marzo to leave after dropping West off at the sidewalk, the Daniels men jumped him when he walked toward the Shack's rear entrance. He'd gotten in a few good hits before Cliff pulled out a gun. Then he'd realized the danger he'd brought to Angel's front door.

He couldn't look at Angel, refused to chance his heart being torn from him. Rome needed their help. If—when—they got out of the bakery, away from the mess of their father, West was going to put his foot down and demand Angel and Rome stay with him. He'd had enough of being alone, of not waking up to a stormy-eyed, dark-haired Angel in his bed. He liked going downstairs for his morning coffee and finding a pair of brothers arguing over the merits of crispy rice cereal or if blue gummy bears were really necessary.

Angel was going to have his four walls of home, and West intended to be the man who gave it to him.

As soon as he beat the shit out of Angel's father and their bastard cousin.

"Fucker! Time for you to die," Byron growled, swinging his gun around.

The weapon barked once, but the bullet went wide, shattering one of the display cases. His finger twitched again, but it was too late for Byron to do more than backpedal a step because West's hands were clenched, already moving to pound at Byron's face.

His thumb ached, and his chest burned a little from the searing terror of seeing Angel fall. Shifting his feet, West planted himself and swung, putting his weight into the punch. Byron jerked his head to the side, trying to avoid the hit, but West connected, grazing his knuckles across the man's mouth. His hand rocked with the impact, and a tooth's edge nicked West's skin.

Fight dirty, Deacon'd told Zig one day when they'd sat down to a dinner and she'd complained about a pack of older boys picking on her friend, a friend who'd turned out to be Rome. His brother-in-law didn't blink when he answered her about what to do if the boys got physical with them. *Fight dirty*, he'd said. *The point of a fight isn't to inflict pain. It's to end the fight. Don't dance around it. Someone comes up and tries to hurt you, you take them down. Then you go find help.*

Help wasn't going to come. No one was going to save them from the bogeymen wearing parts of Angel's face. West was on his own, and he had to take care of Byron before he could choke the hell out of his lover's father.

Byron shoved West into the counter, spitting blood onto the floor. The spittle barely missed West's foot, and his ankle twisted under him, the strained tendons giving in under the pressure of being bent sideways. Grabbing at Byron's filthy shirt, West shoved back, slamming the man into the broken display case.

Knickknacks flew from a table next to the case, falling to the floor with a loud rattle. A long black cylinder landed near West's foot, and he caught on its square base when he took a step forward. He fought to regain his balance, and Deacon's words resonated once more in his mind. Heavy and thick, the battered old tchotchke was going to come in handy. Scooping it from the floor, West grinned at its weight.

Dirty in this case meant a black iron candlestick and the side of Byron's head.

He came at West again, stretching up with his hands clenched together into a meaty doubled fist. Byron'd lost the gun somewhere, hopefully under a couch or behind a table. Either way, West knew the blow coming at him was going to hurt a hell of a lot less than a bullet.

West lashed out, holding the candlestick at its thinner end. Its base was chunky, squared off into a faux Art Deco design. It was hideous, profane in its design, and at any other time of his life, West would have gladly turned his nose up at the thing. At that moment, he sent a brief, silent thanks to the candlestick's probably deceased creator's lack of taste and buried a base corner into Byron's gaunt face.

Someone with wings and divine grace must have been paying attention, because West watched in horror when the candlestick's base bounced off Byron's cheek and lodged into his right eye. Howling, the man spun about, covering his face with his hands. Blood gushed from between his fingers, and he turned, a wicked fire burning in his one good eye, glaring at West standing numbly with the candlestick still in his hand.

"Going to fucking kill you, asshole," Byron promised. "Then I'm going to fuck your mouth with my dick."

West lifted the knickknack up, prepared to defend himself, when another boom drowned out their labored breathing, and Byron's head blew out onto West's face and chest, powdery bloody flecks coating his skin and thickening the spit on his lip.

Byron's eyes widened, either in shock or perhaps his mind refused to believe he was dead. The hole wasn't big enough to see daylight through, but there was no mistaking the brain splatter oozing from the wound or the slacking droop of his jaw muscles loosening. He staggered, taking a fumbling step. Then Cliff fired twice more, shearing chunks off of Byron's skull.

The man finally fell, his body hitting the floor with a wet splat. Blood oozed from his mangled skull, and a dribble of mucus and spit drained from his nose, his good eye rolling back in its socket.

"He was taking way too fucking long there. Now, why don't you put that candlestick down?" Cliff smirked, aiming his gun at Rome's head. "Then we can head to that bank, Harris."

"Let them go first." West refused with a shake of his head. "You don't get shit without them getting out of here."

"Don't push me, asshole. I've only got one son left to shoot, and I don't give a rat's shit about him. They're not worth crap. Neither of them. You're an idiot if you think the older one wasn't going to screw you out of some money. I'm just doing it before he can get to you." Cliff motioned to the door. "Now get moving, because after the brat, there's only you. And I care even less about you."

The boy shuffled back, keeping away from his father, but the distance wasn't going to matter. All it would take was one well-placed bullet and West's world would crumble under him.

He hadn't done the right thing by Lang growing up. They'd never been close and fought more than they'd talked. In the rare times they'd reached out to one another, it'd been too hard, or so West thought. Being with Angel and Rome gave West a scrap of hope he and his brother could have what the Daniels boys had, a teasing, argumentative, loving relationship, and all West had to do was survive Angel's father.

He needed them—both—because as much as he loved Angel, as much as his soul belonged to the older Daniels, Roman'd captured a piece of his heart. And he was going to be damned if Angel and Rome didn't survive along with him.

"You didn't have to do any of this. I'd have given you what you wanted from the beginning. You didn't have to hurt Angel," West offered. "Let them go and I'll give you as much money as we can get out of the bank."

"He can't do that." Angel lurched to his feet. "We're the only ones who know he's here. He can't let us go. And he shouldn't, because as long as he's out there, he knows I'm going to hunt him down, because I'm going to kill him before I let him hurt my brother."

Movies had it right… or wrong… depending on how West looked at it. There might not have been scores of white doves or singing rodents celebrating Angel staggering across the floor, blood seeping out of a wicked-looking gouge in his side, but West felt the sweet chorus of woodland animals echoing in his heart. Especially when Angel gave him a wan smile before taking another unsteady stride toward his father.

"Think I won't blow his head off?" Cliff threatened, waving his gun at Rome. "Or yours?"

"You can't."

Rome's reedy voice quivered, fright bleaching the color from his face. He'd moved a few feet, standing not far from where Byron lay. West hadn't seen Rome reach Byron's side, but he had. His young face was damp with snot and sweat, and his sneakers were coated in the man's drying blood, but it was the snub-nosed black revolver he'd aimed at his father that gave West pause.

"I know you can't."

"You don't have the balls, kid," their father laughed, an uproarious mocking boom nearly as loud as the gunshots he'd let loose in the tight space. "Put that fucking thing down! You don't know what you're talking about."

"You're holding a Rossi Centerfire. It's only got five shots. You taught me that, Dad."

The gun in Roman's hand shook, bobbling about as he tried to hold it steady. West carefully laid the candlestick down, then took a step toward the boy. He shuffled away, but his eyes never left his father's face.

"You've only got one bullet left. I counted."

"Rome!" Angel winced, bending over as he clenched at his ribs. The blood dripping from his side ran down his leg, a dribbling river of red splattering the fabric and the floor by Angel's feet. "Dude, give the gun to West. We'll take care of this. Don't—"

"No, Angel," Rome argued softly. "You take care of everything else. Sometimes I've got to take care of you. He hurt you. I can't let him hurt you."

"Fucking kid, you better—"

Cliff lunged at Rome, and it was all West could do to not fall apart when Roman pulled the trigger as Angel pitched forward, screaming his brother's name.

Epilogue

"HE IS possibly one of the worst drivers I have ever seen." Lang's eyes went wide when a Lexus sedan lurched into the cul-de-sac. The sleek black vehicle jerked and stopped, threatening to stall before lunging forward a few feet, much to the amusement of Zig and Rome, sitting in lawn chairs on the sidewalk in front of Deacon's shop.

"How the hell is he doing that? It's an automatic!"

"Told you," Marzo muttered over the rim of his coffee cup. "He's a menace. It's like he's the Hindenburg and the Titanic wrapped up in one skinny disaster."

"We are *not* skinny," Lang sniffed. "It's that you're the size of a small mountain."

"Never insult a man when his identical twin is standing right next to you. Shit, why didn't we have him learn in some beater?"

Angel winced when the Lexus came to a shuddering stop. He got withering looks from Marzo and Lang, and he sighed heavily when the kids cheered at the car's gunning engine.

"Yeah, sorry. What was I thinking? West Harris wouldn't be caught dead in a Ford Focus."

"Oh, he'd be caught dead in it," Lang muttered. "Then he'd drag his decaying body around until he found a BMW to crawl into."

On a lazy Sunday afternoon, Half Moon Bay was a subdued murmur of activity, lulled into naps, quiet times at home, or lolling about on the shore's broad expanse of glittering white sand. The historic district with its tiny specialty shops was closing down, business coming to a crawl, then petering out the closer it got to dinnertime. There were a few restaurants doing a brisk trade near the main drag, but on the far end of Main Street where a cul-de-sac led to an overworked auto shop, a comfortable bookstore with its two cats-in-residence, and a hair salon filled with laughter and gossip, Sundays usually meant a meandering time spent doing mostly nothing in particular.

The cul-de-sac's indolent afternoons became a thing of the past, and the slow, painful, jittering progress of an expensive sedan moving up and down the street was less of an event over the last few weekends and more of a hazard when crossing the road.

"This is too painful to watch." Marzo crumpled up his cup into a ball, then tossed it into a recycle bin on the edge of the sidewalk. "You two can suffer through this. I'm going to see what the bookstore's got."

"Tell Chris he needs to take his break if he hasn't already," Lang called out after the bodyguard. Turning to Angel, he asked, "Do you ever have that problem? My employees keep forgetting to get off the floor and take their lunches and breaks."

"I tend to employ stoners and slackers." Angel shrugged. "They take breaks they're not even supposed to take, but they make a hell of a great pastry."

The Lexus inched forward, then sped up, careening toward the auto shop's driveway. Rome and Zig shouted encouragement, laughing uproariously when Deacon pressed his face against the passenger window and slathered the glass with his tongue.

"Great, now West is going to have to burn the car. He knows how West is about spit," Lang grumbled. "I can't believe Deacon's doing this."

"He pulled the short straw, and West's overcome a lot of his body-fluid issues," Angel reminded him. "Besides, they're actually doing pretty good together. This is what? Their fourth lesson? Marzo said most instructors don't last two trips with West. And he's mostly driving in a straight line now."

The Lexus hit the curb, jumping the concrete lip running along the edge of the street. The car hung at an angle for a second, then slid back down, shaking when the tire hit the asphalt. Rome groaned and scribbled something down in a notebook he and Zig were passing back and forth. Angel didn't want to know what the kids were writing down. If he knew his brother, he'd taken bets from everyone up and down the block on how often West did something and was running a gambling pool from his yellow-and-white-plaid beach chair.

"Is he doing okay?" Lang asked quietly. "Nightmares? Anything?"

"Rome or West?" Angel teased back, and the silent reproach in Lang's achingly familiar blue eyes was enough to sober him. "He's had some rough nights. Thank God he missed Dad by five miles, or it'd be worse."

"I can't believe… I can't imagine being in a position where you needed to shoot your father." Shaking his head, Lang angled himself away from the kids, keeping his voice low as he spoke. "I mean, I've wanted to. Our father wasn't any treat, but he was mostly cold, unfeeling. What the two of you had to deal with is… unimaginable. And I know that sounds privileged, but I really can't imagine it. It's like Deacon and Zig. They have this experience they share, a life language only they can speak, and it's because of where they came from, how they grew up. It's not anything I can comprehend, and I feel so ignorant, but at the same time—"

"You're glad you don't know?"

"Oh, hell yes," Lang confessed with a wide grin. "And it sounds condescending to say I admire them for who they are, because it sounds like I'm spitting on where they came from."

"I'd be the first one to tell you Deacon's come a fuck of a long way from where he's supposed to be. Zig too. No shame is saying that," Angel replied. "I want more for Rome than how the rest of our family lives, and I'm not going to say I'm sorry about that. If he grows up and lives in a house with a white picket fence and has a wife and two-point-five kids, I'm good with that."

"Somehow, I don't think that's going to be the case." Lang eyed the kids. "God help the world."

"Yeah." Angel shrugged. "But at least we'll probably have bail money for them. I just have to make sure he gets through this shit he's going through and comes out the other side as whole as he can get. Dad's not seeing the light of day ever again, and Rome knows that. Adoption papers were signed last week, so he's stuck with me now. His therapist says it's normal for him to have bad dreams, but you know—"

"You worry," Lang finished, nodding. "Zig has them sometimes. Less and less, but once in a while, they're bad."

"Yeah, they're shitty because I don't have any goddamn way to fix it for him." Angel jostled his coffee cup, wondering if he could get in a refill before Deacon called an end to the lesson. "Doctor says it'll take time. I get that."

"Is he happy?" his lover's twin asked, gently prodding at the scab of Angel's worry. "Is Rome happy?"

Thinking back to the frightened, angry young child he'd first ushered into his apartment and the fierce battles he'd had with Roman in the time since, it was hard to believe the lanky, guffawing boy sitting a few feet away was the same kid. He'd filled out, shot up nearly half a foot, and was slowly—very slowly—learning how to be a decent human being.

"Yeah, he's happy. He likes having West around. The two of them cackle over profit margins and argue about what makes good art. Kid's got champagne tastes, but we're on a Kool-Aid budget. Typical Daniels."

"And what does West think? About the two of you being together?"

"Right now? Nothing." Angel tossed his cup into the bin. "But it's something we've got to talk about. The Moonrise is done with its renovations, and I've got to figure out what we're going to do. He loves me. He says it all the time. But I can't assume—"

"Do you love him, Angel?" Lang's assessing look would come in handy once Zig was old enough to date. It was quelling and awe-inspiring all at the same time. "Do you love my brother, Angel?"

"Truth?" Angel returned Lang's glare with a soft chuckle.

"Where my brother's concerned, the truth is not only welcome," Lang replied, "it's a necessity."

Angel could see West's determined face through the Lexus's windows. He adored that face, reveled in the feel of West's hands on him, and every morning he wondered when he was going to wake up from the dream he'd fallen into. His heart skipped when he saw West for the first time every morning, and its beat lulled him to sleep when Angel fell over, dead tired and happy after a long day.

The sky couldn't be as blue as West's eyes, and he'd bathed in the sweetness of West's kiss every chance he could get. There were times when he only had to look up and he'd find West watching him, a quiet, semishy smile on his face, and Angel lost himself in the emotions only West could pull out of his soul.

"The truth is, Lang," Angel whispered, "your brother hangs the stars in my goddamn sky. It sounds stupid and maybe corny, but when he's around me, it's like the night's full of light. So yeah, I love him. I love him pretty hard."

"Good, then tell him. And *now* the lesson is over. Deacon's face is white." Lang nodded as the Lexus bolted across the street, shot up the shop's driveway, and came to a stop a few feet from the front door. Clapping loudly, he shouted at West as he extracted himself out of the driver's seat. "Good parking! You're in the lines."

"Well, he's in some lines at least," Deacon grumbled loud enough to be heard over the kids' babble.

Zig and Roman bounced over to the car, grabbing at Deacon's arms.

"Yeah, yeah, I'm alive. So's Satan. He'll live to terrorize another circle of Hell later. Just you wait. God, I need a drink."

"I've got cocoa and coffee at the store," Lang offered.

Deacon and Lang exchanged a look. Then the gruff mechanic beamed a wicked smile.

"Okay, grab the kids and we'll head in. I owe them two books each. I bet West would take out the bushes again."

"This is why I don't have faith in my family," West groused, stretching his long arms above his head.

Ambling behind the kids, Deacon snorted, patting Lang's butt as he passed by.

"And no groping my brother."

"Fuck you, he's my husband," Deacon shot back. "And after having my life flash in front of me three times in the last half hour, I'm going to grab his ass as many times as I want."

"Can I go get my books?" Rome stood in front of Angel, practically vibrating with excitement. "I did a double or nothing with Lang about the trash can."

"Can we maybe not fleece people for one Sunday?" Scowling, Angel stared down at his brother. Roman blinked, but none of the fake innocence he'd slathered on drained from his face. "Fine. And then later, we'll talk about that game you're running out of that notebook."

"You're *no* fun," his brother grumbled, but he shot off after Zig, yelling at her to wait up for him.

"Really? He's running a betting book now?" West lifted a saturnine eyebrow, its point nearly buried under the shock of black hair lying on his forehead. "On what? Me?"

"Your driving, what you'll hit, that kind of thing," Angel sighed. "From what I gather."

"I am so proud." Beaming, West leaned into Angel, kissing him soundly. "God, he's like if you and I had a kid. Most of your looks and all of my brains."

"I'm trying to make sure my brother doesn't end up in jail, Harris."

"Please, like that'll ever happen. He's too smart to get caught. And if he does get caught, it'll be a learning experience on what not to do the next time." Sniffing at his shirt, West wrinkled his nose. "I sweat more driving than I do horseback riding. I swear it's the stress. Deacon said he'd take the kids to the movies tonight, so if you want to try that new Indian food place without a lot of *icks* and *eeews*, I can make a reservation."

"Actually, what we need to do is talk," Angel said quietly. "Because I've got to—"

"Because the motel's done?" West grabbed Angel's waist, pulling him in tight. "You think you've got to go off and leave me?"

"Crossed my mind." He nodded, not sure if he wanted to have his heart broken in the middle of the street. "Maybe we can talk about this later. At the house."

"Nope, we're going to deal with this right now, Daniels," West disagreed.

"Can we at least get off the street?" Angel asked.

"How about this?" West laid his hands on Angel's shoulders. "I'll go tell Lang to hold on to Rome for us, and you drive us down to the first place I knew I was in love with you."

"The bathrooms down at the old football field?" He grinned at West's exasperated sigh. "What? That's the first place we—"

"The beach, you asshole. I want to go to the beach." West shoved the Lexus's keys into Angel's hands. "See if you can get that thing to listen to you and pointed towards the ocean. I'll be right back."

NOT SURPRISINGLY, the ocean was exactly where they'd last left it, a seemingly endless shifting churn of white-capped blue water and bits of floating kelp. The area was deserted, the air brisk with a slight chill growing deeper as the sun sank closer to the horizon. A seagull circled them twice, probably debating its odds for scoring food, but winged off in search of better prospects once Angel laid a blanket down on the shifting sands.

The late afternoon sun did little to warm the beach, and the wind smelled of slightly overripe seaweed and salt, but the fragrance was a familiar comfort. About two hundred yards away, a few teenagers were digging out a hole, intent on erecting an illegal fire pit where they'd drink stolen warm beers and tell jokes everyone'd heard a million times before.

"Were we ever that young?" West asked, staring at the laughing pile of teens halfway down the beach.

"Did we ever get any older?" Angel shot back, patting the blanket. "Come on."

West'd snagged a bottle of wine from his brother's office, promising Lang he'd replace it, and while it seemed a shame to pour the fine red into a pair of paper coffee cups, it was all he'd found in the liquor cabinet. As far as seductions went, it was a piss-poor attempt, but it was the best West could do on such a short notice.

Especially since it seemed Angel was forever trying to leave him.

"I'm not trying to leave you," Angel said when West sat on the blanket next to him. His eyes were the color of the sky, hints of blue on dove behind thick black lashes. "I know that's what you're thinking, but you're wrong. I love you, West. I just have to figure out how to live with you and not lose myself in the process."

"I don't want to… absorb you, love." West leaned on Angel's shoulder, nudging him. "I just want to… love you. If I've got to live in a run-down—"

"It's sparkling and clean now. Very retro, though. Looks like your designers watched one too many episodes of the *Avengers*."

"What? Like Mjölnir?" West scrambled through what he'd seen in the apartments. "That Avengers?"

"No, like Steed and Peel," Angel sighed. "Swear to God, you have huge gaps in your pop culture education. It's like you were raised on Masterpiece Theatre and PBS."

"This coming from the man who didn't know who the Kimba was," West shot back. "And I'll watch… whatever show you're talking about. Just so long as we do it together. Don't go back to the Moonrise, Angel. Stay at the fortress with me. Your brother's all settled in, and Marzo's finally got someone who'll let him boss him around."

"That's only going to last a couple more years. Then shit's going to hit the fan with that kid," Angel warned. "It's going to be a rough ride."

"It'll be a rougher ride without you," West admitted. "I've missed you next to me, Daniels. And maybe there was a reason we needed to be apart then, but now I can't see going a day without touching you, without holding you. And if you love me like you say you do, as I believe you do, you'll know that. You'll feel that. Look me in the eye and tell me you can wake up to an empty bed every morning when you can wake up to me."

"I've seen how you look in the morning." Angel smirked. "You're not making a great case here, Harris."

"I'm doing the best I can, Daniels." His heart squeezed in his chest, roiling around in the emotions crashing over him, and West took Angel's hand, holding it in his lap. "Stay with me. Live with me. Love me. Like I love you. Tell me you love me every morning and then grumble at me every night when I drop my towels on the floor. I want to hear you mutter about how spoiled I am when I ask Marzo to do something for me and complain loudly when I teach your brother how supply and demand works.

"For fuck's sake, Angel," West growled. "Stay and I promise to make your life as miserably happy for as long as we both are alive and probably for a little bit past that too. Just... fucking marry me already."

Angel said nothing. Silent, he stared out over the sea, just breathing while West's heart crackled and spat. It seemed like an eternity passed, aging the tension between them until it was brittle enough to break if a single word was spoken.

"There's a part of me that's always been yours, West." Angel pressed into him, his eyes still on the horizon. "This past month has been... a dream. I keep expecting to wake up from it, but every morning, there you are. I feel like I've been running my whole damned life. Running to places. Running away from people. Maybe just running away from myself. But then suddenly you were there, right in front of me, and I didn't want to run anymore.

"So, just so you know, Rome's going to want you to adopt him, because he thinks he's going to get a brother who'll let him get away with shit. And I'm going to be the bad guy and tell him no," Angel replied gently. "You sure you're ready to take this all on?"

"Never been surer. Just so long as *you* say yes." He swore. "How many more times do I have to say yes before I hear one from you, love?"

"Just that once." Bending over, Angel captured West's mouth in a fierce kiss then murmured softly, "So yeah, West. You've got yourself a family. May God have mercy on your soul."

RHYS FORD admits to sharing the house with three cats of varying degrees of black fur and a ginger Cairn terrorist. Rhys is also enslaved to the upkeep of a 1979 Pontiac Firebird, a Toshiba laptop, and an overworked red coffee maker.

Rhys can be found at the following locations:

Blog: www.rhysford.com
Facebook: www.facebook.com/rhys.ford.author
Twitter: @Rhys_Ford

A HALF MOON BAY MYSTERY

FISH STICK FRIDAYS

R H Y S   F O R D

Half Moon Bay: Book One

Deacon Reid was born bad to the bone with no intention of changing. A lifetime of law-bending and living on the edge suits him just fine—until his baby sister dies and he finds himself raising her little girl.

Staring down a family history of bad decisions and reaped consequences, Deacon cashes in everything he owns, purchases an auto shop in Half Moon Bay, and takes his niece, Zig, far away from the drug dens and murderous streets they grew up on. Zig deserves a better life than what he had, and Deacon is determined to give it to her.

Lang Harris is stunned when Zig, a little girl in combat boots and a purple tutu, blows into his bookstore, and then he's left speechless when her uncle, Deacon Reid, walks in hot on her heels. Lang always played it safe, but Deacon tempts him to step over the line... just a little bit.

More than a little bit. And Lang is willing to be tempted.

Unfortunately, Zig isn't the only bit of chaos dropped into Half Moon Bay. Violence and death strike, leaving Deacon scrambling to fight off a killer before he loses not only Zig but Lang too.

www.dreamspinnerpress.com

FISH AND GHOSTS

RHYS FORD

Hellsinger: Book One

When his Uncle Mortimer died and left him Hoxne Grange, the family's Gilded Age mansion, Tristan Pryce became the second generation of Pryces to serve as a caretaker for the estate, a way station for spirits on their final steps to the afterlife. Tristan is prepared for challenges, though not necessarily from the ghosts he's seen since childhood. Determined to establish Tristan's insanity and gain access to his trust fund, his loving relatives hire Dr. Wolf Kincaid and his paranormal researchers, Hellsinger Investigations, to prove the Grange is not haunted.

Skeptic Wolf Kincaid has made it his life's work to debunk the supernatural. After years of cons and fakes, he can't wait to reveal the Grange's ghostly activity is just badly leveled floorboards and a drafty old house. More than a few surprises await him at the Grange, including its prickly, reclusive owner. Tristan Pryce is much less insane and much more attractive than Wolf wants to admit, and when his team releases a ghostly serial killer on the Grange, Wolf is torn between his skepticism and protecting the man he's been sent to discredit.

www.dreamspinnerpress.com

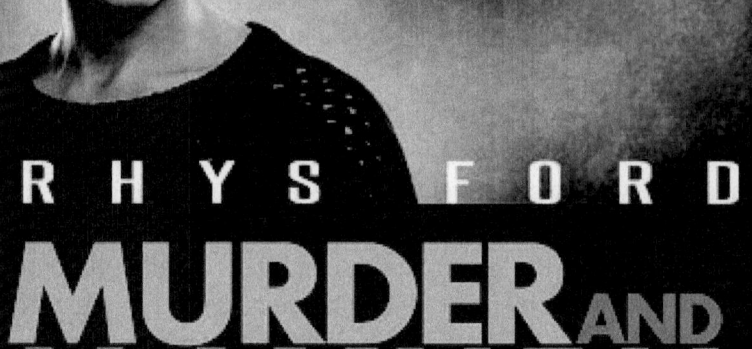

RHYS FORD

MURDER AND MAYHEM

Dead women tell no tales.

Former cat burglar Rook Stevens stole many a priceless thing in the past, but he's never been accused of taking a life—until now. It was one thing to find a former associate inside Potter's Field, his pop culture memorabilia shop, but quite another to stumble across her dead body.

Detective Dante Montoya thought he'd never see Rook Stevens again—not after his former partner falsified evidence to entrap the jewelry thief and Stevens walked off scot-free. So when he tackled a fleeing murder suspect, Dante was shocked to discover the blood-covered man was none other than the thief he'd fought to put in prison and who still makes his blood sing.

Rook is determined to shake loose the murder charge against him, even if it means putting distance between him and the rugged Cuban-Mexican detective who brought him down. If one dead con artist wasn't bad enough, others soon follow, and as the bodies pile up around Rook's feet, he's forced to reach out to the last man he'd expect to believe in his innocence—and the only man who's ever gotten under Rook's skin.

www.dreamspinnerpress.com

.

CPSIA information can be obtained
at www.ICGtesting.com
Printed in the USA
LVOW01s1613130317
527032LV00011B/1292/P